To Die Alone
in
the Yukon

Lynn M. Berk

To Die Alone in the Yukon

Copyright © 2017 by Lynn M. Berk

For my husband Toby.
I am deeply grateful for his boundless
moral support and his editorial
and technical expertise.

In memory of Bobo Larocque,
whose contribution to this book will be obvious
and
Gord Downie, beloved Canadian musician and
activist.

Lynn M. Berk.
Lynn@LynnBerkBooks.com

PROLOGUE

The church and the priest had both grown old. The building looked smaller than he remembered, but then he was smaller now, too. The place was sadly disheveled. Candy bar and gum wrappers clung to the sticky foxtail weeds growing in the yard. The few remaining uprights in the picket fence hung at cockeyed angles. The gate was gone and the narrow sidewalk had disintegrated into bits of rubble, which skittered ahead of him as he walked. Dirty white paint was peeling off the wooden steeple, and the blue, red, and gold of the stained glass windows had been rendered a muddy grey by accumulated grime and mildew.

The old priest put one shoulder to the heavy cedar door and pushed. It stuck just as it had in the old days. He pushed harder. Suddenly it flew open, almost catapulting him into the sanctuary. He steadied himself and stepped into the gloom. His shuffling gait raised a thin cloud of dust as the door closed softly behind him. The church smelled faintly of mold and incense. It was a familiar smell.

He walked slowly up the aisle, steadying himself on the pew backs. He paused midway and worked his finger under his stiff white collar. It didn't fit anymore and it was chafing his neck. But the invitation had been explicit. *Please wear your clerical collar*, it had read.

As he made his way to the front, the priest noticed that one beam of sunlight was falling directly on the altar, casting a rosy glow on the tarnished brass cross affixed to the back wall. He looked across the room and stared at the stained glass window that depicted the temptation of Adam in the Garden of Eden. A single piece of red glass had been wiped absolutely clean. How strange, he thought. Someone has polished the apple.

The old man made his way toward the altar. He was surprised that no one else had arrived yet. The invitation had said that five of his old students would be there to greet him, but the sanctuary was silent. There were no signs of a celebration. All the surfaces were dusty and big, loopy cobwebs hung from the beamed ceiling.

When he reached the front row of pews, he noticed a book lying open on the floor. It was a pulpit-sized, leather bound bible. As he stooped to look at it, he saw the muddy foot print which spanned both pages. "Sacrilege," he muttered. "What swine would trample the holy word?" Steadying himself with one hand on a pew seat, he knelt. He picked up the book in both hands and inspected it. The muddiest part of the footprint had obliterated one his favorite *New Testament* passages, one he had tried to live by. *Suffer the little children to come unto me, and forbid them not; for of such is the Kingdom of God.* He tried to scrape the mud off with his index finger. It just made matters worse.

Then the old man heard a floorboard creak behind him. Ah, one of the students at last. He turned with a smile on his face. But the face that greeted his was invisible behind a bandana, the kind that robbers wore in old westerns. The hair was long and dark and had been pulled into a ponytail. The old man was puzzled. No one had said this was a costume party. It was clear that the face wasn't smiling behind that scrap of red. The eyes were cold and angry.

Before the old man could speak, the figure grabbed him under the arms. The bible fell to the floor with a thud. The masked person pulled him to his feet. The priest closed his eyes and his breathing grew shallow. He felt dizzy. He could feel his wrists being bound loosely together with something stiff and sticky. Then his assailant hooked elbows under his arms and dragged the old man across the wooden floor. A door creaked on rusty hinges and the priest was pulled into a small, windowless room. A voice that was neither male nor female muttered, "Say hello to Joshua's ghost." The door slammed shut and the room went black.

CHAPTER 1

The river bank was littered with the dead ones. Some had been picked clean by ravens and eagles; some still had bits of intestine or stomach wrapped around the bones. The mouths were half open and the eyes had the consistency of egg whites. It was a warm day and there were flies everywhere. The carcasses were beginning to smell.

It was a common enough scene along the rivers of the far north. The ritual seldom varied—decapitation, a neat cut up the spine, and an incision from the anus to the gills. Proper protocol dictated that the skeleton and guts be tossed into the river to be carried away by the current, but not everyone complied. A long string of roe lay coiled on a rock, an amber double helix, fish DNA rotting in the summer sun.

This spot was remote, accessible only by boat or bush plane. A Piper Cub and two Cessnas were parked diagonally next to the gravel runway. A DeHavilland Beaver sat twenty yards away behind a battered tool box. The cowl was off and two Sourdoughs were cursing and sweating as they peered and poked at the nine-cylinder engine. "Goddam it," said one of the old men. "I ain't adjusting those goddamn valves again." He smacked the side of plane with his open hand.

As the old men groused and spat tobacco juice, two women wended their way through the guts and gore and headed for the Cessna 182. They had fishing rods over their shoulders. One had a stringer and a camera around her neck and a small tackle box in one fist. She was tall and sturdy with short, bright red curls that bounced with her long, purposeful stride. The other was six inches shorter with a thick salt and pepper braid flowing down her back. Periodically she took little running steps to keep up with the redhead. A small cooler bounced against her leg as she jogged.

The tall woman was clearly the pilot. She walked around the plane checking the tires, looking for oil leaks, and inspecting the ailerons. The other woman crawled into the passenger seat and stowed the cooler and fishing gear in the rear. The pilot climbed in and slowly ran her eyes down a laminated checklist. Then they both donned headsets. Finally the pilot cracked the window and yelled "Clear!" She started the engine. It thumped softly as the propeller strobed across the windshield.

The little Cessna bumped down the runway on fat tundra tires, its rear wheel shimmying in the loose gravel. It was a battered rental plane, its fuselage and wings scratched, pitted, and dented by countless bush landings. Its original owner had painted a big toothy smile on the nose under the air intake—a comic homage to the Fighting Tigers. The lips had faded to puce and the teeth were cracked and flaking.

The two old bush pilots shook their heads and clucked. This scenario did not bode well. They had seen their share of plane crashes and they were certain that the Cessna's pilot was too young, from the Outside, and inexperienced in bush flying. Worse yet it was a girl. A girl!

"You gotta have balls to fly in this country," one said, cupping his hands in front of his crotch.

"This ain't no business for broads," was the reply.

The Sourdoughs were wrong on all counts but one. Theodora Gianopoulous had 1,000 hours flying experience, much of it in the Rocky Mountains. At forty six, she was much older than she looked. She was muscular and fit and had done a brief stint as an amateur boxer when she was young. She may have been a broad, but she was a damn tough one. Yes, she was from Outside.

Teddy's passenger was her old grad school chum, Lydia

Falkner. She was not an Outsider. She had lived on and off in the wilds of the Yukon Territory for many years and planned to apply for Canadian Permanent Resident status in six months. She loved the Yukon and there was nothing in the States to lure her back. She had no siblings, her father was dead, and her mother was shrill, judgmental, and a pain in the ass. Worse yet, she had recently moved to Florida, land of hurricanes, cockroaches, and giant pythons. Lydia's love of wildlife had its limits.

Lydia grinned as she peered out the passenger window. The skepticism of the sourdoughs was written on their faces. First they grimaced and then they smirked as Teddy positioned herself for take-off. The nose is high on a tail dragger. Teddy had to look out of the right window, then the left, then the right again to locate herself on the runway—standard procedure. She picked up speed and the plane rose sharply. Teddy executed a graceful turn and gained altitude. She waggled her wings at the old men and headed north. The Sourdoughs looked astonished as if they had believed the Cessna would stay forever earthbound.

As the plane climbed, spindly spruce trees became an open forest and then a blanket of deep green, marked in a few places by narrow game trails. Below them the Klondike Highway bisected their path as it twisted and turned. Lydia could see a line of RVs and trailers moving slowly up a steep incline. She could imagine the honking and cursing of those stuck behind the caravan of giant rigs.

"Doesn't anyone sleep in a tent anymore?" she groused into her headset.

"Tents mean sleeping on the ground and pooping in a privy. Your modern camper refuses to suffer such indignities."

"Poop," yelled Lydia into the headset. "Did you really say poop?"

"Give me a break," said Teddy. "I'm trying to clean up my friggin' language."

At Carmacks the Yukon River came into view. Teddy flew

low over Five Finger Rapids, the only fast water on the Yukon. The massive columns of basalt in the middle of the current were the stuff of science fiction. Millennia before, molten lava had broken through the earth's crust and as it cooled, it twisted and swirled into balls and knobs. These in turn hardened into discrete layers divided by ragged crevices. Today the distant rocks glistened copper and gold in the late afternoon sun. Nothing green could gain purchase on the steep, basalt slopes but a little forest of spruce sat atop each monolith. Fat white gulls waddled perpetually among the trees, their thick white droppings enriching the rocky soil. When the plane reached Pelly Crossing, Teddy headed northwest toward the Stewart River.

The landscape was beautiful until it wasn't. Lydia and Teddy were not prepared for the abrupt and startling transformation. They frowned in unison. It was as if someone had drawn an imaginary line in the wilderness. To the west was beauty untrammeled by civilization; to the east lay environmental carnage. Roads had been cut into the forest, ragged tan scars on a field of black and white spruce. Log piles a story high lay rotting in the sun. There were huge mounds of dirt and rock everywhere. A bulldozer lay cockeyed in a deep ditch and a backhoe sat rusting in a creek bed.

"What the hell is that?" yelled Teddy into her headset. 'It looks like a post-apocalyptic movie set."

"That," said Lydia, her jaw clenched, "is the infamous Bad Axe Mine. My old neighbor Frank Johnson wrote me about it when I was still teaching in Colorado, but I've never seen it."

Frank's rage had been captured by his thick black script. He was one of the old timers who remembered the pollution generated by the Faro lead/zinc mine and the Elsa silver mine up on the Campbell Highway. The anti-mine coalition of First Nations, homesteaders, full-time Dawson residents, and environmentalists had been no match for the big guns supporting Bad Axe. Their profits were enormous, but very little of that money was being ploughed back into the economy of the Yukon Territory. Most of the principal players had never been to the Yukon. The mine was owned by an Ontario consortium, the senior managers were from B.C, and all the heavy equipment came from Alberta. But the mine did employ some Yukoners and that income was a boon to those families and their communities.

Teddy throttled down and flew as low as she dared. A high, chain-link fence, concertina wire festooning the top, stretched for more than a mile. There were no trees, no bushes, no cotton grass within. There was nothing below but a grey and tan moonscape of rock tailings and containment pools. The stagnant pond water was a bright turquoise tinged with yellow at the edges. Just beyond the pools was an enormous open pit. Teddy circled it twice. It was impossible to tell how deep or wide the hole was, but each strata of rock had a different texture and a different hue. The rock just below the rim of the mine was dark red, but as the hole deepened, the pigment seemed to leach out; the last layer was the color of ash. The bottom was a muddy pool.

The digging process had ringed the pit with symmetrical terraces, creating an inverted, inside-out version of Machu Picchu. A rock road corkscrewed down to the bottom. Enormous Caterpillar front-end-loaders and diesel powered shovels scooped up loads of dirt and rock. These loads were dumped into even bigger Caterpillar off-road trucks, the tires of which were the height of two men. Dust and smoke swirled in the air as the trucks chugged up the steep, spiral road with their loads. These bright yellow vehicles were the only spots of color in this devastated landscape. There were no people to be seen.

"Mel Gibson is down there somewhere," muttered Teddy.

An enormous metal building came into view. It resembled an old steel factory as it belched smoke and steam. It was surrounded by bizarre machines that looked like the work of a child with a giant Erector Set. These were crushing enormous rocks. The resulting gravel was piled onto wide conveyor belts. The plane's engine and 500 feet of air space drowned out the noise, but it must have been deafening on the ground.

About a mile from the rock crushers stood a cluster of sea containers that had been turned into dormitories. There were no outdoor amenities—no picnic tables, no lounge chairs, no volleyball nets, no shade. Blackout curtains hung at the windows, a necessity in the land of the midnight sun. The late shift snoozed inside these giant metal boxes as the steel roofs winked in the afternoon glare. A few dusty mountain bikes were parked in a rack next to the entrance.

As the Cessna headed toward the northern perimeter of the compound, Teddy abruptly pointed the nose downward. The altimeter plunged to 400 feet. Lydia threw Teddy a look of alarm. Teddy jabbed her finger at the windshield in response. Lydia looked and was astonished to see that the barren, surreal landscape was now full of people. All of them were running back and forth and gesticulating. There were vehicles, too, but they were all human-scale, ordinary. An SUV sat with its side doors open. A van was pulling up behind it. A pickup truck was parked at a precarious angle at the edge of a berm. The red emergency lights of an ambulance flashed. Two men climbed over a pile of rocks, carrying a stretcher. A uniformed man looked up at the plane. He waved his hand, palm out, in front of his face and then pointed north repeatedly. His gestures were emphatic. Teddy shrugged, pulled back the yoke, and headed toward Dawson.

CHAPTER 2

Lydia had been thrilled when Teddy Gianopoulous had appeared unannounced on her doorstep that morning. She hadn't seen Teddy in six years. They had met at the University of Michigan a long time ago. Older than the other graduate students, they had established a special bond. Along with their close friend Anna Fain, they took English classes together, gorged on pizza together, and drank at the venerable Brown Jug. Teddy invariably attracted a bevy of tipsy undergraduate men, who didn't realize she was ten years older than they were. With her Amazonian stature, red curls, startling green eyes, and a deep dimple in her right cheek, she was an exotic magnet for twenty-one year olds. But once they were exposed to her biting wit and strong opinions, once they noted the rainbow tattoo on her inside forearm, most refocused their attention on the sorority girls who congregated in small gaggles around the bar.

Teddy was funny, profane, and loud. Her laugh could rattle the windows. A rumor had circulated among her classmates that she had been a drill sergeant in the army. It wasn't true. The closest Teddy had come to the army was four miserable months in the Girl Scouts at age nine. She had assumed that the girls would hike, canoe, and camp just like the boys did. She was in no way prepared for sewing lessons, cooking demonstrations, and door-to-door cookie sales. Much to her mother's dismay, she invited her friends over and, in a ceremony complete with Kool Aid and thin mints, burned her uniform in the living room fireplace. Unfortunately, she forgot to open the damper. It took her mother two days to get the smell of smoking polyester out of the house.

It was the smell of grilling bratwurst that wafted through the screen door of Al Cerwinski's house the following afternoon. Teddy was snapping photos—Anna waving a pickle like a cigar, Lydia weeping over chopped onions, Al carrying a platter piled high with sausage to the dining room table. A feeding frenzy ensued during which four people devoured eleven brats, two quarts of potato salad, one quart of coleslaw, and innumerable dill pickles.

When everyone was sated, Al went into the kitchen to make expresso. In the living room three excited voices vied for air time, interrupting, increasing in volume, stopping for the occasional breath. The din subsided somewhat when Al walked to through the kitchen door, carrying a tray bearing, sugar, a coffee carafe and four small cups. His giant hands dwarfed the cups as he handed one to each woman. "Perfect timing. We're done talking about you," said Anna.

"You're sure? I am very easily humiliated."

"See," said Lydia. "He's the perfect man. He makes coffee, he cooks, and he's humble."

"Yeah, but how is he in the sack?" asked Teddy, a twinkle in her big, green eyes.

Lydia offered a double thumbs-up while the unflappable Al Cerwinski blushed right up to his thinning hair line. The conversation resumed. Al sat quietly with a bemused smile on his face as the stories poured forth. He had met Teddy for the first time the day before, but over the last year he had heard wonderful tales of her daring-do and chutzpa. Anna was saying, "We did a lot outrageous stuff in Ann Arbor. Remember the time Teddy crashed the Chamber of Commerce parade on her Honda 125 dirt bike."

"Yup," said Lydia. "She snuck in behind the tubas. She was wearing short-shorts, a chain-mail bra and a Viking helmet with horns."

"And when a campus cop tried to chase her down, she drove up the steps of the Union, straight into the ladies' room," added Anna.

"Hey," said Teddy, "I had to pee."

"Speaking of urination," said Lydia, "there was the time we carried that old commode to the front of Angell Hall just before the homecoming game."

Anna broke in. "We had painted it gold with a sign that said *Go Blue*."

Breathless with laughter, Lydia added, "A couple of drunk frat boys unzipped and peed in it right in front a cluster of ancient alums." She paused to catch her breath. "One old lady moved in close, pointed to the drunkest kid and said, 'You call that a dick?'"

Al howled. "So why this trip to the Yukon?" he asked when he finally composed himself. "Did you come up to fish or to see these charming lunatics?"

"Both and neither," said Teddy. "My primary reason was a job. A year ago I got a second master's degree. This one is in ichthyology. I traded in *The Old Man and the Sea* for his marlin. I finally got a short-term gig. I'm working on a salmon count on the Yukon River near the Alaska border. They gave each of us a week off to take whenever we want over the summer; I decided to use it all up at once. I did some fishing on Lake Laberge, checked out the attractions in Whitehorse, and then came up to Dawson to see my friends."

"Why in the hell are you counting salmon?" asked Lydia.

"Turns out that salmon counting is a very big deal. You probably know that the Alaskans and Canadians have been fighting for decades about who catches which fish and where during the salmon run."

Al broke in. "You got that right." His voice boomed. "Those Alaska fishermen are greedy bastards. They've been taking more than their share of fish for sixty years. By the time the salmon get to Canada, their numbers are seriously depleted. It's bad for

the salmon stock and the Canadian fishermen don't get squat."
Lydia's mouth opened in surprise. Al was not prone to public
emotional outbursts. "I can't tell you how much time and money
has been spent on treaties and agreements." Al's voice grew even
louder, his faced flushed, and he waved his big hands in the air.
"We make 'em; the Alaskans break 'em."

Lydia raised her hand. "Chill, Sergeant. Seafood is not in
your job description."

"Sergeant!" said Teddy. "Lydia never told me you were in the
military."

"I'm not," said Al. "I'm a Mountie.

"Recently promoted," said Lydia proudly.

"As in Royal Canadian Mounted Police?" Al nodded.

"You mean to tell me Sergeant Preston is real?" said Teddy
with a grin.

"Honest to God," said Al, raising his right hand. "I've got
the red outfit, the shiny black boots, the Smokey-the-bear hat—
everything."

"And," said Lydia, "on Canada Day he gets to ride a horse
with a Maple leaf shaved on its ass."

"How humiliating for the horse," said Teddy.

"I'd rather talk about your job, Teddy. Are you working for
some sort of agency?" Al asked.

Teddy nodded. "It's a joint project, Fisheries and Oceans
Canada and Alaska Fish and Game. We've got researchers from
both sides of the border."

"So how do you actually count the salmon?" asked Lydia.

"We catch them in fish wheels." The others nodded. Fish
wheels are part of the landscape on northern rivers. Constructed
of wood, metal, and chicken wire, they look like small Ferris
wheels on stationary rafts. The principle is simple–the current
rotates a wheel, which scoops migrating salmon into a basket,
then drops them into a holding box. Most of the fish wheels
on the Yukon belong to subsistence fishermen but a few were
managed by government agencies for research purposes.

Teddy continued. "We can't count every fish, of course. It's a sampling process. They're tagged at one of the counting stations downstream in Alaska."

"What exactly do *you* do?" asked Lydia.

"My specialty is determining age." She cocked her head and gave Lydia a long stare. "I'd say you're a forty-five year old Lake Michigan largemouth bass." Al grinned. Lydia ignored both of them.

"So how do you tell the age of a fish whose driver's license you've never seen? Count the rings like a tree?" Lydia laughed at her own joke but Teddy nodded vigorously. "That's it! That's exactly what we do."

Lydia snorted. "Come on! You're pulling my leg. That's impossible."

"No, really," said Teddy. "Fish have this ear bone. It's called an *otolith*. It's near the fish's brain and over time it gets bigger and bigger as calcium carbonate crystallizes. The calcium leaves rings. You can actually cut the otolith and count the rings."

"That's amazing," said Al. "I had no idea." He paused and grinned. "So, if you swallow an ear bone, does that improve your herring."

A huge smile spread over Teddy's face. "Oh my cod, that was bad," she replied.

"Mullet over," said Al.

"I bait he can't keep this up," said Teddy. "He's floundering."

Lydia put her hands over her face. "Why did I ever introduce them," she muttered between her fingers.

"Anyhow," said Teddy, "one of the goals of our site is to assess the health of the fish we catch. The health assessment is really about the health of river. Are the fish being affected by toxins in the water, that kind of thing. There are other fish counting stations along the Yukon, but we're the only one checking on the condition of the fish."

"What do you do when you're not torturing salmon?" asked Al.

14

Teddy smiled broadly. "I motor over to Fools Gold Village and look for old mining artifacts. I'm told it was a very active mining community at the turn of the twentieth century. It's quite wonderful."

"I've never been there," said Lydia, "but Al has a big, coffee table book about it. The pictures are amazing. I gather that a lot of the old buildings are still standing."

Teddy nodded. "There's a bunch of old mining artifacts strewn around the woods, too." Al's eyes narrowed and Teddy picked up on it immediately. "Oh, I don't take anything, but I photograph it all. I've already got about five hundred pictures stored on my laptop."

"You've got a solar powered laptop?" said Anna.

"We have a generator in camp, you numbskull. How do you think we keep our champagne and caviar cold?"

"There's not enough champagne in the world to make me cut open fish heads," replied Anna.

"Enough about me," said Teddy. She pointed at Anna. "I can see that Lydia is doing fine in the love-life department. How about you?"

"At the moment," said Anna primly, "I am between men."

"That's because she's used them all up," said Lydia. There was some truth to this. At forty five Anna was still adorable. She was small, trim, and athletic with an Audrey Hepburn face, big brown eyes, and Harpo Marx hair.

"I still can't believe you moved up here," said Teddy. "A Brooklyn Jew in the sub-arctic. It's too damn funny. Has your mother come to terms with your moving to the wilds of Canada?"

Anna snorted. "She can't stand the fact that I'm dating nothing but *goyim*. Mom was ecstatic while I was dating Jack Shapiro, but when she found out that he was a Cambodian adoptee, she gave up on me. And she can't imagine how anyone can survive without a good Jewish deli. The last time she came to visit she almost got busted for bringing lox and creamed herring in her carry-on luggage."

"You're kidding," said Al.

"Airport Security said she couldn't take the herring aboard—something about gels and three ounce containers. They confiscated all of it. Mom yelled bloody murder and pulled everything out of the trash bin, screaming *gonif* at the top of her lungs. TSA agents began to assemble. There was going to be a showdown between a ninety five pound Jewish matron and two federal officers the size of Volkswagons. Mom stuffed the food back into her carry-on and stalked off to find a more accommodating TSA agent. Luckily, she found one named Finklestein, who knew exactly what creamed herring costs at Zabar's."

Al chuckled. "I can't believe your mother brought lox to the smoked-salmon capital of North America."

"My mother thinks New York is the smoked-salmon capital of the universe."

"Troy, he's a little boy at the camp, would be outraged," said Teddy. "He built his own salmon smoker. His fish is to die for."

"A kid at a research camp? Isn't that a bit odd?" asked Al.

"Oh, he doesn't belong to a researcher. Turns out there aren't many good places to establish a camp along that stretch of the river, so we're sharing an area with a group of five mushroom hunters. They were there first. The child belongs to one of them. It works out well. We share our tent kitchen and privy with them, and they help with the cooking and other chores. Turns out that morel season and the summer run of chum salmon more or less coincide."

"So you're cleaning up your language for the kid," said Lydia

"Fuckin' A," replied Teddy.

"Do you like your campmates?" asked Anna.

"We all get along pretty well."

Teddy paused and then chuckled. "Well, that might not be strictly true. One of my campmates may have a problem with my sexual orientation."

"How so?" asked Al.

"For a short time I was finding wonderfully silly notes in my tent—cut and paste jobs. Real junior high stuff. One called me a *Diesel Dyke*. Dainty little ole me. Can you imagine!" Teddy lowered her chin to her chest, made two fists, raised her arms into goal posts, and flexed her impressive biceps. "Another one said *Vagaterian* with three exclamation points. I love that one. Whoever left them was a bit unclear on the terminology though. One called me a *fag hag*." Teddy snorted.

Lydia wasn't smiling. "Doesn't that make you nervous, knowing there's somebody there who's hostile to gays?"

"Nah. I've been listening to this kind of crap since I was fourteen. It's so silly and antiquated that it doesn't feel like genuine homophobia. It seems more like a prank. If somebody gets in my face, I'll just hit 'em with a good dose of bear spray." She flashed Lydia a broad smile. "I sure wish I'd had some of that when Professor Warnicke grabbed my tits in his office way back when."

"Oh," said Lydia. "I think stomping on his instep and breaking his metatarsal was punishment enough."

Al's eyes widened. "You really did that?"

"It wasn't the first time I've resorted to brute force, darlin'. You wouldn't believe how many Neanderthals think that all a lesbian needs is a good lay." Al blushed again and Teddy laughed merrily.

Anna looked at her watch. "I promised to take Teddy up to Midnight Dome this evening so we should shove off."

"I have to go back to camp tomorrow," said Teddy, "so this is our last hurrah. But I think you guys should come up and visit for a few days. The summer chum salmon run is winding down, and things will be slow for a couple of weeks. No one will mind."

Anna sighed. "My work schedule is too tight right now. Maybe later in the summer."

Lydia grimaced. "Damn. I really want to get back to my cabin; it's been so long." She pressed her lips together and paused for a long time. She put her hand on Teddy's arm and squeezed. "But who knows when I will see you again." She paused again and then pulled Teddy into a bear hug. "I'll come, but I need a few days in Dawson first." A shadow passed over her face. "I haven't been on that stretch of river since Dad died." "I'll draw you a map," said Teddy. "Show up anytime. There's almost always someone in camp." Al provided paper and pen and Teddy drew a crude rendition of the Yukon River with various landmarks indicated."

After hugs all around, Anna and Teddy departed. An hour later Al went out to pick up a *Yukon News*. When he returned, he slapped the paper on the dining room table with a grim look on his face. Lydia gave a sharp intake of breath when she realized that the aerial picture on the front page was the same hideous landscape she and Teddy had witnessed the day before. Somehow the fact that the photo was black and white made everything look grimmer, more ominous.

The article noted that the person who had been carried away on the stretcher was a woman. She did not work at the mine and mine security had no idea how she had gained access. No one knew her or knew why she was there. The mine authorities knew only that a truck with a payload capacity of two-hundred-fifty tons had run over her, crushing her abdomen and legs and severing her femoral artery. The coroner said she died instantly. The woman had apparently been crouching behind a small rock pile and the truck driver said that he had not seen her. He didn't realize he had hit her until he saw her lying in the dirt on his return trip.

The article went on to say that the victim had carried nothing on her person and was as yet unidentified. The story was accompanied by a morgue photo and a plea for anyone who recognized her to come forward. The picture showed a middle-aged, first Nation woman, slight of build, with high cheekbones and a sharp chin. Her hair was long and straight. Her mouth was partly open and her teeth were crooked and stained. There were deep furrows in her brow and around her mouth. What struck Lydia most was how sad and used-up she looked. She was very thin and, even in death, she looked exhausted. Lydia shuddered. She folded the paper to hide the photograph and looked at Al. "What if no one ever identifies her? What if there is no one to grieve for her? To die alone is a terrible thing."

Al put his hands on Lydia's shoulders. "Worse than that, in a few days everyone will have forgotten about her.

CHAPTER 3

It was true. Three days later even Lydia had forgotten about the dead woman. She had spent the last five months in Fairbanks, Alaska teaching. Now she was busy catching up with friends, gorging on lamb souvlaki at the Drunken Goat, and listening to the Pointer Brothers play at the Arm Pit Lounge.

On day four she was ready to visit Teddy. Since it made no sense to motor sixty miles south to her cabin and then travel one hundred miles back north to the camp, she would leave from Dawson. Al drove Lydia, her duffle bag, a canteen, and a cooler packed with sandwiches and fruit down to the river. Lydia's battered metal thermos sat in her lap. It was filled to the brim with Colombian Supremo and she could feel its warmth through her jeans. Lydia's battered old skiff rattled and bounced behind Al's Explorer on a flimsy, borrowed boat trailer.

Al backed the trailer to the edge of the river and slid the boat down the rails and into the water. He threw Lydia's duffle bag into the bow while she climbed into the stern. He handed her the cooler and shoved the boat into an eddy. She lowered the engine and hit the starter. The first spark caught. Al blew her a kiss from the bank as she steered her mottled old craft into the current. She turned, waved to Al, saluted the old landslide scar above Dawson, and gunned the throttle.

Most of Lydia's time on the Yukon River was spent motoring between Dawson and her summer cabin. She rarely went north so this trip had the feel of an adventure. Within a few minutes she reached what remained of Moosehide. Once a thriving Indian village, Moosehide was reduced to a ghost town in the 1950s when the schoolteacher left and funding disappeared. The only permanent residents were those who lay under the white wooden crosses dotting the hillside.

Through the brush on the other side of the river, Lydia could see another graveyard. This was the final resting place of the old riverboats which, for ninety years, had provided a lifeline to Dawson and other river towns. A few were eventually restored as museums, but others were laid to rest here on the banks of the Yukon. The two-story paddle wheels were still visible among the trees, but the cabins, decks, and wheel houses had been reduced to rotting lumber long ago.

As the riverbank slipped by, Lydia drank coffee, ate a roast beef sandwich, and enjoyed nature's show. She reduced her speed to watch a black bear ambling aimlessly along the river's edge. When he reached a spot where the current cascaded over a pile of rocks and pooled at their base, he paused. He peered into the pool and cocked his head. Suddenly, he leapt into the water and began to slap it with his front paws, turning the pool into a fountain. When he returned to the shore, Lydia could see that he had a huge salmon in his jaws, a chum who was late for the run.

The bear dropped the fish and pinned its head with one paw. The salmon's tail continued to flap and the gills continued to pulsate as the bear systematically stripped off the skin and ate it. Then he bit off the head and sucked out the brains. Finally, he stuck his nose into the fish's belly and wrapped his tongue around a long strand of golden roe. When he raised his head to glance at Lydia, a ribbon of fish eggs hung from his muzzle. When the bear ambled away, a bald eagle flew down to inspect the eviscerated fish. It plucked an eyeball from the severed head and swallowed it.

As Lydia gunned her engine, a large flock of Canada geese appeared overhead. They passed over the boat and she tilted her head back to get a good look. Wings out, necks stretched long, feet tucked in, they were graceful and elegant in flight—except for the incessant honking, which sounded like a truck engine that had run out of oil.

That's when Lydia became aware of another noise upriver. She turned and saw something that resembled a large building bearing down on her. She was almost blinded by the sunlight reflecting off its front windows. "Oh, shit," she yelled. "It's the goddam Queen." The Yukon Queen (Yukon Queen II, to be exact) was a high speed, two story catamaran, a jet boat that carried tourists from Dawson to Eagle, Alaska and back. The damn thing was almost a hundred feet long and, despite Holland America's claims that it created a minimal wake, it routinely flipped canoes and washed small boats right out of the river.

Before Lydia could reach the relative safety of a deep channel, the Queen passed her, creating a rolling wall of water that slammed her boat into the rocky shore, again and again. Passengers waved at her from behind the tinted windows. Lydia shook her fist at the cat's retreating stern. "Slow down, you son of a bitch," she screamed. A fish wheel creaked and moaned at the river's edge when it, too, was buffeted by the Queen's wake.

As Lydia approached the old mining camp at Fools Gold Creek, she could see the roof line of a tall building. Most of the village was obscured by small spruce forest and a low thicket of alders. She'd check this place out before she returned to Dawson. A few minutes later she heard the roar of water. She rounded a bend and quickly moved river right to avoid the turbulence created by a log jam at the mouth of a fast tributary. A few minutes after that there was flash of white above the trees which quickly morphed into a Maple Leaf flag. She rounded a curve and the mushroom camp came into view.

It was a compact little settlement close to the riverbank. Five boats were pulled up on the gravel. One was relatively new and sported an *Alaska Department of Fish and Game* seal. The other four wore signs of long hard use on shallow rivers and rocky shores. Lydia landed her boat beside the others, tied it to a clump of alders, grabbed her duffle and cooler, and traversed a well-worn path. She stood at the edge of the little encampment and looked around. There was no one in sight.

She wandered through the campsite. The place was a study in contrasts. At one end of the clearing stood five faded nylon tents and one ancient umbrella affair. The rain flies on two of the tents had been patched with duct tape and a pole on another had been repaired with a tiny hose clamp. The four dome tents at the other end were large and new. Four folding lounge chairs sat basking in the afternoon sun. Laundry flapped on line that had been suspended between two trees. The clothes were secured by old fashioned, wooden clothes pins. Some of the shirts and pants were stained with resin and pitch and all of the clothes wore a rusty cast, tannin from Yukon River water.

Two screen houses had been erected beyond the residential area. Both were large and sturdy with metal screen doors and clear flaps that could be lowered in heavy rain. One contained three long worktables, folding chairs, and metal storage trunks. The second was a kitchen equipped with three large propane burners, a plastic sink with a long drain hose that ran along the ground, more folding tables and chairs, and a strange looking appliance powered by a quiet gas generator. Crates of pots and pans sat under long wooden tables and propane canisters littered the ground behind the tent. Two shotguns and a rifle leaned against a pile of crates near the entrance. At the very end of the clearing Lydia could see a tall, narrow white canvas structure with a tin stack—a portable privy.

The camp seemed deserted. Only the sound of the river and the buzzing of mosquitoes broke the silence. Lydia called out a few times but no one answered. She dropped her load, pulled a book out of her bag and an apple out of her cooler, and settled into one of the folding camp chairs. She had finished the apple and was looking for her place in a Patrick O'Brien novel when she heard a sneeze. She looked up. There was no one there. Then she heard another sneeze followed by the sound of someone blowing a nose.

"Hey," she said. "Is somebody here?"

A voice emanated from the canvas umbrella tent. "I am," it said. Lydia couldn't tell if the speaker was male or female.

Lydia got up and approached the tent. "I'm looking for Teddy Gianopoulous. Do you know where she is?"

"The tent door zipper moved up and a head and pair of shoulders pushed through the opening. They belonged to a young boy. He looked to be eight or nine. The child crawled out of the tent and zipped the door behind him. He stood slowly and gave Lydia a wary stare with large hazel eyes. He didn't return her smile.

The boy was small and wiry. His face and arms were deeply tanned. His brown hair was streaked with auburn and it had been inexpertly bowl-cut, making him look like an early Beatle. "Are you a friend of Teddy G.'s?" the child asked.

Lydia nodded. "Yes. We went to college together."

Are you a *ikiologist*, too?"

"No, I'm a teacher."

The boy's wariness gave way to curiosity. He inspected Lydia closely, then cocked his head. "You don't look like a teacher. I had a teacher once and you don't look anything like her."

Lydia looked down at her rumpled shirt and her oft mended jeans. Her hiking boots were filthy and she could only imagine the condition of her windblown hair. "No, I suppose I don't. I'm Lydia Falkner. What's your name?"

"Troy Sherman. My dad's a mushroom picker." The boy stuck out a grimy hand and shook hers.

"Do you know when Teddy will be back?"

The boy shrugged. "Nope." His mouth turned down into a small pout. "She went 'sploring and I'm a little mad at her."

"Why?" asked Lydia.

"She usually takes me 'sploring, too, but she wouldn't today."

"Do you hang out with Teddy a lot?"

Troy nodded and gave Lydia a soft smile. "She's nice to me and she treats me like a grownup. Some of the people here treat me like I'm a little kid. Teddy, she don't do that. She listens to me. I like her a lot. I don't care if she's a *letsbean*."

Lydia stiffened. "Who told you that?"

Troy shuffled his feet in the dirt. "Sam made a joke about it. My dad says I shouldn't listen to Sam, that he's an *egoramus*."

Lydia breathed out.

The child walked around Lydia, inspecting her clothes and her boots. He took a long look at the small fanny pack Lydia wore at her waist. "How come you got a purse?" he asked. "It's dumb to have a purse on the river."

"This isn't a purse. This is my Bobo bag."

"Huh? What's a bobo?"

"Bobo was a friend of mine. He told me about a guy who stepped out onto the riverbank without grabbing his bowline and his boat caught a wave."

Troy immediately grasped the implications of the story. "And everything floated away, right? He didn't have no clothes or food or a tent or nothin'."

"Exactly," said Lydia. "He almost died in the wilderness. I didn't want that happen to me, so I put together this little pouch and I wear it whenever I go out on the river. It's got matches in waterproof container, fire starter, a space blanket that folds up to nothing, a signal mirror, some cord, and iodine tablets for water."

Troy nodded with approval. "That's a real good idea." He paused and then grinned. "Hey, you wanna see the burn? The pickers are all done with the worst part. It's real cool and kinda spooky."

Lydia knew that morel mushrooms were the fruit of forest fire. By word of mouth, by phone, by e-mail and web postings, mushroom pickers learn about areas that had burned the previous year. One by one, they converge on the remotest of sites. Navigating a landscape of ash, charred brush, and downed trees, they uncover morels, a commodity which per pound is often the most expensive item at the supermarket.

"I'd love to see the burn," she said.

"We'll need some energy for the walk. Do you like salmon?" Lydia nodded and Troy pulled a small paper bag from his pocket. He extracted two stiff pieces of dried fish. Bits of lint and sand clung to them. Lydia took a bite. Her eyes opened wide. Nothing in Brooklyn could compare with this confection. It was tender and chewy and tasted like honey and wood smoke.

"I made it myself," said Troy.

"It's the best I've ever had," said Lydia. "Would it be rude to ask for more?"

Troy grinned and handed her the bag. She limited her intake to two more strips but it wasn't easy. She returned the bag with regret. Troy took her hand and led her toward a trail. The taste of smoked salmon lingered on her tongue.

After a five minute walk through a lush spruce forest, they came upon the first signs of fire. Small pieces of charred wood lay in the path and bits of grey ash clung to sedges and cotton grass. In another five minutes they encountered significant fire debris—small, blackened trees that had toppled like pick-up sticks, huge nests of charred alder and willow, piles of incinerated pine needles, and leaves reduced to skeletons. A few shriveled morels were scattered among the needles.

The more Lydia and Troy walked, the more surreal the landscape became. Cracked and blistered, the bark on the tall white spruce trees looked like alligator hide. Some trees had been shorn of limbs, their tops forged into spear points by flames. Many trees had fallen. Those remaining upright leaned against each other at crazy angles.

As Lydia looked around her, the entire landscape was black and shades of grey. She felt as though she were standing in the middle of a charcoal drawing. But when she looked down, she was greeted by a palette of magenta, green, and yellow. The fireweed was true to its name; its underground rhizomes had survived last year's conflagration and now the leggy flowering stalks were reclaiming the forest floor.

"Let's sit," said Lydia. She crossed her left ankle over her right and lowered herself to the ground. A little plume of soot rose, tickling her nose. Troy plopped down with less ceremony. Fireweed towered over his head. Lydia picked a purple flower and chewed on it. It was sweet. She pushed the fireweed aside and gazed intently at the ground. The forest floor was teeming with life—fragile grasses, sturdy little sedges, and tiny green shoots that might become baby alders or birches or even spruce.

Lydia had expected silence in this wasted land but she had been wrong. With her head this close to the ground, she was enveloped in sound. The metallic buzzing of bees came in waves, waxing in one ear, waning in the other. A small dragon fly with diaphanous green wings hummed softly as it flew past Lydia's nose and landed on her shoulder. She could hear the skittering of a large black beetle as it chewed into a blackened log just beyond her knee. The sharp rat-a-tat-tat above proved to be the work of a flicker chiseling out a hole high in a dead spruce. Little warblers wearing various shades of brown chirped thinly as they scampered in the new growth looking for seeds.

"It's beautiful in here," said Lydia.

Troy nodded and gave her a satisfied smile which was almost immediately supplanted by a look of panic. "Uh, oh" he muttered.

"What's wrong?"

"We gotta go back. I promised Bob I wouldn't leave camp. There's nobody else there and sometimes porcupines come and chew on stuff."

Lydia stood up and brushed ash off her butt. "You lead. I'm utterly lost."

"I know a short-cut," said Troy.

He took Lydia's hand again and they bushwhacked through high grass and alders. At one point Lydia stopped and sniffed the air. "Something smells bad."

"It's a dead animal. Things die in the wilderness, you know," said Troy with a hint of condescension.

"This is a particularly stinky thing," said Lydia, wrinkling her nose. She looked up. Ravens were circling high above them. Did they smell it, too? Lydia scanned the ground for the carcass of a hare or ground squirrel, but the area appeared corpse free.

The camp was porcupine free when they broke through the woods, and Bob was nowhere in sight. Troy heaved a sigh of relief. "You won't tell on me, will you?"

"Cross my heart," said Lydia.

Troy broke into a big grin. "Bob doesn't get mad like other people. He doesn't get all red and yell and stuff. Instead, he snaps his suspenders. One time he snapped them so hard his pants fell down."

"I'm glad we didn't give Bob any reason to snap them at us," said Lydia.

Troy went to wash his hands. Lydia was about to lower herself into a folding chair when she heard something crashing through the wood, something much larger than a porcupine. A moment later a tall, slender man broke into the clearing. He was carrying a tower of plastic crates in a backpack frame. His clothes were black from the crown of his hat to the tips of his gloves to the soles of his hiking boots. His face was virtually invisible behind a mask of dirt and soot; the hair that lay in a ponytail on the back of his neck was stiff with grime and sweat. As he approached the center of the clearing, the filthy man fixed his large blue eyes on Lydia and broke into a smile, cracking the dirt around his eyes and mouth. "Oh, my God," he cried with just a trace of a foreign accent. He shrugged one shoulder, sloughed off one pack strap, and lowered his burden to the ground. Then he loped to Lydia's side and enveloped her in his long arms.

Lydia stiffened. She turned her face away from his grimy shirt and began to push him away. Then she remembered the voice. "Oh my God, it's Karl!" She wriggled out of the man's arms and looked up at him. "Karl Kovacs!" This time Lydia did the hugging. When she stepped away, Troy giggled and pointed at her shirt. Lydia looked down. Karl's grimy embrace had left a black smudge on each of her khaki-clad breasts.

Lydia walked over and inspected the crates that Karl had been hauling. They were filled to the brim with mushrooms. Plump, triangular, and deeply ridged, the morels looked like tiny faceless gnomes. "Wow," she said. "They're perfect."

"Yup," said Karl. "We've got a good crop in there. I may be able to eat this winter."

"I can't believe you're here," said Lydia, squeezing his arm.

"Hey, this is a mushroom camp and I'm a mushroom picker. But why in heaven's name are *you* here?"

I'm here to visit Teddy Gianopoulous for a few days. She's an old college pal of mine."

"You're kidding! You know Teddy?" Lydia nodded. "She's a great gal. We spend a lot of time exploring the river together. I've been showing her how to navigate the side channels. We make music together now and then, too."

"Ah," said Lydia. "So you're the harmonica player she told me about."

Karl bowed. "That would be me. We also team up for cooking. She makes a morel stew that's *finom*."

"What's *finom*?" asked Troy. "I thought morel stew was just mushrooms."

Karl rumpled the boy's hair. "*Finom* is Hungarian for delicious."

"What's *Hungarian*? Is that like being hungry?"

Karl rolled his eyes at Lydia. "Troy has been the recipient of some spotty home schooling."

"Ah, that explains his 'I had a teacher once' remark," said Lydia.

"I *did* have a teacher once," said Troy. "Her name was Mrs. Prinzing. She was mean. I hated her. I like being home schooled."

"Does your mom teach you while your dad is picking?" asked Lydia.

"No," said Troy, looking down at his shoes. His voice became a whisper. "My mum's gone." Then he looked up, his face angry, his mouth set in a hard line. "She ain't never coming back."

Karl put his hands on the boy's shoulders and massaged them.

"Troy's dad and grandmother teach him. Apparently, they haven't gotten to geography yet." Karl left his hands on Troy's shoulders as he described the glories of his Budapest childhood.

By the time he was done, Troy had relaxed. "But how come you don't live in Hungary anymore?" he asked. "Didn't you like it?"

"I did like it. But when I was younger than you, my grandfather bought a picture book about the Yukon River. I was fascinated. The book inspired me to learn English and then I read everything about the Yukon I could get my hands on. I decided that when I was grown, I would come here. And I did."

Troy nodded. "Yeah. I'd rather be out here in the woods than anywhere in the world." He raised his eyes to the sky and pointed at an eagle circling high above the camp. "You can't see that in any damn ole school."

Karl swatted the boy gently on the back of his head. "No cursing in front of ladies."

Lydia snorted. "Lady, my as ... uh, foot."

Troy pointed at Lydia and stamped his own foot with glee. "You were going to say ass. I knew you weren't a real teacher."

CHAPTER 4

Lydia and her father had met Karl Kovacs nine years ago when Karl was working a burn near Otto's property. Karl had approached the cabin one rainy afternoon in search of fuel for his boat. Otto had invited the picker in for lunch and the next thing Lydia knew the two men were laughing and swapping stories like old friends. The picking season was nearly over, so Karl had stayed for four days. From then on Karl would appear on the Falkner doorstep once or twice a summer with a bag full of moose jerky in one hand and a jar of gravlax in the other.

"You and I have a lot of catching up to do," said Karl. He squeezed Lydia's shoulder. Her stomach tightened as she nodded. Catching up would include sharing two pieces of terrible news. "I'll get cleaned up and then we can talk." He checked his watch. "I wonder where Teddy is. She's usually back by now."

Karl pulled his toiletry kit, clean clothes, and a towel from the tent. As he headed for the river, Lydia checked her own watch. It was 4:30. Where *was* Teddy? She plopped into a deck chair and opened her book. Troy sat cross-legged on the ground next to her, pulled a small knife out of his pocket, and began whittling on a thick stick of alder. Lydia could hear Karl bellowing the refrain from *Whiskey River* as he splashed in the 55 degree water. She had just finished the first chapter of *HMS Surprise* when Troy tapped her on the knee and presented her with the product of his labors, a perfect old-fashioned clothespin.

A few minutes later Karl climbed back over the river bank. He was wearing a clean T shirt and jeans and his boots were mud free. His wet hair was the color of daffodils.

"How about a beer?"

"Sure," said Lydia.

"Come on over to the kitchen. You can choose what you want from our splendid stash of brews. Troy, would you go find Bob and tell him that we have a guest for dinner?"

"Sure, I will," said Troy. He trotted off toward the trees.

Lydia settled into one of the metal chairs under the kitchen canopy. Karl pulled a crumpled pack from his shirt pocket and extracted a cigarette. He put it into his mouth without lighting it. "I'm trying to quit," he explained as he opened the door of the odd appliance. He extracted two Labatts. He patted the refrigerator door. "This is a bear-proof refrigerator. Oceans Canada had it specially designed.

"You know," he said, settling back into his chair, "I stopped by your cabin two summers ago and it looked abandoned. I was afraid Otto had sold it."

Lydia's looked down at her beer bottle. She picked at the label. "You haven't heard about my dad." It wasn't a question.

Karl frowned and leaned forward. "No. Did something happen to him?"

"He's dead, Karl."

Karl lost his grip on his beer bottle, spilling its contents on his freshly cleaned boots. The bottle landed in the dirt with a gentle thud. "Dead," he whispered. "Jesus."

"He died on the river five years ago. Our boat turned over in a storm. He drowned. I didn't go back to the cabin for three years after that. Last summer was my first trip back to the Yukon."

Lydia took a deep breath. "I've got more bad news." Her voice cracked. "Frank—Frank Johnson was murdered last year."

"Mary, mother of God," muttered Karl. He clutched the seat of his chair and his face went white. It took Lydia half an hour to tell Karl the story of Frank's murder and its aftermath. When it was over, Karl simply stared at her and shook his head. There was nothing to say.

Their silence was punctuated by the arrival of more mushroom pickers. One by one they emerged from the trees, gray ghosts in muddy hiking boots. Their faces were unreadable under the patina of dirt and ash, their clothes were stiff with sweat, and their halting gaits reflected exhaustion.

They shrugged off their backpack frames outside the kitchen tent. Lydia could see that the crates they were carrying were decorated with flagging tape; each picker's crates flew a different color.

"What happens now?" asked Lydia.

"We wait for the buyers," said Karl. "They fly into Eagle and then come up here by boat. They'll be here in about an hour. I'd better go get my mushrooms."

As Karl exited, he was greeted by three newcomers as they entered the kitchen tent. The last one in let the door bang and in unison they turned to face Lydia. Their faces were not welcoming. Lydia suddenly realized that they had no idea who she was or why she was there. She smiled. No one smiled back.

"Who are *you*?" asked a man in a bright red sweatshirt as Karl opened the door and reentered. "We already got all the pickers this patch can support." He took a few steps closer to Lydia. "There ain't no room for you."

Karl glared at him. "Sam, where are your manners? She's not a picker. This is Lydia Falkner. She's an old friend of mine, but actually she came to visit Teddy G."

The man named Sam was tall and solidly built with a long nose and large, dark eyes. He was hatless and his thick brown hair was festooned with bark and bits of soot and ash. His hands were large, calloused, and scarred. "Why? Is she her girlfriend?"

Lydia smiled. "No, we're just old friends. I like men." At this Sam stood up straighter and tried to comb the bark out of his hair with his fingers. "Besides, I thought it would be interesting to see the salmon counting operation."

Sam's look was contemptuous. "Shit, that's not interesting. We're the ones with interesting jobs. Why I could tell you things that would make …"

Karl interrupted him. "Sam, let me introduce Lydia before you get started." The guy with the stories was Sam Avakian. The other two were Bob Dunlap and Liz Nguyen. Their hair was covered by broad brimmed hats and their faces were invisible behind a crust of grime.

Just then the screen door slammed and a fifth picker entered the tent. He looked to be in his early forties. He had already washed and Lydia could see that his face was deeply lined from many years in the sun. "This is Red Sherman," said Karl. "He's Troy's dad. Red, this is Lydia Falkner. She's come up to see Teddy." Red gave Lydia a curt nod as he fixed his startlingly blue eyes on hers. She was surprised to find that Red's name had not been inspired by his hair. It was brown and, like Troy's, inexpertly cut.

"Okay," said the oldest picker, Bob Dunlap. He was a plump man with a grey beard and a long, white pony tail speckled with soot and streaked with ash. He wore his pants below his substantial gut and held them up with wide, purple suspenders. "We'd better get our asses in gear. The buyers'll be here soon."

There was a flurry of activity. Liz, Bob, and Sam trooped down to the river to wash hands and faces. Then three folding tables and six chairs were carried down to the bank. Three balance scales appeared from somewhere. Sam grabbed a cooler of water and some plastic cups. In fifteen minutes, the bank of the Yukon looked like a street market.

Lydia followed Liz Nguyen, who had changed into clean jeans and a tank top featuring a scowling Scrooge McDuck. Liz was Asian and slight of build, but a summer of picking and carrying had given her impressive shoulder and arm muscles. Her straight black hair was evenly cut just below her ears and parted on one side, the perfect hairdo for wilderness living.

Liz sat down on the river bank and patted the ground next to her. "Join me," she said.

"What do you do in winter," asked Lydia as she plopped down.

"I'm a grad student at Simon Fraser University. Picking pays my tuition."

"How does this work? Do you need a permit? Liz nodded.

"Do the buyers always come to you?"

"Yeah, it's a lot more efficient this way. These mushrooms will be on a plane to Vancouver or Seattle in less than twenty four hours, where people will pay outrageous prices for microscopic plates of morels in wine sauce. This is an especially good year. For some reason this patch is producing mushrooms later than usual." Liz put her hand to her ear and cocked her head toward the river. "Here come the buyers now."

Lydia threw Liz a skeptical glance; she couldn't hear any sign of a boat. But sure enough, a few moments later the breeze carried the low rumble of an outboard. She heard the crunch of gravel as a boat landed on the riverbank just out of sight. A moment later, she heard the engine again and saw an old aluminum craft head back into the current. Liz frowned and put her hand over her eyes to block out the sun. "Who the hell is that? It's certainly not the buyers."

Lydia shaded her eyes as she watched a tall individual wearing a broad brimmed hat trudge up the embankment. The hat covered the hair and shadowed the face. Could it be Teddy? No, this person was too slender and the gait was wrong.

"Jesus Christ," said Liz, shielding her eyes against the sun. "That's Gretchen but where's her boat?" Lydia could see that the woman walking toward them looked exhausted. Her mouth was set in a grim line and her eyes narrowed a she scanned the group milling around the bank. Lydia noted that her clothes were full of snags and there were twigs in her hair. Her high rubber boots were caked with mud.

"Has Teddy come back to camp?" she asked Liz. Her voice was tight and angry.

"Not as far as I know. I thought she supposed to pick you up at the number one fish wheel."

"She was. Six hours ago. She never showed. I hitched a ride

with that fisherman."

Lydia's chest tightened. "She dropped you off and never came back?"

The woman glared at her. "Who the hell are you?"

"My name is Lydia Falkner. I'm an old friend of Teddy's."

The woman's voice lost its edge. "Oh. I'm Gretchen Lawler. I'm Teddy's supervisor on the salmon project. Teddy said she was going exploring. She didn't say where. She dropped me off at seven and promised to be back by ten thirty, but she never came. I spent hours walking up and down the bank looking for that bitch. I climbed over a million logs and waded in some nasty muskeg. I've got blisters on my blisters. I could just kill her."

Lydia bit her lip. "I hope nothing has happened to her."

"Nothing happened to her," said Gretchen sharply. "There's no wind, no rain, no fog. She forgot, that's all. She forgot." Gretchen's face went red.

"Maybe she got stranded somewhere," said Lydia. "Did she have any emergency supplies?"

Gretchen took a few deep breaths and thought a moment. "As far as I know all she had was a day pack and a water bottle. Oh, and she had her camera, like always."

"She was in a Fisheries and Oceans Canada boat," added Liz. Gretchen nodded. Her face was grey with exhaustion now.

"Maybe we should go look for her," said Lydia.

Gretchen shook her head. "Feel free, but I'm not going *anywhere*."

Lydia stood up. "I'll go and take Karl Kovacs with me, if he's willing."

"Fine with me," said Gretchen. "But when you find Teddy, tell her she's fired."

Gretchen and Lydia trudged up the path toward camp, while Liz resumed her wait for the buyers. As Lydia worked to keep up with Gretchen's long stride, she studied the younger woman. Gretchen looked to be in her late-thirties. She was close to six feet tall. Even in loose nylon pants and a baggy long sleeved T shirt, she looked fit and strong. Gretchen's long blond hair was contained in two thick pigtails which reached the middle of her back. Her blue eyes were framed by long lashes and her flawless complexion was set off by rosy cheeks and a small, straight nose. She looked more like a model for L.L. Bean than a researcher in the bush.

The two women parted when they reached camp. Gretchen went to her tent to clean up and Lydia headed for the kitchen. Karl was alone in the tent, pouring himself a cup of coffee. Lydia repeated Gretchen's story. "I'd like to look for her but I don't know the area. Will you go with me?"

"Of course," said Karl. "Liz will sell my mushrooms for me."

"Do know where the number one fish wheel is?

Karl nodded. "Yeah. It's downstream. Not far."

"Let's go," said Lydia.

During the next ten minutes, Karl and Liz struck a deal over mushrooms sales. Then Lydia and Karl loaded water, a medical kit, and a sleeping bag into her boat in case Teddy had capsized. Lydia had just maneuvered the skiff into the current, when she heard another outboard. She turned in her seat to see it. It was a large boat and it slowed as it approached the mushroom camp. Lydia's heart leapt until she realized that the boat held three people. The buyers.

"Crap," she whispered.

CHAPTER 5

It only took Lydia and Karl a few minutes to reach the fish wheel where Gretchen had waited. There was no sign of Teddy. Then they headed for the flags the marked the boundary between Canada and Alaska. A boatload of tourists had stopped to photograph the border but there was no Teddy. Lydia and Karl made a U turn and retraced their path, this time with eyes peeled on the opposite bank.

They passed the camp and a few minutes later Lydia heard the roar of the logjam she had passed earlier in the day. She backed off the throttle and steered the boat toward the middle of the river. On their right side, hundreds of tree trunks and snarls of brush had piled up at the mouth of a wide, fast tributary. The river held the debris in the crook of the sharp bend. Logs were scattered like giant pick-up-sticks and clods of dirt and dry weeds lay atop the scrum. Such jams were common on the Yukon. Every spring the melting snow filled the creeks and rivers to overflowing. The rushing water captured everything in its path. Eventually, logs, branches, and clods of dirt accumulated at a bend in the river or at the mouth of a creek. Over time the Yukon would disassemble this jam, as it pulled one log after another into its mighty current.

Lydia was about to give the boat more throttle when Karl stabbed the air with his forefinger. Peering through the tower of spray, Lydia could see that the logs had captured an aluminum boat, its stern end partially submerged in the frothy current, its bow tilted upward. Lydia took a sharp breath.

There was a large eddy upstream and Lydia steered her skiff

into it. Her glasses were covered with spray and she could barely see the other boat much less make out any details. Karl wasn't wearing glasses and his head moved slowly as his eyes scanned the errant boat from bow to stern. Very carefully, he stood and scanned the boat again. Then he got down on his knees, and crawled back to Lydia. His face was grim. He cupped his hands around his mouth and yelled into her ear.

"It's the Canadian Fisheries boat," he yelled. "There's nobody in it. I do see a day pack on the seat though." He scowled and said something Lydia couldn't hear. She shook her head at him.

By the time they rounded the next bend, the noise was reduced to a soft roar. Lydia slowed the boat and Karl turned around and leaned toward her. "Teddy has a lot of boating experience. She always coils the bowline neatly and puts it on the bottom. But that rope was floating in the water. If Teddy had been piloting that boat, the line would be inside. I think that boat was tied up somewhere and then broke free."

Lydia sighed with relief and nodded. "That makes sense. Besides, if the day pack stayed on the seat, the boat probably slid up those logs at a pretty slow speed." She thought a moment. "Maybe the Yukon Queen unmoored it with its wake."

"I bet that's what happened," said Karl. "That means that Teddy's boat was tied upstream of the log jam."

"At Fools Gold Creek," said Lydia. She relaxed. Teddy was merely stranded. She grabbed the gunwale as Karl gunned the engine.

Fools Gold Creek was the site of a 2,000 year old Indian village, as well as an eighteen nineties mining community. The area was an historic treasure trove, filled with ancient First Nation artifacts and the more recent detritus of the gold miners. Abandoned for over a hundred years, the site had recently become a territorial park operated jointly by the Yukon government and the Han Gwich'in First Nation.

Lydia and Karl turned into the creek and landed on a stretch of gravel a few hundred yards from its mouth. As Lydia was tying off her boat, Karl tapped her on the shoulder and pointed. A sleek red boat had been partially dragged up onto the bank. "I wonder who that belongs, too," said Karl. "It's expensive. Twenty five thousand dollars at least." The Lund was empty. The owner had tied the line to a tall stump using a bowline knot that had not been pulled tight.

Karl shook his head. "A high wind comes along and that boat is gone."

The old town site was not accessible by road but it was a popular stop for canoeists and boaters. A well-worn path led from the river bank to a cluster of old buildings, most more or less intact, a few collapsed and rotting in the weeds. The village appeared to be deserted. The only sound was the wind rustling through birch leaves and the ever present hum of mosquitoes. Suddenly Lydia stopped walking and sniffed the air. "Hey, somebody's cooking." She stopped and pointed at a little cabin fifty yards down the trail. "Look, there's smoke coming out of that stack."

Karl and Lydia approached. Although this was one of the original mining cabins, it was in excellent shape. The logs were freshly stained and the chinking was in good repair. The tin roof looked new. There was heavy mesh wire over the windows and two heavy sliding bolts on the front door, bear deterrents suggesting that someone actually lived there.

Lydia banged on the door. It was opened by a well built, middle aged man with a thick thatch of salt and pepper hair. With his square chin and high cheekbones, he resembled Charlton Heston in his prime. He was dressed in fashionable khaki pants and a shirt bearing the Ralph Lauren Polo icon, an odd wardrobe for wilderness living. The prep school look was undercut by his beaded leather moccasins and a turquoise and silver earring. A sprinkling of old acne scars on his cheeks did not detract from the man's craggy good looks. Reading glasses were perched on his nose and he held a thick book.

"Can I help you?" he asked.

"We're looking for someone," said Lydia. "A woman of about forty five, big, tall, bright red hair. She might be wearing a blue Alaska Fish and Game shirt. Have you seen her today?"

The man shook his head. "I haven't seen anybody except my own grad students. I'm an archeologist and we're excavating the old First Nation village on the other side of the creek."

"Is that your boat pulled up on the bank?" asked Karl.

The man nodded. "Yes, it is."

"Have you seen any other boats near here today?" asked Lydia.

"No but I heard one this morning."

"What time?" asked Lydia.

"I don't know. I was still in bed, so it was before seven." The man caught the worried look Lydia flashed Karl. He frowned at her. "What's this about anyway?"

"We're looking for a friend of ours. We found her boat in a log jam downriver. It looks like it became unmoored and got caught. She likes to come here to photograph artifacts, and it's possible that she fell and broke her ankle or something."

"Let me help you look for your friend," said the man. "I've been here for two summers. I know the area." With that he held out his hand. "I'm Jack Marsh, by the way."

Lydia shook it. "I'm Lydia Falkner and this is Karl Kovacs."

"Come on in while I put some boots on," said Marsh. He waved them through the door. The cabin was a surprise. It had once been a general store but now it was a pleasant one room house, complete with crisp cotton curtains at the windows, a rag rug on the floor, and a double bed covered with a bright handmade quilt. There were three straight chairs, a kitchen table piled with books and papers, and open shelves filled with dishes and cooking implements. Three bottles of Dewars stood tall among the cans of corned beef hash, chicken soup, garbanzos, and green beans. Something was spitting and sputtering in a frying pan on the small wood burning stove.

"Oh, hell," muttered Marsh. He grabbed a rag and removed

the pan as he inspected the contents. "Anybody want a piece of blackened sausage?" he said grinning.

"I'm sorry we ruined your dinner," said Lydia.

"Don't worry about it," said Marsh. He dumped a smoking black lump into a small garbage can. "I'll be ready in a jiffy." He pulled a pair of hiking boots from a cupboard and sat down on the bed to put them on.

"The gal we're looking for, what's her name?" asked Marsh.

"Teddy Gianopoulous," replied Karl.

Marsh smiled. "That's a mouthful." He stood up and smoothed out the bed quilt.

When Lydia stepped over the threshold of the little cabin, she was surprised to find that in the short time they'd been inside, it had clouded over and the temperature had dropped. She was chilly in her flannel shirt. She hoped Teddy had something warm to wear.

"I'll check the cabins" said Lydia.

"I'll check the trails behind the buildings," said Marsh.

"I'll walk along the creek," said Karl. The three separated. Soon Karl and Jack Marsh were out of sight but Lydia could hear them calling Teddy's name, Karl's high clear tenor sailing over Marsh's booming baritone. Lydia called, too, but her voice sounded thin and tight in her own ears.

The cabin next to Marsh's retreat was unrestored but intact. The logs were the color of lead and the rounds were rotten on the ends. The walls leaned inward but they still supported the peaked tin roof. Pieces of one by eight had been nailed over the windows and the door frame. These boards had been bleached grey by sun and wind. The thistles and devil's club ringing the building were window-high and a spruce sapling was growing just inches from the front door. No one had entered this structure in years if not decades.

The next cabin was both intact and accessible. There was no glass in the two small windows and no door in the frame, but the metal roof had protected the interior from rain and snow. It was a one room structure with a narrow bunk built into one corner. Three long shelves still clung to a wall next to a ragged stove pipe hole. A firebox door was all that remained of a cast iron stove. Lydia brightened when she saw four waffle-soled footprints just beyond the threshold. Her heart leapt when she caught sight of a camera lens cap lying on the weedy floor. The cap was dust-free. When she picked it up, her heart sank. The logo read *Leica*. Teddy carried a *Canon*.

Becoming more discouraged with each step, Lydia passed two cabins that had collapsed years ago and headed for the old dance hall. It was the only two story structure in the village and, unlike the others, it had been built of milled lumber. It stood tall and solid, its empty window frames staring blankly out at Fools Gold Creek. A second floor door that led out into thin air bespoke a missing balcony. That door was boarded shut, while the first floor door had been removed from its hinges and was nowhere to be seen.

Tall balsam poplars and cottonwoods towered over the roof of the dance hall, blocking the afternoon sun. A gust of wind raised tiny dust devils in front of the empty door frame. Lydia stepped over the threshold and shuddered. It was cold in the building; the light was dim and the air dank. The first floor of the hall was cavernous, an empty shell with no interior walls. The iron staircase to the second floor was in the process of rusting away; the middle section was missing altogether while at the top and bottom, the steps hung crazily from their risers.

Lydia gave her eyes a minute to adjust to the dimness and then took a few steps forward. The room was empty. Not one stick of furniture, not one shelf or chair remained. Yet, this building had been the entertainment hub of the Fools Gold mining community in the 1890s. Histories of the gold rush were filled with old photos of this dance hall and its patrons. Grizzled men, wearing looks of sensual abandon, clutched elegantly, if immodestly, dressed young ladies as they danced to fiddle and accordion. Gloomy landscapes in gilt frames and oil lamps housed in elaborate sconces hung on the rough walls between skins of bear, wolverine, and lynx. The now inaccessible second floor had held six tiny rooms where the dancing girls had plied their second, more lucrative, trade.

Gazing upward at the decaying staircase, Lydia started across the old plank floor. When she looked down again, she realized that just a few feet ahead of her hiking boots the floor disappeared entirely. She stepped carefully to the edge and looked over. She wrinkled her nose at a smell that was at the same time musty and dusty. Far below was a dirt floor littered with broken glass, rocks, lengths of rotting lumber, and pieces of scrap metal. Lydia squatted and peered more closely at this desolate landscape. She could make out two large ceramic crocks, a rusty Dutch oven, a set of old fashioned bed springs, and the toe of a crusty boot.

She had gotten up and brushed herself off when she realized something was wrong with the tableaux below. She lay down on her belly again and pushed herself over the edge until her upper torso was hanging in mid-air. She curled herself down and took a closer look at the boot. Suddenly, it hit her. This was no artifact. It was a modern hiking boot with a modern lacing system. She scooted forward another couple of inches and looked again. There was a sock in the boot and a khaki-clad leg in the sock.

Lydia's head swam and her stomach clenched. "Teddy?" she called quietly. "Teddy, is that you?" There was no response. "Teddy!" Her voice was a hoarse croak. She pulled herself up and stumbled to the door. She steadied herself on the doorframe a moment and then stepped out into clean, cool air. "Karl," she yelled. "Karl, come to the dance hall. Come quick."

A few moments later, she heard someone scrambling through the brush down by the river. Karl was breathless when he reached Lydia's side. Her voice was tight when she pointed to the dance hall and said, "There's somebody—." She cleared her throat. "There's somebody in there. In the cellar." Her shoulder muscles contracted and she shuddered.

"Is it Teddy?"

"I can't tell." Her voice caught. "All—all I could see was a boot and a leg."

At that instant Jack Marsh trotted down the path. "I heard you calling. Is everything okay?"

"No," said Lydia, swallowing hard. "Is there a caretaker here?"

"I'm afraid right now that's me," said Marsh. "The real caretaker is recovering from a heart attack."

"Do you have a flashlight, Mr. Marsh?" asked Karl.

"And a ladder?" added Lydia.

"I have both," said Marsh. "I'll be back in a jiffy."

Marsh was true to his word. A few minutes later he came down the path carrying an aluminum extension ladder in both hands. Lydia could see a flashlight protruding from his pants pocket. She helped Marsh carry the ladder into the building. When she put her end down, Karl put his hand on her shoulder. "I'll go see if it's Teddy," he said. "You don't need to subject yourself to that."

"No. We'll go together."

Marsh and Karl worked to stabilize the ladder on the rocky cellar floor. Karl descended first and then held the light for Lydia. Her hands were shaking as she clutched the uprights and hunted for the rungs with her feet. When she reached the bottom, Karl moved the beam toward the form lying in the debris and rubble. He breathed in sharply. Lydia could barely hear him when he said, "It's Teddy."

"What did you say?" called Marsh. "Is it your friend?"

Neither Karl nor Lydia answered him.

Lydia's breath was shallow and rapid as she looked down at the form on the cellar floor. It was lying face down in the dirt; it was hatless and Teddy's red curls were unmistakable in the small circle of light. Her arms were spread above her head and her fingers were bent as if she were attempting to clutch the dirt clods that littered the floor. Karl moved his flashlight over the body and Lydia saw that Teddy's hands were almost blue and her fingernails had lost all color. There were cuts and scratches on her arms and abrasions on the one elbow visible to Lydia. One of her legs was cocked as if she were in mid step. Teddy's torso had taken on the contour of the rocks beneath her, her head low, her chest high, her pelvis nestled in a shallow hole. That must be uncomfortable, thought Lydia, even though she knew Teddy was dead.

Karl knelt and pressed his fingers into Teddy's wrist. He kept them there a long time. Then he looked up at Lydia and shook his head. His lips were quivering.

Marsh peered over the edge of the floor and called again. "Is it your friend?"

"Yes," said Lydia."

"Is she okay?"

"No," Lydia shouted. "She's dead, damn it. She's dead."

Lydia's eyes burned and her heart pounded. *Who knows when I will see you again*, she had said to Teddy just a few days earlier.

"Poor thing," said Marsh. "She must not have seen the hole. Probably broke her neck when she fell."

Karl knelt on the cellar floor. He looked up at Lydia and motioned to her. She knelt, too. Karl pointed to the side of Teddy's neck. Clots of coagulated blood had left a trail that ran down her jaw bone. Another trail ran into her ear. Her shoulder was soaked in blood. There was a large dark stain in the dirt. Karl lifted Teddy's hair. There was a wide, ragged wound in the side of the neck. "Do you think she hit a rock when she fell?" asked Karl. He spoke softly.

Lydia whispered. "She fell face down." Then she looked up at the first floor and scowled. "Wait. No. She couldn't have fallen into this spot. She's too far under the floorboards."

Karl cast the light in circle around Teddy's body. When he reached Teddy's feet, he moved the light behind them. Two shallow furrows ran out beyond Teddy's boots, one narrower than the other. They terminated in a swath of disturbed earth about two yards away where there were more dark stains.

"Oh, God," whispered Lydia. "She fell and then she crawled. She crawled and then she died." She began to cry softly.

"What should we do with her?" said Karl.

Lydia wiped her eyes with the back of her hand. "Nothing. We need to call the Mounties. Don't tell Marsh about the wound." Suddenly a wave of dizziness hit. Lydia took a number of fast breaths and steadied herself against Karl. "I've got to get out of here."

"Hold the ladder," yelled Karl to Jack Marsh. Marsh grabbed the uprights from above and Lydia and Karl ascended.

When Marsh began to pull the ladder up, Lydia grabbed his arm. "Leave it," she said sharply. Marsh started and removed his hands as he gave Lydia a quizzical look. "The Mounties will need it and this will save them having to bring one from Dawson."

"The Mounties! You're calling the Mounties?"

"Yes," said Lydia. She did not explain.

Lydia turned and headed for the door. "I need some fresh air and some light." The men followed her out. Lydia sat cross-legged in the weeds and bent over. She closed her eyes and tried to breathe normally. There didn't seem to be enough air in the universe.

Karl gently placed his palm on her back. His breathing was shallow, too. "How am I going to tell Troy about this? Or Gretchen? It's unbelievable."

Lydia nodded and looked up at him. "Is there a satellite phone at camp?" Karl shook his head.

Marsh raised his palm. "I've got a *sat* phone here."

Lydia blew out air and stood up. "Thank God. Let's call Dawson right now."

Marsh nodded and the three of them trudged back to the cabin. After Marsh retrieved the phone, he led Lydia and Karl to a large clearing where, he assured her, reception would be good. Lydia knew the number at the Dawson RCMP detachment by heart.

After the call, Marsh invited Karl and Lydia into his cabin and insisted on providing a food and coffee. He bustled around, removing books from chairs and clearing the table of folders and papers. After seating his guests, he brought out a loaf of bread, a wheel of Gouda still in its red casing, a thick stick of hard sausage, and a jar of spicy mustard. Then he reheated coffee in a well-used blue enamel pot. He poured them each a cup. Lydia drank it without tasting it.

"I bring this stuff up from Vancouver," said Marsh cheerfully. "It's a special grind. I teach at Simon Fraser University and it's a hop, skip, and a jump over to the city. What do you two do?"

Lydia closed her eyes and tried to remember what it was she did.

Karl answered. His voice was low and tight. "I'm a mushroom picker. She's a teacher."

"A fellow slave to students," chirruped Marsh. "What grade?"

"Community college mostly," said Lydia, her voice flat.

"Hey, it doesn't matter where you teach. It's all about students and knowledge."

Under any other circumstances, Lydia, who had lost her job to cost-cutting, would have launched into her diatribe on the corporatization of higher education, but right now all she could think about was Teddy crawling to her death in the dirt.

CHAPTER 6

Time crawled and Jack Marsh never stopped talking. Lydia's head was pounding and she could manage only the occasional monosyllable. Karl was completely silent. Finally a soft hum caught her ear. The noise grew louder and soon turned into an insistent thrumming. It was a jet boat; the RCMP had arrived.

Karl and Lydia reached the creek just as the boat operator backed off the throttle and the craft rounded the bend downstream of the Fools Gold settlement. As it headed for the bank, Lydia could see that the Mountie at the wheel was Al. Next to him was an officer she didn't know, a middle aged First Nation woman. Wilbur Rogers, a veteran Mountie, was sitting behind them. The female constable's long pony tail bounced when Al cut the engine and the boat came to an abrupt stop. Rogers threw the bow line to Lydia, who tied it around a big cottonwood tree.

The three Mounties clambered over the side of the boat, each of the men carrying a bulky waterproof bag. When they reached the path, Al opened the smaller of the two bags and extracted a camera and a hard plastic case. These he handed to the woman. Then he removed two large battery powered spot lights and gave them to Karl. In the meantime Rogers was wrestling with a body bag.

Al pulled Lydia away from Karl and spoke softly. "I prefer that no one at the village or the mushroom camp know about our relationship."

"Karl's an old friend. I told him about us earlier."

"Okay. He'll get the same instructions." Al spoke briefly to

Karl.

Jack Marsh trotted up and introductions were made. Lydia learned that the woman was Constable Bonnie Snowshoe, a new addition to the Dawson RCMP detachment from Inuvik. The party walked down the path toward the old dance hall in silence.

When the group reached the building, Lydia hung back. She didn't want to reenter this gloomy old whorehouse; she didn't want to smell decay more than a century old; she didn't want to gaze into the hole that had claimed Teddy's life. She closed her eyes and willed her feet to step over the threshold. She stood just inside the door. When she finally opened her eyes again, she was surprised to see that the room was much brighter than before. The sun was low enough to send beams through the leaves of the birch trees and into the empty window frames. Small splotches of golden light danced on the walls and the floorboards. Illuminated dust motes swirled in the wake of the Mounties' footsteps. The effect was a kaleidoscope of gold and silver. But the back of the room where floorboards gave way to air was as dark and forbidding as it had been two hours earlier.

Lydia noted that Karl had not come in. She heard the faint crinkle of cellophane and a few moments later smelled cigarette smoke. She stuck her head out the door and saw him sitting on a rock looking sad and pensive. He gave her a wan smile and held up a cigarette. "I'll quit again tomorrow."

Marsh lowered himself to the ground with his back to a fallen log. He pulled a small notebook and pen from his pocket and began writing.

Lydia thought about retreating and joining Karl on the rock, yet she was torn. She didn't want to see Teddy's wounded and twisted body again, but she needed to bear witness, to be there for her old friend. Al barely knew her and the others didn't know her at all. She couldn't leave Teddy alone with strangers. She thought about the woman at Bad Axe Mine. No one should be alone in death.

Lydia took a deep breath and walked slowly across the

planks. Al was shining a light on the floor near the edge. He knelt down and motioned to Snowshoe. A large stain was almost invisible on the moldy, old spruce boards. Snowshoe took a series of photos and then she sliced off a long sliver of wood, which she placed in a plastic evidence bag. Al descended the ladder with the other spotlight. When he reached the bottom, he turned it on. Everyone squinted as pupils tried to adjust to the sudden, harsh light. Rogers and Snowshoe followed Al into the cellar. The three Mounties cast enormous shadows on the wall as they inched along the dirt floor.

Lydia descended the first three rungs. Holding on with one hand, she turned her head slowly. Bonnie Snowshoe was snapping more pictures; she took photos of the body, photos of the area around it, photos of the entire cellar. Wilbur Rogers searched the floor and took notes. Periodically, he squatted, picked something off the ground, and put it into one of the many small bags he carried in his shirt pockets. At one point he scooped up dirt and bagged it.

Only then did Al examine Teddy's body. First he picked up one hand and attempted to bend the fingers. He said something to Snowshoe, who wrote a few words in a notebook. Then he turned his attention to the wound. At one point he gently turned Teddy's head sideways. Al leaned over until his own face was just inches from Teddy's neck. Then he motioned to Constable Snowshoe who knelt next him. She snapped five close-ups of Teddy's neck and skull.

Finally, the two Mounties nodded at one another and Al began to turn Teddy over. Lydia couldn't take any more. She turned away and quickly ascended. She sat in the doorframe of the dance hall, her knees pulled up, her forehead against them.

A few moments later, she heard the rattle of someone handling heavy plastic, then the sound of stones rolling, followed by the rasp of a long zipper. One of the Mounties grunted and there were heavy footsteps. Lydia heard hard breathing as the two men pulled and pushed the unwieldy body bag up the ladder.

Rogers and Al were sweating when they finally laid the body on the ground. Rogers pulled out a bandana and wiped his face. Constable Snowshoe followed the two men with the camera and the lights.

Al turned to Lydia and Karl. "I need a firm identification. I know you've identified her from the back but I need for you to see her face." They both nodded. Lydia clenched her hands and held her breath.

As Al lowered the zipper, a ray of sun caught the top of Teddy's head and moved slowly down her face. The light illuminated a shallow cut on her forehead and a deep, ragged gouge on her right cheek. Dried blood had pooled in her dimple. Her whole face was caked with dirt mixed with blood; the spray of freckles across her nose was almost invisible. One eye was half open and a milky film obscured the bright green of her iris. Her lips were parted and her mouth was set in a rigid line, as if she were in great pain. Lydia had to take a deep breath before she could say, "Yes. It's Teddy Gianopoulous.

Karl nodded. "Yes, it is."

Marsh was standing next to Lydia and she felt him stiffen as he looked down into the body bag. He grunted and grabbed Lydia's arm. "Oh, my God, *I have* seen her."

Lydia scowled at him. "You told us you hadn't."

"I didn't recognize her from your description. Whenever I saw her she was wearing a hat, so I didn't notice the red hair you mentioned." He paused, looking slightly embarrassed. "And, frankly, I thought she was a guy. I guess it was the way she walked. I saw her on the edge of the village a few times, poking around in the ruins. She smiled and waved at me." Marsh paused and frowned. "I also saw her quite recently on the trail that goes up toward the gold mine."

A look of surprise crossed Al's face. "There's a mine here? An active mine?"

"It's a tiny placer operation. It belongs to a couple of old hippies. I came across it last year when I was out hiking. I can't imagine that they get anything out of it"

"Do you know anything about these miners?" asked Al.

"They're both in their late fifties, early sixties. The woman's kinda fat, got greying hair. Wears it in braids. The guy's tall and thin as a rail. Sort of Jack Sprat and his wife. They're not friendly. I don't know their names. They live about three klicks up Fools Gold Creek. The creek's only navigable for one or two clicks at the best of times. This year there's so much deadfall that the miners tie their boat down here and hike all the way up."

"So they're not up there now?"

Marsh shook his head. "They left three days ago. If they were back, their boat would be tied up next to mine."

"Who else is in the immediate area?" asked Al.

"Just my grad students. They camp at the dig. It's just two clicks away. I'm the only one here at the village. Oh, and there's that mushroom camp downstream."

Al nodded. "I'll have one of the constables to talk to your graduate students this evening. I'd like a few words with you right now, Mr. Marsh."

Marsh looked surprised. "Uh, okay."

Al moved away from the group and beckoned Marsh to follow. The two men talked for about ten minutes. Al's contributions were short; Marsh's were longer. Marsh's facial expressions ranged from concern to surprise to indignation and back to concern. Finally he nodded at Al and the two men shook hands. Marsh headed down the trail toward his cabin.

As soon as Marsh was out of site, Al put his hand on Lydia's arm. "Teddy was stabbed." Lydia closed her eyes and nodded. "I'd say she's been dead for more than twelve hours."

Al fixed his eyes on Lydia and then on Karl. "You must keep this to yourselves. You can tell the people at the camp that you found Teddy in the cellar but don't mention the wound. I don't want them to know any particulars." Lydia and Karl both nodded.

Al asked Rogers and Snowshoe to check the surrounding area, to talk briefly to the students at the dig, and then ferry the body back to Dawson. "I'll go over to the mushroom camp with Lydia and Mr. Kovacs. Call the detachment and have them send another boat to pick me up there about midnight."

"I could take you back to Dawson," said Lydia. "I've got no reason to be at the camp now that Teddy's gone."

"No. I want to pick up Teddy's boat tonight and check it for evidence. I'll need a powerful craft to get it off the logjam." Al turned to his colleagues. "Let's get moving."

On the way back to the mushroom camp, Lydia asked Al about the murder weapon. "It's a strange wound," replied Al. "It wasn't a knife. It looks like the killer used something thick and blunt. It left two little semi-circles in the flesh. The weapon was short but it went in with a great deal of force. The edge of the wound is ragged. It looks like the weapon caught the edge of the carotid artery, thus all the blood. Had the killer hit the artery dead center, Teddy would have died almost instantly.

Lydia gave a small groan. Bile rose in her throat. She pressed her lips together for a long time. Finally, she said, "Does Marsh have an alibi?"

Al nodded. "He said he was entertaining a lady friend and she didn't leave until lunchtime. We'll follow up, of course."

Lydia swallowed hard as the camp can into view. It was late. Everyone would be there. Troy was already on the bank when Lydia steered the boat onto the shore. "Did you find Teddy?" he yelled. "Did you find her?"

As soon as Karl disembarked, he put his arm around the boy and asked him to go find Red. "But did you find Teddy?" said Troy.

"Just get your dad, Troy. Tell him I need to talk to him."

Karl met Red at the top of the bank. They spoke briefly. When Red approached the group, his face was tight and pale. Red took Troy's hand and led him to a large cottonwood log. He sat down, pulled the boy onto one knee and began talking. Suddenly Troy's mouth opened wide. Lydia could hear his agonized, "No! No way!" She could hear his sobs and watched his tears make tiny brown rivulets on his dirty face. Red wrapped his arms around him and Troy buried his head in his shirt. They sat like that for a few moments and then Troy broke free. He ran to his tent, crawled in, and zipped the door behind him.

Red followed and Lydia watched as he talked to the boy through the canvas door. He returned a few minutes later. "Troy said he needs to be alone for a while."

Al had decided to wait down by the boat while Karl broke the news. Lydia followed Karl into camp and into the kitchen. He approached Gretchen who was standing at the make-shift sink washing dishes. He took the sponge from her hand and laid it on the drain board. "I have something to tell you."

Gretchen scowled at him. "Are you going to tell me that Teddy cracked up my boat?"

Karl shook his head. "It's much worse than that."

Astonishment and then shock registered on Gretchen's face as Karl told his story. By the time he had finished, her rosy cheeks were the color of putty. Gretchen grabbed Karl's shoulders and shook him. "No," she cried, "it's not true. It can't be true!" When Karl failed to respond, she turned to Lydia. "Tell me it's not true," she pleaded. "Tell me."

"I'm afraid it is," said Lydia.

Gretchen began to sway. Lydia grabbed a folding chair and helped her into it. She opened the refrigerator and took out a bottle of water. Gretchen waved it away. She emitted a sob. "I was such an idiot," she said, her voice cracking. "How could I have believed that Teddy would leave me stranded?" She began to cry.

As Lydia patted Gretchen's shoulder, Karl picked up the dinner bell and shook it hard. "Everyone in the kitchen," he called. "I've got bad news." One by one the pickers walked into the screen house. Then two men appeared whom Lydia hadn't seen before. They were young. Both wore blue polo shirts; one sported a Fisheries and Oceans Canada logo and the other an Alaska Fish and Game seal. The Fisheries Canada man was tall and lithe with pale blue eyes, pale blond hair, and a neatly trimmed blond mustache. Lydia wasn't surprised when Karl introduced him as Lloyd O'Hara. Charlie Stafford, the American, was skinny, already balding, and had a receding chin and an overbite. His prominent Adam's apple bobbed whenever he swallowed.

When everyone except Troy had assembled in the tent, Karl gave them an abbreviated account of the search for Teddy and Lydia's discovery of the body. Reactions varied. Liz gasped and put her hand over her mouth. Bob emitted a yelp and grabbed his suspenders. Lloyd uttered a low "Jesus H. Christ." Charlie Stafford went pale; his top teeth bit into his bottom lip. A moment later he rushed from the tent and vomited in the bushes. Red's face revealed nothing.

Everyone's eyes were on Karl and no one saw Al approach the tent. But when the screen door banged behind him, all eyes were on the Mountie.

"Fuck," said Sam softly "It's the cops. This ain't good."

Charlie re-entered the tent. His face was ashen. He collapsed into a chair and fixed his eyes on the ground. Al introduced himself to those assembled and asked everyone to please stay in the kitchen so he could speak to each of them individually in the research tent. He explained that circumstances surrounding Gianopoulous's death were odd and that he had some questions. Everyone nodded except Red. People who had looked exhausted ten minutes ago were now alert and attentive. This was high drama.

One by one, Al interviewed both researchers and pickers. As she sat waiting her turn, Lydia heard a multitude of theories. *Maybe she was stoned and tripped. Maybe she was witness to a crime. Maybe some nut case was stalking her.*

"I think she jumped," said Sam Avakian as he stared at the ground. Gretchen gave a small gasp and buried her face in her hands.

The RCMP boat came to pick up Al at 1:15 A.M. The sun had just set but it would be twilight until it rose again three hours later. Karl helped Lydia pitch her tent. She wanted it far from the others so she wouldn't be disturbed. She crawled into her nylon cave and fell asleep fully clothed on top of her bag. She slept fitfully, her sleep punctuated by dream fragments—Teddy doing wheelies on her little Honda, Teddy snapping photos of everything in sight, Teddy crawling in the dirt calling Lydia's name.

Much later, Lydia was awakened by something, probably the patter of rain on her tent fly. Damn it, she thought, I'm on low ground. Then she heard splashing and irregular breathing just outside her tent. Her chest tightened. Was it a caribou, a bear, Teddy's killer? She lay perfectly still as the intruder gently pushed on the tent wall and then retreated. There was more splashing and a series of deep moans. These were followed by the sound of soft chewing. Utterly perplexed, Lydia slowly unzipped her door. As the zipper descended, a long hairy nose pushed its way into the opening. A pair of large brown eyes met hers. That's when Lydia heard Troy shout, "Hey, there's a moose." The bull jerked his head upward, caught his antlers in the tent fly, and shook his head vigorously. In moments the fly was in tatters. Long blue streamers hung from the points of his antlers. As the bull jerked away from the tent, he pulled up four stakes and broke three fiberglass poles.

"Dammit," yelled Lydia as the tent collapsed and water seeped through the walls. She dug through her duffle bag and found her fleece jacket and her rain suit. She put on her boots and crawled out through the flaps. The tent had been reduced to a puddle of blue nylon. She checked her watch. It was 6:30.

As Lydia pulled her rain hood tightly over her hair and dashed for the kitchen, she saw Troy following the moose up the creek. Apparently, he was the only one who had witnessed the demolition. The three researchers and Liz were drinking coffee in the tent. If this weather held, the pickers wouldn't go out. Finding morels among the roots, burned branches, and ash was hard on a sunny day; ground fog would render it impossible. It could be a long, tense day in camp.

Lloyd handed Lydia a cup of steaming coffee as soon as she burst through the screen door. Then the two of them joined the others at the table.

No one spoke. The only noise in the kitchen was the pinging of rain drops on the empty propane canisters outside and the hollow thrumming of water hitting the heavy plastic sheeting on the screens. Wood frogs chortled in the distance and a pair of ravens squabbled behind the privy. Gretchen traced the edge of her cup with her index finger and Lloyd stared blankly at the coffee urn. Lydia couldn't handle the tension. She said the first thing that came into her head.

"Liz, you go to Simon Fraser. Did you ever encounter Professor Jack Marsh?"

"Sure. I took a course with him, a course on indigenous culture. He's famous."

"For what?"

"He's an expert on First Nation history and archeology. He's part First Nation himself, you know." Lydia didn't know and was surprised. Despite his high cheekbones, Marsh looked thoroughly northern European to her. Liz went on breathlessly. "Anyhow, he's made some astonishing discoveries in the last few years. His work is forcing the archeology community to revise some long-held beliefs about migration patterns and dates. He has a dig just up the river."

"I know. I met him at Fools Gold Creek."

Liz winced. "Oh, yeah. When you found Teddy."

"So Jack Marsh is a highly regarded scholar."

"Absolutely," said Liz. She paused. "He does have detractors, archeologists who say his migration dates aren't supported by the data, but they're just jealous. Marsh is hot shit, the real deal. He's incredibly smart, a terrific speaker, and on top of everything, he's pretty damn good looking."

"Did Teddy ever talk about him?"

"No. Why would she?"

"Oh, she was interested in the gold rush artifacts and Marsh was an archeologist."

Liz shook her head. "No. The gold rush isn't Marsh's thing. He's all about ancient First Nation stuff. All that gold rush junk just gets in his way."

Gretchen had been frowning throughout the entire conversations. She looked at Lydia. "Do you think Marsh had something to do with Teddy's death?" Gretchen's voice was low and she was clutching her cup so hard her knuckles were white.

"No. I'm just curious about Marsh."

"He was there," said Gretchen.

Liz touched Gretchen's hand. "Jack Marsh would never hurt anyone. He has a gentle soul."

"How in the hell can you know anything about his soul?" said Lloyd, throwing Liz a contemptuous look. "What crap." He turned to Gretchen. "Let's get to work." Lloyd, Gretchen, and Charlie left the kitchen tent. Liz and Lydia refilled their coffee cups and sat in silence until Red and Troy entered.

"Did you see that moose?" asked Troy.

Lydia mustered a smile. "Did I ever."

Red poured cereal and milk for both of them and coffee for himself. He sat down next to Liz. Troy took the seat next to Lydia and touched her arm.

"Are you sad?" he said.

"Yes. Are you?"

Troy nodded and tears filled his eyes. Red pulled a ragged bandana out of his pocket and handed it to Troy but his eyes were fixed on Lydia. His voice was deep and resonant like an old time radio announcer. "So you're a friend of Teddy's, eh?"

"I'm an old roommate," explained Lydia. "We met in college."

"There's something odd about all this," said Red.

"What do you mean?" asked Lydia.

"Teddy was careful and she was agile. Troy told me that she always carried a flashlight when she went to Fool's Gold Creek."

Troy nodded. "She always did. And she put on gloves before

she touched anything."

Red continued. "Teddy took Troy into that old dancehall. Right, son?" Troy nodded again. "Troy said she was extremely careful. She showed him how to test the old floorboards and made him stay well away from the edge." He paused and rubbed his bare arms. "Hey, Troy. Would you go get my jacket? It's colder than I thought." Troy nodded.

As soon as the kitchen door banged, Red pressed his lips together. Then he said softly, "Teddy didn't trip and fall into that cellar. Somebody pushed her."

CHAPTER 7

Lydia hung around the mushroom camp until after lunch, waiting for the weather to clear. By 2 PM the clouds were starting to move north. Lydia jammed her wet sleeping bag and damp duffle into a stuff sack while Karl tossed the ravaged tent into the trash.

Things were miserable on the river. It continued to drizzle. The rolled collar on Lydia's rain suit allowed a small rivulet of water to meander down her sternum and pool in the center of her bra. Worse yet, it became increasingly clear to Lydia, that the coffee Lloyd served her at lunch had been decaffeinated. The man was either illiterate or sadistic.

As the air warmed, steam came off the water and there were moments when Lydia could see only a few feet in front of her bow. Periodically the boat collided with one of the small logs that danced on the waves. The steam dissipated just before Lydia approached the log jam that had captured Teddy's boat. Lydia backed off the throttle and rode as close to the jam as the turbulence would allow. After wiping raindrops from her glasses, she could see that the Canadian Fisheries boat was gone.

As Lydia approached Fools Gold Creek village, she recalled Jack Marsh's words. He had seen Teddy on the trail that led to the placer mine. The miners had been gone for days when the murder happened. But maybe Teddy had befriended them. She was a gregarious soul. Maybe they knew something useful. Maybe they had returned to their cabin.

Lydia knew she was grasping at straws. She knew she wasn't

being rational. She knew she was interfering with a police investigation. She knew Al would be pissed. But she had to do *something*. It might be days before the Mounties got around to interviewing those miners. She'd be careful. She wouldn't tell them that Teddy was dead. She'd simply find out if they had known her. What harm could it do?

Lydia executed a fast, hard right turn. She steered the boat up Fools Gold Creek and landed on the bank above the dance hall. As she tied the bow line around a sturdy cottonwood, she noted with satisfaction that there was a battered aluminum skiff equipped with a small outboard moored among the alders. Jack Marsh's fancy red boat was gone.

The trail was steep in spots and narrow and muddy everywhere. Branches grabbed at Lydia's rain suit; twigs scratched her face and hands. She kept her eyes on the ground watching for logs, rocks, and holes. As the trail grew rockier, a new hazard emerged, pine needles. Wet with rain, the needles were as slick as silicon and they slid downhill with every step Lydia took. It was like walking up a water slide.

Suddenly Lydia cocked her head. There was a rustling in the bushes to her right. She stood motionless and peered into the woods. The rustling stopped. Then the bushes in front of her were in motion; branches shook; twigs crackled; something emitted a soft grunt. A moment later an enormous porcupine ambled onto the trail, a leafy branch protruding from his mouth. He stopped in mid chew and peered at Lydia with myopic eyes. It took him a moment to register her presence, then she saw his spines rise. He turned and presented his backside. Lydia stepped away, just in time to avoid being lashed by a powerful, barbed tail. His path successfully defended, the porcupine waddled across the trail and disappeared into the woods. The area behind him was littered with five-inch gold and black quills. No wonder Bob worried about porcupines.

In another quarter mile the path widened. Multiple footprints were visible on the trail. They were rendered oversize by the sliding of boots in the muddy terrain. The trail dead-ended at a small clearing, which contained an old army wall tent and a rickety shed sitting high in the air on wooden stilts, a food cache. Lydia watched with amusement as a red squirrel scrambled up one pole and squeezed through a large gap in the logs. It emerged a moment later with cheeks bulging. A homemade ladder lay on the ground under the cache.

The area looked like a salvage operation. A pile of rebar, angle iron, and metal pipe was stacked at one end of the clearing. Lengths of old PVC pipe had been bound together with wire and lay in a patch of fireweed. Galvanized buckets and rusty shovels had been stored under the food cache.

One flap on the canvas tent was open and a thin plume of smoke spiraled from the galvanized stove pipe sticking through the tent roof. Lydia stepped into the clearing and called out, "Do you have a few minutes for a visitor?" The crack of a bullet answered the question as it splintered the bark on a young birch about two yards away. She screamed and hit the ground. When she finally caught her breath, she yelled, "Stop it! Stop! I'm harmless."

Using her elbows for propulsion, she crawled on her belly back into the shelter of the trees. Lydia had been shooting since was a teenager and knew that the bullet had come from a small caliber rifle, probably a .22. Her assailant was shooting from the other side of the clearing. It would take an expert marksman to hit a target at that distance in this wind. From the look of it, this was not an expert marksman.

Lydia decided not to test her own theory. She stood slowly and backed down the trail, keeping her eye on the clearing as best she could through the trees. A few moments later, she saw someone emerge from behind the tent. It was a woman. She was short and stout. A long rainbow colored skirt fell below her purple rain jacket. Twin braids fell over her breasts. In her arms she cradled a long gun.

Curiosity skirmished with fear in Lydia's consciousness.

Should Lydia try to talk to this woman or get the hell out of there? Lost in internal debate, Lydia did not hear the footsteps behind her until it was too late. Large hands clamped over her arms and a hoarse male voice commanded, "March." The man pushed her down the trail toward the clearing. "I got her," he yelled to the woman.

"I'll make coffee," the woman yelled back.

Coffee? Lydia felt hysterical laughter building in her chest. She who was being taken prisoner was to be served coffee? Would there be doughnuts as well? She choked the laughter off with a soft cough.

Lydia was gently pushed across the clearing and into the army tent. She was surprised to see that the front was framed, screened, and boasted a screen door. The inside was as cozy and almost as well-equipped as her own cabin. There was a plank floor, a wood burning stove, a table with four chairs, a free-standing kitchen cabinet, a platform bed, a bookcase made from crates, and an old fashioned wardrobe. An aluminum coffee pot sat on the stove, the metal plinking softly as the contents heated.

Lydia's captor led her to one of the kitchen chairs and turned to face her. "Sit," he said. She sat. The man was indeed Jack Sprat, very tall and reed thin with a long untrimmed beard and his thinning hair pulled into a pony tail. He pulled off his raincoat and hung it neatly on a clothes tree. He wore Carhartt overalls over a tie-dyed T shirt and wire-rimmed glasses on his long, straight nose. Lydia felt as if she'd been dropped into a time warp.

Jack Sprat sat down on the bed and fixed his eyes on Lydia. "What're you doing, poking around our place?"

"I'm looking for someone named Teddy."

The woman leaned forward. "Is she that tall, red-headed woman? Got a Greek last name?"

Lydia swallowed hard. "Yes. We were supposed to meet at that mushroom camp and she didn't show up. Have you seen her lately?"

The two shook their heads in unison. "We've been away," said the woman.

"Were you friends with her?"

"No," said the woman emphatically. "She was up here, snooping around, looking for our mine. She loves mines, she said. She's never seen a placer mine, she said. We were nice the first time, gave her coffee. But then she came back again and we didn't like it. This is private property and we don't want anybody snooping around. We're sick and tired of trespassers."

"I assume most of the trespassers are people who stop to see the Fools Gold mining settlement?"

"Yeah," said Mrs. Sprat. "And then they see our trail and up they come. We've had some problems. Somebody broke into our food cache one time. Another time somebody stole an axe."

"Trespassing isn't Teddy's style," said Lydia.

Mr. Sprat looked at her sheepishly. "Well, she didn't exactly trespass. She called out and knocked, but we thought we made it clear the first time that we weren't going to show her the mine. And we didn't."

Mrs. Sprat got up and took a wash cloth from a hook. She moistened it in a basin of water and handed it to Lydia. "Wash your hands. They're filthy." Lydia scrubbed the mud off while Mrs. Sprat poured coffee into three enamel cups. Lydia accepted hers gratefully. "Thanks for showing mercy to an interloper," she said. "The coffee is wonderful."

"You'll drink it and then you'll go," said Mr. Sprat. He shook an index finger at Lydia. "And you won't come back."

Lydia nodded. As she slowly sipped her coffee, she surreptitiously scanned the Bullocks' bookcase for evidence of extreme views on politics and/or homosexuality. What she saw instead was a stack of *Mother Earth News*, a few copies of *Organic Gardening*, an ancient *Whole Earth Catalog*, three small volumes on placer mining, and a bunch of mysteries. All of the magazines and book covers were curled with moisture. Lydia looked over at the rifle, which Mrs. Sprat had parked behind the door next to a twelve gauge shotgun. "You weren't really trying to hit me, were you?"

The woman flashed Lydia a genuine smile. "No. If I'd wanted to hit you, I would have."

CHAPTER 8

Al Cerwinski gasped when Lydia appeared on his doorstep. Her hair was in tangles, her boots were soaked, and her rain suit was covered with mud. He hovered over like her mother never had—unlacing her boots, drawing a bath, laying out clean clothes. He refused to let her talk until she was clean and fed.

When Lydia emerged from the bedroom, dressed and pink from a thorough scrubbing, Al brought her freshly brewed coffee. She smiled when saw it was in his special *Mountie Python* cup, which featured a snake wearing a snappy red coat and a Dudley Do Right hat. He returned to the kitchen and reemerged with an enormous ham sandwich on rye. She accepted the offerings gratefully. When she was done eating, he slapped his hands on his knees. "Okay," he said. "Tell me why you walked in here looking like a mud wrestler."

She began. As she heard herself talk, she knew she was exaggerating the details just the tiniest bit–the slipperiness of the trail, how close the bullet had come, the stern demeanor of her captor-hosts.

Al's solicitousness gave way to irritation. He shook his head and sighed. "Goddam it, Lydia. You've got to stop playing cop. You could have screwed things up." He stared at her hard, his face tight. She quickly finished her coffee, afraid that Al might wrest Mountie Python from her grasp.

"Did I screw things up?" she asked in a small voice.

Finally his mouth relaxed. "I guess not. We've already got witnesses placing these people in Whitehorse over the past few days, so they're not murder suspects. But we will need to talk to them, and now that they think Teddy is missing, they'll be on their guard." He sighed. "Please. Think before you act. Think!" He tapped his temple.

Lydia lowered her eyes and bit her lip. They both knew her contrition was an act. Finally Al smiled and said, "For your penance, you will make me bacon, eggs benedict, and French toast in the morning." Lydia nodded vigorously, relieved that Al hadn't blown up at her.

"Okay, let me tell that your kidnappers, Adam and Eve Bullock, have a legitimate claim on Lanier Creek. They filed three years ago but they've found very little gold. Mostly they've mined pyrite, fool's gold. The Bullocks seem keep to themselves and shop in town only occasionally."

Al was interested to learn of their encounters with Teddy. "I wonder why they ran her off. Teddy struck me as a charmer, not one to piss off the locals. Why won't they let anyone see the mine? They've staked their claim; nobody can steal it; and it doesn't seem to be worth anything. This makes the Bullocks a lot more interesting."

"Did you find Marsh's lady friend?" asked Lydia. "Does his alibi check out?"

"Yes," said Al. He didn't elaborate.

"So what did Marsh's graduate students have to say about Teddy?" asked Lydia.

"They said she had come up to the dig three or four times. She'd come late in the day and they'd all sit around and have a few beers. They said she was interested in the history of the area and how archeologists work."

"Then Marsh is lying about how well he knew Teddy. He must have seen her at the dig."

Al shook his head. "The students said Marsh seldom comes to the site. In fact, he leaves Fools Gold Creek for days at a time. One of them said that she was frustrated by the lack of supervision. Apparently, this is the first dig most of them have worked."

"That's odd," said Lydia. "If he's as great as Liz Nguyen says he is, you'd think he'd keep close tabs on his work, especially if he's challenging the archeological establishment."

A strange look passed over Al's face, then he shrugged and grinned. "Well, you know the old saying. 'Those who can't do, teach.'" Lydia raised her middle finger but her heart wasn't in it.

"What about Teddy's camera? Was there anything on the memory card that might help?"

Al scowled. "We didn't find a camera. There was a laptop in her tent with a lot of photos on it, but no camera."

"That's weird," said Lydia. "She never went anywhere without her camera. She took pictures during our barbecue, remember? Maybe she left it in the boat and it fell out when the boat hit the logjam."

Al shrugged. "Maybe, but her backpack and water bottle were still in there."

Lydia dropped her head to the back of couch and got a far-away look in her eyes. She gave Al a half-smile. "Teddy was always a shutter-bug. She loved doing portraits. In grad school she made her friends pose in front of crumbling brick walls, or cockeyed fences, or rusty, wrought iron gates. She loved interesting backdrops. There was this one hilarious picture of Anna …." Lydia took a deep breath and closed her eyes. "Oh, God, Anna doesn't know. I have to tell Anna."

"Do it tomorrow," said Al. "I'll release you from your Benedictine penance and you can go over first thing in the morning."

"Anna will be a basket case."

"Go to bed. You'll need your strength."

Lydia nodded. "Good idea. Turns out interfering with a police investigation is tiring work." She gave Al a wan smile.

Teddy was Lydia's dear friend but Anna was her soulmate. Like Teddy, Anna was tough, out-spoken, and very funny. Thoroughly urban, Anna had come to the Yukon one summer to visit Lydia and Otto Falkner in their river cabin. Much to Lydia's amazement, Anna had fallen in love with Dawson City. She gave up her spacious rent-controlled apartment in Brooklyn and moved into a small two bedroom on Fourth Avenue. Her next move surprised Lydia even more. The ex-English teacher from the exclusive Dalton School in Manhattan took a job as a waitress at Dawson Dolly's restaurant. Eight years later she was still waiting on table and still living in the Blue Moose Apartments. Her master's degree in American literature adorned the wall over her toilet and her collection of Hemingway and Faulkner collected dust in the bookcase.

Anna was supremely happy. After spending much of her life in New York City, she found the intimacy of a small town protective, reassuring. She knew all the permanent residents and was invited to every barbecue, every birthday party, and every beer bash. Dawsonites appreciated Anna's directness and loved her Brooklyn accent. The tourists who flocked to Dawson Dolly's liked her efficiency and tart sense of humor. Anna made far more schlepping plates of macadamia nut halibut and capered salmon than Lydia had ever made teaching.

Lydia didn't call Anna in advance of her visit. She knocked and waited anxiously on the apartment's catwalk. She waited a long time. Finally Anna opened the door wearing nothing but flip flops and a towel. Droplets of water dripped from her short brown curls.

"Jesus," said Lydia as she pushed her friend back into the apartment, "I could have been the UPS guy."

"Would that you were," replied Anna. "He's hot."

Lydia knew she should tell Anna about Teddy straight-away, but breaking this news while Anna was half-naked seemed wrong somehow. Lydia forced a bemused smile and said, "Yeah, yeah, I'm sure he's adorable. Go get dressed. We have to talk."

"That sounds ominous," said Anna. "Am I in trouble?"

Lydia forced another smile. "No more than usual."

Anna went into the bedroom and returned a few minutes

later dressed in black jeans and a black T-shirt. She's wearing mourning, thought Lydia.

Anna scanned Lydia's face. "Something's wrong."

Lydia's vocal cords seized as she closed her eyes and croaked, "Anna, Teddy G. is dead."

Anna dropped into a chair. She didn't speak; she didn't blink; she didn't move a muscle. Her mouth was half open and she began to take short, stuttering breaths. There were no tears, just a far-away stare as if invisible shades had fallen over her eyes. Lydia gathered herself, squatted in front of Anna, and put her arms around her. "I'm sorry I didn't tell you immediately, but I couldn't make the words come."

Finally, Anna spoke. Her voice was a whisper. "What happened?"

Lydia clutched Anna's hand hard when she said, "She was murdered."

Anna's intake of breath sounded as though she'd been punched in the gut. She shook her head wildly. "No, no, no. Nobody would kill Teddy." Her voice rose until it was a high, keening scream. "Nooo!" She began to cry—hard, gut-wrenching sobs that shook the chair.

Lydia held Anna until the sobs had turned into a series of whimpers. Finally, Anna was able to speak. "Who did it? Where did it happen?"

Tears streamed down both their faces as Lydia told her story. When it was over, Anna shook her head in amazement that Lydia had found Teddy's body, just as she had found Frank's the year before. She held Lydia's face in her hands. "I'm so sorry you had to be the one."

"It was best. Otherwise, Teddy would have been alone with strangers."

Lydia and Anna held each other for long time. When the tears had subsided, Anna wiped her eyes and said, "Our hike up the Midnight Dome really was our last hurrah—forever and ever."

Lydia stood and pulled Anna to her feet. "I need a cup of coffee." Lydia raised her hand as Anna started to speak. "No instant. No coffee bags. The real thing."

"We'll have to go out then."

Lydia said, "That's fine. I think we should eat, too. We'll feel better if we do."

Anna gave Lydia a wan smile. "You sound just like my mother. Let me wash my face and get some tissues in case the waterworks start up again." She disappeared into the bedroom.

It was hot in the little apartment and Anna had opened all the windows. Lydia laid her head back on the couch and closed her eyes. The noises of civilization percolated up through the screens—the crunching of bike wheels on gravel, the single *boop* of a car alarm as someone locked a door remotely, the shouts of children playing in the yard below. Suddenly the shouting ceased to be background noise. One of the voices grew loud and angry. Lydia picked up her head and listened. She could hear the words clearly. "You take that back. She ain't. She ain't." There was a pause and then the playground erupted into a cacophony of screaming and yelling.

Lydia jumped up and ran to the window. A small boy had a larger one pinned on the ground. The first boy was pummeling the second with his fists. A circle of children had formed around them but no one was trying to break it up.

Lydia emitted a piercing whistle. The boy on top pulled his punch and turned to look up at the window. He shaded his eyes with one hand in an attempt to see through the screen. The other boy took this opportunity to thrust his hips up, unseating his tormentor. Troy Sherman fell sideways to the ground. His victim sprinted away.

"Troy," yelled Lydia. "Wait there. I'm coming down." Troy covered his face with his hands and rolled over onto his stomach. He lay still. The other kids stood watching him, silent, inscrutable.

Troy was still lying there when Lydia reached the yard. The onlookers scattered as she approached him. She kneeled down beside the boy and touched his back. He didn't respond. Lydia grabbed him under the arms, raised him to a seated position, and put one arm around him. His cheeks were streaked with tears and his breathing was ragged.

"What happened? Why did you beat that kid up?" Troy turned his head away and closed his eyes. "Come on, Troy. You can talk to me. I won't tell anybody."

"Promise?" said Troy. His voice was a whisper.

"I promise," said Lydia. She took Troy's hand and helped him stand. "Let's go sit over there and talk for a minute."

Troy allowed Lydia to lead him to a stone bench which flanked a small garden of annuals. Lydia pulled a clean bandana from her pocket and offered it to the boy. He wiped his eyes and blew his nose but his face remained a mask of anger and pain. She gently sat him down and knelt in front of him.

"So what just happened?"

Troy's lip quivered, he hiccoughed a couple of times, and then began. "That boy, Jared Spolsky, he said my grandma is lazy. She ain't. It ain't true."

"Why would he say such a thing?" asked Lydia.

"Because she's Indian."

"But Indians aren't lazy."

Troy gave her contemptuous look. "I know that. But Jared don't. He says Indians are too lazy to work. But my grandma don't have to work. She used to work and now she's tired."

"You mean *re*tired?"

Troy nodded. "Yeah, *re*tired. Jared Spolsky is a stupid idiot."

"Yes, he is," said Lydia, "and you shouldn't let him get to you."

"But he said …."

Lydia interrupted. "Jared probably believes that mud is chocolate pudding, too." This elicited a small smile from Troy. "So what are you doing here in Dawson, Troy? Why aren't you at the mushroom camp?"

"It was too sad there. Everybody was too sad. Everything

reminded me of Teddy. Dad said that I should come to Grandma's to heal. He brought me here this morning." He dug at his eyes with a grimy hand.

"Your Grandma lives in this apartment building?"

"Sure, she does." Troy paused and frowned at Lydia. "Hey, how come you're here? I thought you lived on the river."

"I'm visiting my friend Anna Fain."

Troy flashed Lydia a real smile. "I like Anna," he said. "She hits balls with me sometimes." Lydia was startled. As far as she knew, Anna had no interest whatsoever in children.

At that very moment Anna called from above. "Hey, I thought we were going for coffee." She peered down through the screen. "Oh, hi, Troy. I see you've met my friend."

"I already knew her," said Troy.

"Oh?" said Anna, obviously surprised by this piece of news. To Lydia she said, "I'll meet you out front."

"Will you be okay now?" Lydia asked Troy.

"Sure, but if that stupid jerk Jared comes around, I'll beat his butt."

Lydia sighed. As a teacher of freshman composition, she was used to her words falling on deaf ears. "I'm sure you will," she said.

Suddenly Troy jumped up and yelled, "Hey, there's Grandma." He waved frantically at a woman who was walking down the street carrying a sack of groceries in the crook of her arm. The woman caught sight of Troy and headed toward him.

Troy's grandmother looked to be in her early sixties. She was tall for a First Nation woman and very slender. Her face was a perfect oval with high, elegant cheek bones and a long straight nose. She wore her hair in a stylish feather cut. Her dark red pant suit complemented her golden skin and jet black hair. She was beautiful.

"What are you up to, Troy?" she said as she approached the pair. "Are you staying out of trouble? Who's your friend?" She put her sack on the bench.

Troy grabbed Lydia's hand. "This is Lydia. Remember, I told you about her. I met her at the mushroom camp. She was Teddy's friend and now she's mine." Then he turned to Lydia, pointed to his grandmother and said slowly and carefully, "Jii shitsuu t'iinch'ùu." He looked up his grandmother for approval and she nodded at him.

"That was perfect," she said. She smiled at Lydia. "I'm teaching Troy a little Gwich'in."

"What did you say to me?" Lydia asked Troy.

"I said, 'This is my grandmother.' Isn't that cool?"

"Very cool," said Lydia.

Troy's grandmother stuck out her hand. "My name is Ethel Haugen. It's nice to meet you. Troy has been talking about you endlessly."

Lydia returned Ethel's firm handshake. "It's good to meet you, too. Troy's a great kid."

Ethel smiled and tousled the boy's hair. "He's my favorite grandson."

Troy gave her a shocked look. "You have another grandson?"

"No. That's why you're my favorite."

"Hey, I see you've met Ethel," called Anna as she approached the trio from the front walk. Anna's face had been scrubbed pink and her hair was combed. She was pale and her eyes were still a bit red, but she had put on a touch of lipstick.

"My goodness," said Ethel. "You know Anna, too?"

"I've known Anna since graduate school," said Lydia. "She moved to Dawson because of me."

"And because of all the single men," said Anna. Lydia could see that she was working hard to speak normally.

"It really is a small world," said Ethel. "You should both come up to my place for tea and cookies sometime."

"We'd love to," said Lydia.

"I have to get these groceries inside. The ice cream is going to melt," said Ethel.

"Ice cream!" yelled Troy. All thoughts of Jared Spolsky

vanished. He began to run toward the apartment. "I hope it's chocolate," he yelled over his shoulder.

CHAPTER 9

Anna and Lydia headed toward Dawson Dolly's cafe. Even in her grief, Anna was unwilling to give up her 40% discount. They were almost to Second Avenue when they noticed a man staggering in their direction. He was waving his arms and weaving the entire width of the boardwalk. A young woman wearing a gay nineties getup—tight red bodice, long purple skirt held out by stiff crinolines, and high buttoned boots—was coming up behind him. As she began to pass the man, he stumbled, lurched sideways, and knocked the dance hall girl to her knees. The momentum propelled him off the boardwalk and he fell onto the dusty street where he remained on his hands and knees, breathing hard with his eyes closed.

"Shit," said the girl as she got to her feet. She grabbed a fistful of velvet in each hand and tried to shake the dust from her voluminous skirt. "This sucks. I go on in half an hour."

Lydia pulled a bandana out her pocket and handed it to the girl. "Here. You can brush yourself off with this. It's clean. Just keep it." Then she stepped off the boardwalk and knelt beside the old man. The dance hall girl seemed to have no interest in his condition or his fate. After a few a quick rubs, she dropped the bandana next to Lydia and hurried off in the direction of Diamond Tooth Gertie's Gambling Hall, where tourists would admire her fish-net clad legs as she danced in the high-kicking chorus line.

As Lydia peered down at the man, she realized that she knew him. He opened his eyes and squinted at her. "Wha happened?"

"Good grief, it's George Jenkins," said Anna.

Lydia grabbed one arm as Anna grabbed the other. "Get up, George," said Anna. "You can't stay here. You'll get run over." After a couple of tugs, they managed to haul the old man to his knees and then to his feet. As he leaned into Lydia, she could smell whisky on his breath and vomit on his clothes. He squinted as he tried to focus on the apparitions in front him.

"I know you," he said. "You're ... you're ... friends ... Katie ... dau ...." His eyes rolled and Lydia thought he was going to pass out. Lydia grabbed him under both armpits and held him upright. He tried to focus again and gave her a crooked smile.

"Goddam it, George, you're drunk!" Lydia had to resist an urge to shake him. George Jenkins was a recovering alcoholic who attended AA meetings every week and had been dry for at least two decades.

"No," said George. "Not drunk. Jus a couple a snorts. Thas all."

"You're drunk as a skunk," said Anna. They hauled the old man back up on the boardwalk and propped him against a wall while they discussed what to do. By the time they had decided to take him Dawson Dolly's, he had one cheek pressed against the window of a clothing store and was staring cross-eyed at a psychedelic tie-dyed T shirt. He didn't respond to the shop owner, who was tapping on the window and motioning him off. A group of teenagers across the street began imitating George's spastic motions.

Lydia grabbed George's arm and pried his face off the plate glass. She led him into Dolly's and pushed him into a chair while Anna went to call his daughter. Lydia sighed as George Jenkin's head wobbled on his long, patrician neck. He didn't look much like the dignified, retired school teacher that she knew him to be. He was in his early eighties but he looked ten years older. His thin white hair was standing out straight from his scalp; his blue eyes were bloodshot and his face was mottled red and grey. He was having trouble breathing and he kept snorting as if he had something caught in the back of his throat. George's clothes were of good quality, carefully pressed, and filthy.

The tourists at the next table shook their heads. The man rolled his eyes dramatically and the woman said in a booming voice, "Pathetic. I've read that alcoholism is major problem up here." She waved her arm as if to embrace the entire subarctic.

"So are obnoxious tourists," said Lydia sharply. The woman gasped and turned her face to the wall. The cashier offered Lydia a big grin.

George closed his eyes, opened them, and then stared blankly at Lydia for a moment. "You ... you ..." but before he could finish the thought, his eyelids closed again and he pitched forward on the table.

Anna returned with a cup coffee and put it on the table. "This isn't going to do him any good. Katherine's on her way. She suggested that we take George outside to wait so he doesn't barf all over the restaurant."

By the time, they had extricated George from his chair and pushed and pulled him to the boardwalk, Katherine Jenkins was driving up to the restaurant. She stumbled as she got out of the car. Her face was grim and her eyes were wet. Lydia helped her cram George into the passenger seat of the Subaru. Katherine slammed the door shut and leaned her back against it. Her face collapsed at the same time her body stiffened.

Lydia put an arm around the other woman and squeezed her shoulder. "What's happened to George, Katherine? What's going on?"

"I don't know," said Katherine, struggling to maintain control. "I wish to God I did. He's been like this for over two months. Dad hadn't had a drink in twenty five years. He went to AA meetings faithfully. He sponsored two other people. Now look at him." Lydia turned and peered through the glass. George's head had fallen against the dashboard. She could hear his snores through the car door.

Suddenly there was a piercing blast. George had shifted in the seat, toppled left, and hit the horn with his head. Katherine ran to the driver's side, yanked open the door, and roughly pushed her father upright. She spoke to Lydia and Anna over the top of the car. "I don't know how much longer I can take this. I can't let him out of my sight. He's got booze stashed all over the house." She pulled a tattered tissue from her pocket and wiped her eyes. "I'm terrified that he'll hurt himself. Or even worse, somebody else." Katherine ducked into the driver's seat and gave Lydia a small wave.

The smell of George Jenkins lingered in the air. Neither Anna nor Lydia had any desire for food. "I need to go lie down," said Anna. "This has been the worst day of my life." Lydia gave her a long hug and headed back to Al's.

She had just poured herself a cup of coffee when the phone rang. The voice on the line was high and tense.

"Lydia, it's Katherine. Can you talk for a minute?"

"Sure. What's going on?"

"When Dad and I got home, the mail had arrived. I picked it up before we went into the house and went through it while we were standing in the front hall. One of the envelopes didn't have a stamp and was addressed to Dad in pencil. The handwriting was strange, like somebody right-handed had used their left hand. When Dad saw the envelope, he gave this little moan."

"Did you ask him if he knew who it was from?"

"Yes, and he just shook his head. He went in the living room and curled up on the couch. He wouldn't even look at me."

"So did you open the letter?"

"Yes. All it said was *The apple doesn't fall far from the tree.* It was the same strange handwriting. There was no signature or anything. But that's not the weirdest part. I went into his bedroom to see if I could find anything that would explain this. What I found was three more of these letters. They all looked pretty much the same."

"That *is* weird," said Lydia. She paused a moment and then repeated the message out loud. "*The apple doesn't fall far from the tree*. That usually means that the child resembles the parent. Do you think it's somebody claiming to be his child?"

Katherine was silent for a moment. "I hadn't thought of that. My mother died young and Dad may have had affairs. I don't remember any girlfriends but that doesn't mean anything."

Then Katherine paused so long that Lydia felt compelled to ask, "Katherine, are you still there? Are you okay?"

Katherine's voice was faint. "Yes, I'm here. What if I really do have a half brother or sister somewhere? Maybe I should try to find out. I have to make him talk to me. I ...." Her voice caught. "I have to." Lydia hung up the phone and shook her head. Katherine certainly didn't deserve this grief. She was what Lydia's mother called a *good person*. She volunteered at the abused women's shelter; she had stray cats neutered; she routinely housed the unemployed in her spare bedroom. The folks in town called her Saint Katherine. Some of them rolled their eyes when they said it.

A children's librarian, Katherine was completely relaxed with kids, but her relationships with grownups were constrained, serious. Katherine rarely joked or laughed with adults and she never seemed completely comfortable with them. Katherine didn't chat, she debated. She was smart, well-read, and opinionated. For her, adult discourse had to have a point and a purpose— politics, literature, culture. She wasn't much for kicking back and hanging out.

Two days later Lydia had finished her list of supplies for the cabin. It was noon and she was ready for a beer, a burger, and a bit of diversion. She strolled downtown. She was about to pass Diamond Tooth Gertie's gambling emporium when two women brushed past her. One was frowning. "Damn it," she said. "I can never remember the hands. A straight beats a flush, right?" Her friend rolled up the right sleeve on her shirt, peered at her arm, and nodded. Lydia stifled a laugh. The second woman had written the poker hands in order on her forearm but she was reading them upside down. Lydia wasn't inclined to come to their rescue. Gamblers like this were good for the economy.

It was a busy afternoon in downtown Dawson. Locals dodged tourists who were clogging the sidewalks as they gawked at restored Victorian architecture dripping with ginger bread. A group of motorcyclists revved their engines as they sat astride their Harleys eating ice cream cones. Melting chocolate splashed on the gleaming black gas tanks. RVs threaded their way through pedestrians as they rumbled toward the auto ferry that would take them across the Yukon to the Top of the World Highway and into Alaska.

Lydia headed for the Downtown Hotel, an establishment dating back to the Gold Rush. It was busy day and night, even in winter. Its big attraction was its world famous sour toe cocktail. For over forty years, this establishment had been home to a series of gnarled, hideous, mummified toes. For an extra ten dollars, Leonard, the toe overseer, would add the toe to any drink. To receive the coveted *Sourtoe Certificate*, the drinker's mouth had to touch the shriveled, blackened digit. On occasion, an especially drunk patron would swallow it. The menu periodically carried this plea.

Got frostbite? The Downtown Hotel in Dawson, Yukon Territory is currently seeking toes for its world famous sourtoe cocktail. Donor will be forever immortalized in the Sourtoe Hall of Fame.

A mix of tipsy patrons clustered around the bar. Most were tourists, some were locals, and a few were wearing *Bad Axe Mine* work shirts. There was a lot of good natured laughing and shouting. In the midst of the commotion, a man wearing a baseball cap came in the back door. He ignored the knot at the bar. He approached a kid wearing a Megadeth T shirt and studded bracelet, who was shooting pool alone. The man spoke softly to the kid and then looked up. Lydia did a double-take. It was Sam Avakian. He didn't see her. He motioned to the kid and they went out the back door. Sam returned a few minutes later and spoke to a miner who was standing apart from the others. The miner nodded, and they, too, went out to the alley.

In the meantime the crowd at the bar was ordering sour toe cocktails. Lydia watched with a bemused smile as a plump, middle aged woman in flowered Capri pants and a floppy orange hat ordered a sour toe scotch. When her lips brushed the toe, she fist-bumped the woman next to her. Leonard grimaced when that woman ordered a sour toe bloody Mary. She, too, successfully navigated the toe. A bald, heavily tattooed construction worker ordered the bar's signature drink, a Yukon Jack sour toe whiskey. He tipped his shot glass slightly and put it to his lips. He started to drink and lost his nerve. "Oh, hell, I ain't doing this. It's disgusting."

"Pussy," yelled a woman on the edge of group. She was young, pretty, and had a voice like Roseanne Barr. "Gimme a sour toe tequila," she bellowed at Leonard. "Make it a double." Leonard complied. The woman drank the tequila down in one swallow—along with the toe.

There was a universal "Oh, shit!" from the other patrons. Everyone's eyes were on the toe overseer.

Sam Avakian re-entered just in time to see Leonard's face go scarlet. "Goddam you. That's our last toe," Leonard yelled. He leaned over the bar and got in the offender's face. "There's a five hundred dollar fine for that. Payable immediately."

"You a cop?" said the woman.

"No. So what?"

"Then fuck you."

Leonard started to walk around the bar with his hands clenched.

"I'll pay her fine," said a voice. Sam Avakian stepped between Leonard and the woman. He pulled five bills from his pocket and slapped them in Leonard's hand. The crowd cheered.

"It's time to leave," he said to the woman as he put his arm around her shoulder. As he led her out the back door, she thrust her middle finger into the air.

Lydia was stunned. Five hundred dollars was a fortune to a mushroom picker. Lydia couldn't decide if Sam was incredibly generous, crazy, or both. Did he know this woman? Was she his girlfriend? A relative? Forget it, she thought. It's his money.

Lydia finished her burger and ordered a second Moosehead. She leaned back in her chair and savored the brew. Tomorrow she would drive to Whitehorse to stock up and two days later she'd head for her cabin. She smiled at the prospect.

She had just emptied the bottle when the swinging doors of the saloon blew open and Anna burst through. She marched over to Lydia's table. "I've been looking all over for you," she yelled.

"Why? What's the matter?"

"Did you hear about George Jenkins?" she asked breathlessly.

"No."

"He's gone missing."

"Jesus. For how long?"

"He got another one of those notes yesterday and disappeared. His car's gone. Katherine's a wreck. I saw her this morning and she said she thinks he might have headed for Ross River. She's going down there."

Lydia scowled. "Why does Katherine think he's there?"

"Those notes. *The apple doesn't fall far from the tree.* She thinks she may have a half-sibling from when George taught there."

Lydia groaned. "Oh, God. This is my fault. I put that idea into her head. Why didn't I keep my mouth shut? Maybe I can talk her out of it."

"Nobody has ever changed Katherine's mind about anything," said Anna through clenched teeth.

"I have to try. This is crazy."

Anna walked Lydia to the Robert Service School, where the public library was housed. She had no interest, however, in trying to talk sense into Katherine Jenkins, so Lydia entered the building alone. Twice she tripped over the muddy Crocs and sneakers abandoned by children who had obeyed the **Please remove shoes** sign.

As she looked around, Lydia heard a voice rising and falling on the other side of room. She threaded her way through the stacks and found Katherine in the children's area. She was sitting in a chair flanked by two dying tropical plants. A group of ten children were on the floor at her feet.

Katherine's face was haggard. Her long hair had been pulled back in two mismatched barrettes and lay lank and dull on her shoulders. A shapeless blue jumper covered a white T shirt which had encountered something new and red in the washing machine. Broken down suede Birkenstocks peeked out from under her long skirt. Katherine had never been a clothes horse but her dress had always been neat and professional; her hair was always carefully braided and coiled on her neck. This current dishevelment suggested extreme distress.

But Katherine's mental state had not diminished her powers as a story teller. The diminutive audience gazed at her with rapt attention. No one fidgeted; no one poked, prodded, or pinched a neighbor; no one whispered or coughed. As Lydia listened, she realized that the story sounded very familiar. Good grief, she thought. Katherine's telling *Beowulf* to nine year olds. And she was. There were monsters, fierce battles, brave warriors, and sumptuous feasts, but the death and dismemberment had been toned down. Katherine's hands danced as she set each scene and her face morphed into that of King Hrothgar, then Beowulf, then the monster Grendel, and then Grendel's vengeful mother.

After the story ended, Lydia made her way through the knot of children and put her hand on Katherine's shoulder. "How're you doing?"

"You've heard," said Katherine.

Lydia nodded. "So there's still no word."

Katherine shook her head. "No." Her eyes filled with tears. She turned away and took a handkerchief from her pocket.

"Anna said you're going down to Ross River. Is that true?"

Katherine nodded. "My father has another child and that's the scene of the liaison."

"How can you be sure?" asked Lydia.

"It turns out that *apple* is another word for a mixed race child. My dad taught at Ross River for a long time. He was a widower for the last few years. I'm sure he had an affair with a First Nation woman."

It was hard to argue with Katherine's logic. "Do you know anyone there?" asked Lydia. "Have you asked if anyone's seen him down there?"

Katherine shook her head as she blew her nose. "No, but I'm going anyway." Then she looked hard at Lydia. "Would you go with me?"

Lydia groaned inwardly. It was the last thing in the world she wanted to do. "When?"

"I'd like to leave this afternoon."

This time Lydia's groan was audible. "Oh, God, this isn't a good time for me." Katherine did not withdraw her request. Lydia thought about telling Katherine about Teddy; she thought about telling Katherine that she desperately needed more time to recover; she thought about telling Katherine she had to get home to her cabin. The word *no* had formed on her lips. But she didn't utter it.

Guilt always seemed to lurk at the edge of Lydia's Midwestern consciousness. She had never been good at saying *no* but neither was she good at suppressing the feelings of resentment that often surfaced after agreeing to inconvenient or unreasonable requests.

"I'll come, but can't we wait until tomorrow? That's a seven or eight hour drive and I'm in bad shape today." She bit her lip. "I recently lost a close friend." Katherine offered no condolences. She seemed oblivious to Lydia's distress.

"I can't wait any longer. I've waited too long already." Katherine's eyes teared. "Please, Lydia. Please," she croaked. Lydia suddenly remembered what it had been like to lose her own father. She would help Katherine find hers.

"Look, I have to go back to Al's and get some clothes. How long do you plan to spend down there?"

"If we find him right away we can come back tomorrow. If we don't …." Katherine shrugged.

Lydia trudged back to the house. By the time she had reached the front door, her irritation had reached its peak. "How do I get myself into this shit?" she muttered. While a fresh pot of coffee brewed, she threw a couple of changes of socks and underwear and a clean T shirt into her day pack. She wolfed down some leftover chili and treated herself to a bowl of chocolate ice cream. Then she drank one cup of coffee and poured the rest into her steel thermos.

Lydia didn't want to make this trip and she most certainly did not want to tell Al that she was making this trip. She called the RCMP detachment at 1:30, certain that he would be at lunch and she'd be transferred to his voice mail. But when the desk clerk put the call through, she was greeted with, "This is Sergeant Cerwinski. How can I help you?"

"Well," said Lydia, "you can help by not accusing me of being crazy for doing this."

There was a long pause on the other end of the line. Finally Al said, "For doing what, may I ask?"

"Driving with Katherine Jenkins to Ross River."

"Ross River," bellowed Al. He paused and composed himself. "This is about her father, isn't it?"

Lydia nodded at the phone.

"Does Katherine have any concrete evidence that her father's actually down there?"

Lydia shook her head at the phone.

"I'll take your silence as a *no*," said Al. Lydia could tell that he was frustrated. "Has she contacted anyone down there?"

"She says she doesn't know anybody."

"Well, I do. Let me make a couple of calls," said Al. "Tell Katherine to wait until she hears from me."

"You'd better call her here," said Lydia. "She's on her way over now."

"Goddam it," said Al. "Don't leave before I call back." He hung up.

The click of the receiver was accompanied by the slam of a car door. A few moments later there was a knock and Katherine stuck her head into the front hall. "Are you ready?"

"No," said Lydia from the living room. "We need to wait for a bit."

Katherine walked into the living room shaking her head. "I can't wait," she said. "I have to leave now."

Lydia told her what Al was doing. "He knows people in Ross River. He might be able to find out for sure whether or not George is there. This is worth waiting for."

Katherine fell into a chair. She put one hand over her face. "I'll give him half an hour," she said through her fingers. "That's it. Half an hour."

Lydia nodded. She grabbed the thermos from the counter and poured them each a cup of coffee. Katherine didn't take her eyes off the phone as she raised the cup to her lips. Twenty three minutes later it rang. Lydia and Katherine jumped up at the same time.

Lydia waved Katherine back into her chair. When she picked up the receiver, she was greeted with, "I'll be damned. It looks like Katherine was right."

"George is in Ross River?" Lydia was incredulous. Katherine gave an audible gasp.

"It sure sounds like it. One of the guys I called was in the café yesterday morning. He said an old white guy came in, drunk on his ass. The physical description he gave me certainly fits. Let me talk to Katherine a minute."

When Katherine hung up the phone, she was smiling.

"He's there. He's alive."

Lydia nodded. Alive, yes. But living? Hardly.

CHAPTER 10

As Katherine and Lydia headed south on the Klondike Highway, Lydia asked, "What will you do when you find George?"

"Make him come home." Katherine replied firmly as if this would resolve everything. It suddenly occurred to Lydia why Katherine was so desperate for her company. If George was drunk, and the odds were good, he wouldn't be able to drive. It would be Lydia's job to bring his car back to Dawson. This epiphany didn't improve her mood one bit.

Fortunately, Lydia was not required to be civil. Katherine had no interest in conversation. The bubble of fear and dread in which she had enveloped herself was impenetrable. She sat tall and rigid in her seat, eyes straight ahead. She gripped the steering wheel so hard that the veins stood out on the tops of her hands. She was driving too fast.

The words to Stan Roger's powerful ballad *Canol Road* floated into Lydia's consciousness. Roger's driver stares unblinking into the dark; his shoulders are tensed; his hands clutch the steering wheel. Crazed by cabin fever, he kills a man in Whitehorse and freezes to death on the Canol Road. The Canol Road passes directly through Ross River.

As the afternoon wore on, Lydia became grumpier and grumpier. She slouched in the passenger seat and sulked for a while. When her lower back began to protest, she removed her boots and put her stocking feet on the dash board. She silently dared Katherine to make an issue of it. Katherine didn't even look in her direction as Lydia wiggled her toes at on-coming traffic.

Shortly before Stewart Crossing, three cars in front of Katherine came to a complete stop in the middle of the southbound lane. "What the hell is their problem?" muttered Katherine beating her palms on the steering wheel. There was a blind curve ahead and she didn't dare pass. Lydia smiled and pointed. There was a grizzly sow with two cubs just a few yards from the road. Mama bear was large and magnificent. She was dark blond with a massive hump between her shoulders. As she watched the cars, her tiny round eyes seemed too small for her broad, flat face. Convinced these hunks of metal were harmless, she turned away from the road and approached a rotting birch log with her lumbering, pigeon-toed gait. She sniffed it and then tore into it with teeth and claws. Wood chips flew.

The cubs were this year's babies. They were very small with button noses and bright, curious eyes. Their fur was still dark brown and fluffy, and they sported the tiniest of humps behind their heads. At first they calmly nibbled on flower tops, but then one cub smacked the other and a wrestling match ensued. Standing on tiny hind legs, they batted at each other's heads. Then one grabbed the other in a head lock and they both fell over. As they rolled their way through magenta fireweed, Lydia saw the passenger window on the rental car in front of the Subaru go halfway down. A telephoto lens peeked over the edge.

"Oh, for Christ sake," said Katherine. She laid on the horn. In a flash the sow and her cubs disappeared into the brush. The driver of the rental car opened his window and shook his fist.

"That was uncalled for, Katherine," said Lydia through clenched teeth. "Those folks just wanted to get a couple of pictures.

"I don't have time for that," said Katherine. Lydia couldn't trust herself to respond.

When Katherine slowed for the turn just after Five Finger Rapids, Lydia fixed her eyes on the Yukon. The water sparkled as it washed over rocks and logs; water bugs danced on the surface creating tiny wakes. In a small pond a pair of trumpeter swans swam among the cloven leaves of stiff, pink water lilies. Lydia longed to be down there sitting among the horsetails or wading in an eddy—anywhere but in this station wagon, next to this grim and desperate woman, on the way to collar an even more desperate old man. It was definitely time that she learned to say *no*.

Katherine had packed food for the trip and by 5:00 PM, Lydia was starved. She extracted two sandwiches from the cooler. She passed one to Katherine and unwrapped the other one. She wrinkled her nose as she inspected the ingredients, two slices of processed cheese on airy white bread with a dab of mayonnaise. Although Lydia had contempt for each ingredient, she devoured every crumb. Katherine nibbled at hers for a few minutes and then placed it on the dashboard next to Lydia's left foot. Half an hour later, Lydia finished Katherine's sandwich. Then she insisted on a bathroom stop. When Katherine refused, she threatened to pee on the Subaru's leather seat. It was 10:45 pm when they finally reached their destination.

Ross River is a Kaska First Nation village of less than four hundred people. The sun was just beginning to set and the village had not yet gone to bed. Four elderly women sat on a front porch, knitting and chatting. A lone teen ager shot baskets on the court at the Ross River School. His long baggy shorts hung dangerously low on his skinny hips, and with every jump shot they inched lower. A gaggle of smaller children chased each other through neighborhood yards, causing spasms of barking from a team of tethered sled dogs.

Everything is expensive in a remote, sub-arctic village. There was a General Store but locals hunted, fished, trapped, and picked berries to fill their smokers and freezers. One family exhibited its prowess on the exterior wall of the garage—four sets of moose antlers, a number of mountain sheep horns, even a buffalo skull. Beneath the eaves of an old log cabin, pieces of chum salmon had been hung on a rack to dry. Chow for the sled dogs.

Katherine pulled up to the village's Motor Hotel and Cafe. Katherine insisted on putting the room on her credit card and Lydia didn't argue. But by 2:00 AM Lydia was wishing that she had shelled out for a room of her own. Every time she managed to doze off, Katherine would flail around on her bed sending her springs into a paroxysm of creaking and squeaking. Katherine got up three times in the night and peered out the window at the empty road. She got up twice to pee. She got up once more to get a glass of water. By morning, Lydia was exhausted.

The two women had breakfast at the café attached to the hotel. The place was a period piece, a tribute to taxidermy and knotty pine. Lydia ordered two eggs over easy, brown toast, sausage, and potatoes. Katherine ordered a piece of buttered white toast and a cup of tea. A stuffed wolverine stared at them balefully as Lydia wolfed down her food and Katherine picked at her toast.

When the waitress came to refill their coffee cups, Lydia turned to Katherine. "Ask her," she said.

"Ask me what?" said the waitress.

Katherine took a deep breath. "I was wondering if you'd seen my father in the last couple of days." She described George Jenkins.

The waitress nodded. Yes, she had seen the old white man yesterday morning. She hadn't talked to him. He was way too drunk for conversation; he was almost too drunk to eat. "It wasn't even eight o'clock," she said, giving Katherine a sympathetic look. Then she turned and headed for the kitchen.

"If he was that drunk, he can't have gone far," said Lydia. "I wonder if he has any old friends here." Katherine shrugged.

When the waitress returned with the coffee pot, Lydia said. "We'd like to find someone who might have known Katherine's father back in the early sixties. He taught school here. Can you steer us to some people who were living here then?"

The waitress thought a moment. "Well, we've got a lot of old timers born and raised in the area. Most of the old men are out fishing." Then she raised an index finger. "Mrs. Ellgate. I'll bet she knew this man. She's lived here all her life and she's about eighty. She was a school teacher, too. "

"Where can we find her?" asked Lydia.

"Her house is down the road toward the river. She's painting it and the old paint is half scraped off. You can't miss it."

They didn't miss it. The front of the house had been taken down to bare wood. Huge curls of white latex littered the ground. Someone wearing overalls was standing on an extension ladder removing blue paint from the fascia under an eave. As they walked up the front path, Lydia could see that the woman wielding the scraper was lean and muscular. Iron grey hair peeked below paint spattered baseball cap.

"Are you Mrs. Ellgate?" asked Lydia.

The woman turned to face them. Her face was the color of strong tea, deep laugh lines spread out from her eyes, and crevices in each cheek inscribed parentheses around her mouth. "Yes. I'm Marjorie Ellgate," she said.

Lydia nudged Katherine in the ribs. Katherine cleared her throat. "I'm Katherine Jenkins and this is Lydia Falkner. We were hoping you could help us find my father. His name is George Jenkins."

Mrs. Ellgate's mouth opened in surprise. "George Jenkins! I haven't heard that name in fifty years." She gave a little laugh. "I didn't even know he was still alive." She climbed down the ladder and laid her scraper on the porch railing. She looked Katherine up and down. "You must be little Katie. You've grown a bit since I last saw you." She gave Katherine a penetrating look. "How did you come to lose your father?"

Katherine mustered a small, tight smile. "He took off from our house in Dawson without telling me where he was going. I had reasons for believing he came here. Then we heard that someone actually saw him in the café yesterday. We were hoping that he's still here, that maybe he contacted an old friend."

Mrs. Ellgate frowned. Her face tightened. "We weren't friends and he didn't contact me."

"But you knew him," persisted Katherine. "The waitress said you taught at the school. So did he."

Mrs. Ellgate's mouth opened, then she snapped it shut again. She pressed her lips together and her eyes narrowed. It was clear that she was trying to make a decision.

Lydia decided to push. "What is it? What do you need to tell us?"

The woman pushed a stray piece of hair out of her eyes and looked hard at Katherine. "You don't know, do you?"

"Know what?" said Katherine.

"That your father taught at the Indian school."

Katherine frowned and cocked her head at Mrs. Ellgate. "Yes, he taught at Ross River School."

"No," said Mrs. Ellgate, her face tight. "He didn't teach at Ross River School."

"Well, where did he teach then?" said Katherine sharply.

"At the Salmon River Indian School. It was a residential school run by the Anglicans. It was about fifteen miles up the road." Lydia stared at Mrs. Ellgate. She had heard horror stories about residential Indian schools and she was astonished that George Jenkins had been part of that system.

But Katherine either knew nothing of residential schools or chose to ignore the significance of Mrs. Ellgate's words. "So maybe that's where he went," she said, brightening. "To that school."

Mrs. Ellgate shook her head. "No. I don't think so. It's been gone for decades." She paused and gave Katherine a challenging look. "We burned it down."

Lydia could hear Katherine's intake of breath. Katherine took a step away from Mrs. Ellgate and asked, "But why? Why would anyone burn down a school?"

"Do you really want to know?"

Katherine stared at the woman, mute. Then she shook her

head ever so slightly as she surreptitiously peeked at her watch. Lydia reached over, covered the face of the watch with her palm and said, "Yes, we do want to know."

"Come in then and I'll make some coffee."

As Mrs. Ellgate ascended the steps and opened the front door, Katherine grabbed Lydia's shirt. "Are you crazy? We haven't got time for this," she hissed. "We've got to look for Dad."

"Look," said Lydia, who didn't even try to keep annoyance out of her voice, "we don't know what brought George to Ross River but it's probably something connected with that school. We need all the information we can get."

Katherine closed her eyes and sighed. When she opened them, she said, "Okay, but no more than half an hour. Half an hour max." The thirty minute ultimatum seemed to be Katherine's specialty.

The two women followed Mrs. Ellgate into the house. She directed them to sit at the kitchen table. There was no conversation as Mrs. Ellgate put the kettle on and laid some cookies on a plate. She pulled three sturdy mugs from the cupboard and measured a teaspoon of instant coffee into each. Then she poured in boiling water. Lydia's stomach lurched but she accepted her cup with a smile. "How much do you know about residential Indian schools?" asked Mrs. Ellgate as she seated herself at the table. Katherine responded by looking deep into her coffee cup.

It was Lydia who replied. "I don't know much, but I do know that in the old days kids were sometimes forcibly removed from their families and sent to these places. I know there were terrible abuses. I remember a famous photograph." She paused and looked at the ceiling as she tried to recall the details. "There were actually two pictures, both of the same little First Nation boy. In one he was dressed in skins and fur and beads. He's holding a gun and his hair was in long braids. In the second, his hair was cut short and he was wearing boots and a high collared suit. A before and after study, I guess."

Mrs. Ellgate nodded. "Exactly. That was little Thomas Moore

in 1904, before and after he was taken to the Regina Residential School. He was the government's poster boy for the residential school movement. In the *before* picture he's supposed to be a raw savage." She made quotation marks in the air around the word *savage*. "In the second picture he's been civilized." She inscribed quotation marks again.

"But all that happened a long time ago," said Katherine.

Thomas More was a long time ago, but there have been a lot of abused kids since then," said Mrs. Ellgate. "Do you know when the very last residential Indian school in Canada was closed?" Lydia shook her head and Katherine shrugged.

"Nineteen ninety six. Not so long ago, eh?"

"How bad was Salmon River School?" asked Lydia.

"It was terrible. The food was barely adequate. The dorms were freezing cold in the winter. The kids had to work hard for their keep. We'll never know how much abuse there was. The goal of Salmon River School was the same as all the other residential schools. Assimilation. No Kaska, Tutchone, Tagish, or Gwich'in could be spoken in classrooms or in the dormitory. Any child who disobeyed had their mouth washed out with lye soap. No traditional rituals could be conducted on the grounds. Indian clothing wasn't allowed. The boys all wore military style uniforms and the girls wore plain cotton dresses. The assumption was that if the children looked and sounded like white kids, they'd be white kids. But you know what the worst thing was?" Mrs. Ellgate didn't wait for an answer. "They stripped our children of their language and their culture but they didn't put anything back."

"What do you mean?" asked Katherine.

"They gave them a lousy education. It was a terrible school. Those children didn't learn anything that would help them get ahead in the white man's world and they lost the very things that made them Indian."

Katherine's face was pale. She clasped her hands together and held them to her chest. She spoke in a small, tight voice. "My father was a good teacher. He was popular with the students in Dawson."

"George taught less than a semester at Salmon River School. Then he was made principal. He was the man in charge. And believe me, he wasn't popular."

Katherine gave a small squeak and buried her face in her hands. "Oh, God."

"When did the school burn?" asked Lydia.

"The government closed it in 1971. The Anglicans left it to rot, so six years later we torched it."

"Who's we?" asked Lydia.

Mrs. Ellgate waved her arm in a large circle. "Indians from all over the central Yukon. It was a huge event. Lots food. Lots of dancing. It went on for three days. For us it was a cleansing experience." She offered a small, sad smile. "I suppose you could even call it an exorcism. Anyhow, there's nothing left of the place. It's all gone back to forest. You wouldn't be able to find the grounds. I doubt that I could. Even if George could find the right spot on the road, he wouldn't be able to penetrate the tangle of trees and brush. And trust me, there's nothing to see."

Katherine stood up and brushed her hands over her clothes as if to press out the wrinkles. "Thank you, Mrs. Ellgate. You've been very …." Her voice caught. "Helpful."

"Wait," said Lydia. "Don't you have something else to ask Mrs. Ellgate?"

Katherine shook her head vigorously.

"I'll do it then," said Lydia. Katherine glared but didn't try to stop her. Lydia cleared her throat and tried to think of a delicate way to pose her question. She couldn't. "Do you know if George Jenkins ever had an affair with a First Nation woman which resulted in a child?"

Lydia was startled when Mrs. Ellgate threw back her head and laughed.

"What's so funny?" said Katherine, looking at the same time baffled and offended.

"Your father was the most straight-laced man I ever knew. I can assure you he didn't have an affair with any woman, white or First Nation. Not while he lived in Ross River anyway. And believe me, you can't keep a secret like that in a town like this." She paused and looked hard at Katherine. "So you thought you had a half Indian sister or brother. Whatever made you come to that conclusion?"

Katherine told Mrs. Ellgate about the notes. Mrs. Ellgate shook her head. "You got it wrong, Miss Jenkins. Those notes aren't about a half-breed child; those notes are about an Indian child, one who went to a residential school. That's what the government wanted to do to our children. Turn them into apples. Red on the outside, white on the inside. Somebody from Salmon River School sent those notes to your father and I doubt that it was someone who wished him well." Katherine grabbed Lydia's forearm and held it tight. There was panic in her eyes.

"Do you have any idea who might have sent them?" asked Lydia.

"None at all. Hundreds of children passed through that school. All of them hated it."

Lydia nodded and stood up. "Thank you so much for your time and the coffee."

"I'm sorry that I had to tell you things that were upsetting," said Mrs. Ellgate. "But you asked."

Katherine stood and pulled a business card out of her pocket. "If you see my dad or hear anything about him, will you please call me?"

Mrs. Ellgate nodded and put the card in the pocket of her overalls. "I didn't like your father, Katie, but I don't wish him harm."

CHAPTER 11

Lydia and Katherine trudged back to the motel in silence. Lydia had no idea what their next move should be and Katherine seemed incapable of formulating any sort of plan. Just before they entered, Lydia stopped and put her hand on Katherine's shoulder. "Think hard. If George couldn't visit the school, maybe there's another place that had meaning for him. A place he might be drawn to."

Katherine gave Lydia a hopeless look and squeezed her forehead between her thumb and little finger. Suddenly, she dropped her hand and breathed in sharply. "Yes," she said. "There *is* a special place. I haven't thought about it in years. I know it was on the North Canol Road because I remember taking the ferry to get there. There was this creek where my family went for picnics. We went every Sunday during the summer. Mum always made deviled ham sandwiches. Every week it was the same—deviled ham, chocolate cake, and lemonade." Suddenly Katherine put her hand to her mouth and her eyes teared. "Yesterday was Sunday, Lydia. It was *Sunday*. That's where he went!"

"Can you find it?"

Katherine nodded. "I think so."

"Let's go," said Lydia. They sprinted for the car and drove the few hundred yards to the river crossing.

Fortunately, the little car ferry was on their side of the river. Unfortunately it was 12:50 PM and ferry service was suspended from 12:00 to 1:00. The operator was sitting with his back against a cottonwood eating something out of a little bag. Katherine rolled down the car window to talk to him. He was unmoved by her pleas. He was pleasant but firm, as he pointed to his watch. "We don't go 'til one. Them's the rules. It's posted." He shoved an empty Smarties package into one shirt pocket and pulled a lighter and pack of cigarettes from the other.

"Jerk," said Katherine. He blinked at her but didn't respond.

Katherine looked ready to explode as she raised the window. "Relax," said Lydia. "It's less than ten minutes. No big deal." But after eight minutes of Katherine's sighing, fidgeting, and foot tapping, Lydia was ready to cold-cock the operator and hijack the ferry herself. Finally the young man ground his cigarette out on the sole of his shoe, got to his feet, and motioned them aboard.

Like the Alaska Highway, the Canol Road was a World War II military project. When the Japanese attacked petroleum installations in the Aleutian Islands, the Americans decided it was time gain access to the Norman Wells oilfields in the Northwest Territories. From 1942 to1944 the U.S. military built a road and a pipeline to bring oil south to Whitehorse. The Canadians had not been enthusiastic. The project was a bust. The pipeline leaked and the road fell into disuse. It is strewn with rocks and full of potholes. Many culverts have collapsed, leaving sharp metal edges which can slice through the tread of a tire as it sinks into the mud of a stream. Only the most intrepid travelers drive the North Canol Road.

In the first mile Lydia and Katherine passed two local pedestrians who were gathering herbs and one three-legged dog. Half a mile later they encountered a teenage couple necking in a pickup. A bra hung from the rear view mirror and two T shirts were draped over the steering wheel. The kids ducked as Katherine drove by. Low mountains ringed small lakes, which sparkled blue and silver in the intense light. A man in waders stood at the edge of one, his lime green monofilament inscribing circles in the air.

Soon all signs of current habitation disappeared, but the detritus left by the WW II American military was everywhere.

Old engines, oil cans, huge links of chain, and rusted out truck carcasses littered the roadside. Suddenly, without warning, Katherine braked hard. Lydia's seatbelt dug into her shoulder. "That's it. That's the spot." Katherine pointed to a wide, flat boulder which sat in a meadow filled with pale pink poppies. Lydia could see a small creek beyond.

Katherine steered the Subaru to the side of the road. The two women got out of the car and approached the rock. Water gurgled as it flowed over the rocky creek bed and through the brush tangles that had collected at the water's edge. A lone mallard swam in circles, his bright green head iridescent in the sun.

When Katherine reached the rock, she lay down on it and closed her eyes. Her fingers traced its knobs and crevices. "I can't believe I'm here again after all these years." She sat up, turned to her left, and pointed. "And there's the truck I played in when I was little. It was in much better shape then."

Lydia had to grin at the sight of the derelict US army truck, sitting tireless and almost rimless in a field of vibrant pink fireweed and tall bluebells. It had the look of an old boxer who had lost his last fight. One headlight was gone completely and the other hung from its socket by a single thick wire. The truck's front grill was gone, but four vertical supports remained in the hole, giving the truck a gap-toothed smile. The front bumper had crumpled inward and looked like a split lip. The truck's military paint job had faded to the color of pea soup in those few places where it had not given way to rust.

Katherine sat up and looked wistfully at the creek. "A few weeks after my mother died, Dad and I came out here to build a stone memorial, an inukshuk. I still remember him gathering stones. First he made Mum's legs out of oblongs. Then he found three flat stones in the creek for her torso. The top one was much longer than the rest and it looked like two outstretched arms. It was hard for him to get the big, round piece on top for her head. I piled up a few pebbles for her shoes. The inukshuk looked gigantic to me. I was only six. Some of the rocks sparkled and I thought it was the most beautiful thing I had ever seen."

Katherine slid off the rock. "I wonder if it's still here." She paused and looked around. Then she pointed. "I think it was beyond those poplars. Let's go look."

As Katherine and Lydia rounded the alder thicket which grew beneath the trees, Lydia was astonished to see a green sedan parked in the midst of flattened cotton grass, gouged tree trunks, and battered bushes. Katherine stopped dead. "Oh, my God," she whispered. "That's Dad's car." She began to run.

Lydia reached the vehicle just as Katherine wrenched open the driver's side door and thrust her head and shoulders inside. "He's not here," she screamed. "He's not here." She pulled herself out and clapped her hand over her mouth. She fell to her knees.

Lydia leaned into the vehicle and then backed out immediately. All the doors and windows had been closed and the biting, sour smell of vomit was overpowering. Lydia held her nose and looked in again. The car was empty except for a light weight jacket, two empty whiskey bottles, a small canvas bag, and a set of keys in the ignition. Holding her nose, Lydia reached in and grabbed the bag. It held a wallet and one clean pair of socks. She withdrew from the vehicle and took a deep breath of fresh air.

Lydia pulled Katherine up and put her arms around her. As Lydia held the other woman, she cast a quick glance at the front of the vehicle. A pile of large rocks lay against the tires and the bumper. A long, flat rock glistening with quartz had shattered a headlight. George Jenkins had run over his wife's inukshuk.

Lydia turned Katherine away from the car and began walking her to the road. Katherine continued to sob and Lydia shook her gently. "Calm down. Let's go find him. How far could he go?"

Katherine's sobs turned to hiccups. "I don't, *hic*, know. *Hic.* He's been drinking."

Indeed, thought Lydia. Out loud she said, "We'll find him. You walk north and I'll go in the other direction. I'll meet you back here in ten minutes."

Katherine nodded. She pulled her handkerchief from her

pocket and wiped her eyes. "Here I *hic* go," she said. Lydia watched her pull herself together both psychologically and physically—head up, neck long, body ramrod straight. Katherine took off down the road, her footfalls unnaturally heavy and her arms swinging. Every few seconds she called out. Sometimes it was *George*; sometimes it was *Dad*. Lydia flashed back to when she had Karl had done exactly the same thing except that the name they'd been calling was *Teddy*.

As Lydia headed back down the road, the old army truck caught her eye. It was the perfect place to finish off a liter and have a snooze. She trudged through the meadow. As she approached the derelict vehicle, she was startled to hear noises inside. She had been right! She quickened her steps but her hopes were dashed when two small paws appeared over the front bumper, followed by a grizzled brown head with black eyes and small ears. The marmot took one look at Lydia and scrambled back into the engine compartment. A moment later Lydia heard a soft thump as it jumped to the ground.

Lydia stood on tiptoe and peered over the long hood through the paneless windshield. The sun was in her eyes and the cab was reduced to a dark cave. As she walked around to the passenger side, she noticed that the gravel was scuffed bare in spots. Lydia slowly raised her eyes. The missing door provided her a full length view of the man slumped over on the seat, head jammed against what had once been a storage compartment. A bottle containing a few inches of amber liquid lay at his feet.

Lydia called George's name. There was no movement. With tiny steps she approached the empty door frame and peered at the form. Everything was covered with dried vomit but the smell had been carried away by the summer breeze. George's right arm hung loose at his side. Lydia reached out and touched his hand; it was cold. She pushed up the sleeve of his sweatshirt and pressed her fingers into his wrist. There was no pulse.

Lydia didn't touch him again but she did look closely at those parts she could see without moving him. There were no signs of trauma, no signs of violence. Lydia squatted in the dirt in order to see George's face. It was yellow with jaundice. A rusty stain ran down his grizzled chin and onto his shirt and pants. Blood. George Jenkins had finally drunk himself to death.

As Lydia backed away from the truck, she heard Katherine calling her name. She looked up and saw her heading back up the road. Lydia met Katherine half way. "It's impossible, Lydia. We have to get help. We'll never find him out here."

Lydia put both her hands on Katherine's shoulders. "I just did, Katherine. He's in the truck."

Katherine ducked from under Lydia's hands and began to run. "Oh, my God. Oh, my God," she cried over her shoulder. "That's wonderful."

"Katherine, no!" yelled Lydia. "Don't!" But it was too late.

The noise that Katherine Jenkins emitted when she saw her father's body was feral. By the time Lydia reached her side, Katherine was kneeling in the dirt, breathing hard and sobbing. "Somebody killed him," she gasped.

Lydia shook her head. "I don't think so. I think George died of internal bleeding."

"That's what I said. Somebody killed him." Katherine was yelling now.

Lydia shook her head again. "George drank himself to death. His veins and capillaries have probably been collapsing for months."

She offered Katherine a hand and pulled the other woman to her feet. Katherine, tears streaming down her face, immediately reached into the truck and tried to dislodge her father.

"No," said Lydia. "We have to get the Mounties."

Katherine withdrew her arm and gave Lydia a desperate look. "But you said, you said …." She paused and took a deep breath. "You said he killed himself. Why do we need the Mounties?"

"I'm not a doctor or a coroner, Katherine. The Mounties have to certify his death. Besides, I could be wrong." She took Katherine's hand. "Let's go back to Ross River." Katherine let

Lydia lead her back to the Subaru. She handed Lydia the keys without protest. This time the ferry operator did not make them wait.

CHAPTER 12

After being interviewed for an hour by a Ross River Mountie; after arranging to have George's car towed to Dawson and his body shipped to the Whitehorse coroner; after driving Katherine and herself to Dawson; after helping Katherine arrange George's funeral and attending it, Lydia was ready to sleep for a week. But instead she accepted Anna's lunch invitation because Anna said she had news.

Anna didn't have news. All she had was a flyer. It was identical to a hundred other flyers pasted on lampposts, tacked to public bulletin boards, and piled on counters at restaurants and bars. The graphics were dramatic. At the top the words *Stop Cultural Genocide* were emblazoned in large red type. This line was followed by three photographs. The first was a grainy black and white picture showing a group of First Nation children dressed in European school uniforms standing in front of a stone schoolhouse. It was dated 1909. A faded color photo dated 1977 showed an Inuit woman holding up a chocolate bar in one hand and a doughnut in the other while offering the photographer a toothless smile. The third was a picture of a large, unidentified pit mine.

> *The white man has been destroying First Nation and Inuit culture since first contact. They're at it again. Come to a panel discussion and rally on July 18 at 7:00 PM at the Odd Fellows Hall. Dr. Jack Marsh, a nationally known expert on cultural genocide and Thomas Clark, an elder of*

the Vuntut Gwich'in First Nation will speak on the terrible effects the Bad Axe Mine is having on aboriginal people in western Canada. A representative from the Bad Axe Mining Company will also be in attendance.

The call for action came at the bottom of the flyer, again in big red type. **The Bad Axe Mine is poisoning our children. Let's shut it down!** A small note invited everyone to stay after the panel for refreshments.

Lydia and Anna were sitting at Dawson Dolly's. Lydia was sipping coffee, eating bumbleberry pie, and trying to ignore the toddler screaming across the room. Anna was gorging on a large chocolate brownie and waving one of the flyers in Lydia's face. "Let's go. It's tonight."

Lydia sighed. "I don't know. I'm not anxious to see Jack Marsh. I don't particularly like him and I don't like the idea that he's speaking on behalf of natives."

"Isn't he part Indian?"

"He claims to be and he does have some nice cheekbones, but I'm not convinced."

"You're too cynical for your own good," said Anna as she stuffed the flyer in her pocket. Lydia stuffed her mouth with pie to forego further comment.

Despite her cynicism, Lydia did attend the lecture. There must have been seventy people in the room. This was a good turnout in a town with a permanent population of 1,800. It was clear that the organizers had not anticipated this much interest and too few chairs had been set up in the ballroom on the second floor of the Odd Fellows Hall. Lydia and Anna merged into the throng at the back of the room. This suited Lydia; it gave her an opportunity to examine the audience. She was surprised by how many attendees were unknown to her. Apparently, a number of people had come in off the river and from homesteads up in the mountains. Many in the audience appeared to be First Nation. A few were Inuit.

As Lydia settled in with her back to the wall, she realized that there was something wrong. Instead of standing around in small conversation groups, people were sitting in the unpadded folding chairs, silent, eyes straight ahead. In bush communities events of any kind were an occasion to greet old friends, catch up on gossip, and share stories. Many of these people lived in isolated places and saw one another on very rare occasions. But tonight no one was sharing anything.

The silence prompted Lydia to whisper to Anna, "You could cut the tension in here with a knife."

Anna nodded. "I've heard some heated conversations at Dolly's. Some of my customers say the mine is poisoning the river and killing the fish. Others say that's environmental bullshit. There was a slugfest on the patio one night."

Lydia's eyes widened when she saw two familiar faces. "Unbelievable," she said. "Look who's here."

Anna spotted the McDougal brothers instantly. "Wow. They never come to town. This must a very big deal." Lydia nodded.

Mick and Mack McDougal were identical twins, soft-spoken giants with snow white beards and long white hair pulled back in identical pony tails. They were both wearing tan Carhartt overalls and green camouflage hats. Mack's flannel shirt was red and Mick's was green. Their faces had been scoured by wind and snow and tanned by the midnight sun; they looked more like their Gwich'in neighbors than their Scottish ancestors. The brothers ran a tiny lumber mill, which provided those who lived in Keno, Mayo, and Faro with roof trusses, two-by-fours, and wide boards for doors, siding, and floors. Lydia noticed the tiny clumps of dark sawdust nestled in Mick's hair. A yellow wood curl cut by a hand plane clung to the sleeve of Mack's shirt.

Lydia threaded her way through the crowd to greet the twins. When she tapped Mack on the shoulder, he turned and looked at her with surprise. "Lydia! What are ye daeing here? I didn't know ye had an interest in mining?" Despite having lived in the Yukon Territory, all of their lives, the brothers still spoke the

Scots English of their father.

"Anna dragged me here."

Mick nodded. "Guid. The mine's a huge problem. It's already polluting the whole Yukon watershed. They have tae shut it down or everything will be ruint."

"What about all those promises the company made? What about the studies done by the government?"

"It's all shite," Mack muttered. "I daed not believe them then and I dinna believe them nae."

"Is there any hope of stopping it?"

"Mebbe, mebbe not. There's a lot of money at stake and lots of powerful people involved—bankers, politicians, investors. It's a goddam *fankle*."

A loud "Testing. One two three" echoed in the room. A microphone squealed. "Gotta go," Lydia whispered. She kissed them both and made her way back to Anna.

At that moment the speakers entered the room. There was a smattering of applause, but most of the audience sat impassively as Jack Marsh and a stranger took a seat in the front row while Thomas Clark stepped behind the podium. The moderator introduced Mr. Clark as representative of the Vuntut Gwich'in First Nation and handed him the microphone.

Clark was simply dressed in khaki pants, a crisply ironed shirt, and an unadorned caribou skin jacket. He stood very still and did not gesticulate or pull faces. He fixed his eyes on the back of the room during his entire presentation. Despite his lack of stage presence, he was a compelling speaker. He spoke softly about the ways in which the mine was threatening his people. Articulate and passionate, he talked about how many Gwich'in were subsistence dwellers and depended on the fish in the river and the mammals that roamed its banks. He maintained that the Bad Axe Mine was polluting not only the rivers but the groundwater. Fish were turning up dead in some of the little lakes. Traces of mercury had been found in local wells.

Clark also presented a brief slide show of the effects of

mining contaminants on wildlife—fish with distorted spines and lesions on their eyes and bodies, moose with fist-sized growths on their sides, hares and beavers rendered gaunt by Tularemia, a neurological disease which can be transmitted to people when they trap and clean the animals. He noted that none of this evidence had come from wildlife in the vicinity of Bad Axe, but this was a new mine and he feared that over the next few decades a similar disaster would unfold in the Yukon watershed.

The next speaker was a mine administrator, who didn't look more than twenty-five. He was tall and bony. He walked to the podium with stuttering steps, his mouth set in a grim line. His eyes darted around the room as if he were expecting an ambush. He was the only person in the room wearing a suit and tie and he kept running his finger between his collar and his neck. He cleared his throat four times and finally spoke. His voice cracked with nervousness. He kept his eyes on his script as he talked.

"Hello. My name is Robert Herkle and I'm the Assistant to the Assistant Director of Public Relations for the Bad Axe Mining Company. *Ahem*. The subarctic environment is extremely complicated eco-system. *Ahem*. Contaminants emanate from many sources, not the least of which is global warming. *Ahem*. A well-known researcher from the US Geological Survey has argued that the permafrost has been absorbing naturally occurring mercury for thousands of years. Now that the permafrost is melting, the mercury is being released back into the environment. The mercury in the local watershed is not from mines. *Ahem*. It's been in the ground all this time."

There were snickers and a few boos. A man at the back of the room yelled, "Bullshit!"

Herkle's eyes darted around the room again and he ran his hands through his hair. "Industrial pollution from around the world plays into this as well. The Yukon watershed is a catchment for pollution from Europe and Asia. Coal power plants in Asia produce 860 tons of mercury every year. Winds carry pollution into the Yukon and it winds up in our river systems and all other

North American river systems."

This was greeted snorts and a bit foot stomping from the people in the front rows. "Bile yer heid," bellowed a familiar voice.

"You think we're friggin' morons?" yelled a young woman, wearing a waitress uniform. "We know your containment ponds are leaking into the water table."

An Inuit woman stood up. She had a baby tucked into a shawl that she wore like a bandolier. "Did you know that in Nunuvut they've created a new word? *Hilaupuunnakpallianinga*. It means global warming. The Inuit never needed this word before. It's not just the mine. It's coal and cars that are heating things up, not rocks and contaminated water." Her voice rose. "It's those greedy *Qallunaaq* down in Vancouver who over-heat their houses and drive SUVs to the shopping mall." The baby began to whimper.

The audience wasn't sure how to react to this. On the whole, they didn't care for those privileged white folks down in Lotus Land, but global warming wasn't the issue here. Finally, a young man stood up and shouted, "It's the mine, goddam it! It's not coal and cars that's hurting our kids; it's the fuckin' mine."

The moderator banged her gavel. "There will be no profanity."

"Shee-it," said the man as he took his seat.

Herkle shook his head and gave the moderator a desperate look. His microphone was still on when he said, "I can't do this." He picked up his papers and ran for the stairs. This was greeted by laughter and a few cat-calls.

Jack Marsh stood, turned toward the audience, and silenced the room with a wave his hand. Lydia looked over at Anna and stifled a giggle as Jack approached the podium. He was a vision in turquoise and silver. His belt buckle contained a large stone which was the color of a tropical sea. The clasp on his bolo tie was a heavy silver wedge inlaid with turquoise and coral. He wore a plain, wide silver bracelet on his left wrist. On his feet he wore boots with silver toe tips.

"Good lord" whispered Lydia. "That's all Navaho and Hopi.

Not one of those pieces was made by a Northwestern Indian." Anna snorted.

Years of teaching had taught Marsh how to capture an audience. He had the cadence and timing of a tent revivalist. Heads rose and fell with his voice. He seemed to make eye contact with everyone in the room. He used no notes; he cited no facts or figures. Thomas Clark had already done the heavy lifting. Marsh's message was simple. The mine was destroying a way of life. All the aboriginal people in the Yukon watershed would be affected. The caribou herds would diminish; the salmon would grow sick; native children would develop neurological diseases from heavy metals. Animals would die. People would die.

When he was done, a number of people jumped to their feet and applauded. Jack offered them a self-satisfied smile. When the noise subsided and people sat down again, he said, "I'm glad we've reached consensus."

A young man in worn overalls jumped to his feet. "We *ain't* reached consensus." His voice was strained. "Nobody's talked about jobs. Bad Axe gives us jobs. Good jobs. I got laid off from a cannery five years ago. I was on the dole." He looked at Jack Marsh with contempt. "What does a fancy professor like you know about living on the dole? I got a good salary now. I can take care of my family." There were yells of support from other young men in the audience.

The owner of a local bar stood up. "Those miners come to Dawson for R and R, even in the winter. They dump big bucks into our businesses."

The bouncer at another establishment yelled back. "Yeah, and they get shitfaced, smash mirrors, and ruin the felt on the pool tables."

A young woman near Lydia stood. She kept her eyes on the floor as she said, "I don't believe that the river is polluted. My husband and I have a fish wheel upriver. The salmon we pull out of our baskets don't have any lesions or boils or nothin'. They're perfectly healthy."

A few people nodded at this, but the crowd's attention had turned to an old Inuit man, who was getting slowly to his feet. He leaned heavily on a cane. His deeply lined face bespoke a life lived in wind, sun, and snow. "I live in a tiny village on the Beaufort Sea. We depend on seal and whale meat. But the pack ice is melting and the number of seals is small. We haven't had a whale in three years. Things have been terrible. We were afraid that we would all have to move south and that our way of life would be lost forever. But then my grandsons and some other young men came down here to work at the mine. They make enough to support the village. We don't have move. The boys will work in the mine until the whales return and then they will come home and we will be whole again."

No one seemed willing to challenge this soft-spoken elder until a woman who had been sitting in the second row got up and turned to face the rest of the audience. She was one of the most beautiful people Lydia had ever seen. She wore a calf length dress of tanned caribou hide decorated with glass beads and porcupine quills. Her hair was dark with rich auburn highlights and fell to her waist. Her face was a perfect oval and her dark eyes were rimmed with long black lashes. As she spoke, her slender fingers moved in soft arcs in front of her. Her voice was low, almost seductive. Her words, however, were not.

"You won't be whole. None of us will be. This is about cultural genocide, you fools, not global warming. This is a plot to destroy us. The mines, the oil and gas pipelines—these are all schemes to make white people rich while our way of life withers away." She waved her hand at the elder. "Our children are leaving their ancestral villages and they'll never go back. They'll forget how to fish and hunt and make clothes from caribou skin. Soon we'll be just like the white man, unconnected to the land. We'll be heartless, soulless, and hopeless." She went on, excoriating the audience for its passivity and its complicity. Lydia suddenly noticed that Anna was frowning as she craned her neck to get a better look at the speaker.

Comments flew for another ten minutes. Finally the moderator cut things off and Jack Marsh and Thomas Clark left the room by a back door. Anna grabbed Lydia's arm. "Let's go. I've got something to tell you." As they rushed past the refreshment table, Lydia noted that no one was staying behind for tea and sugar cookies.

When they reached the sidewalk, Anna said softly, "The woman in the caribou-skin dress. That was Beatrice Sherman. Troy's mother."

"Are you sure?"

"Ethel showed me an old picture of her. I'm positive this is the same woman." Anna's gaze shifted and her mouth opened in surprise. "Look at that." She pointed to a couple strolling up Princess Street, the man's hand in the small of woman's back as if he were gently pushing her along. She seemed to be shrinking from his touch. Her gait was stiff, mechanical. It was Jack Marsh and the woman in the caribou dress. The evening sun glinted off Jack's silver bracelet.

"Jeeezus," said Lydia under her breath. "What in the hell is that about?"

"If Beatrice hates white people so much, why is she stepping out with Marsh anyway," said Anna. "Seems pretty damn hypocritical."

"Marsh does say he's part First Nation, even if I don't believe it."

"Hell," said Anna. "Five pounds of turquoise and silver is no substitute for blood."

Lydia watched as the two disappeared around a corner. She frowned. "They don't look like a couple to me." She paused. "Do you think Beatrice's mother knows she's in town?"

"I doubt it," said Anna. "But I suppose we could stop by and ask."

Lydia grimaced. "But what if Ethel doesn't know? Then it would be a mean thing to do. And what if Troy's there?"

"You're right. But we could stop by and if Ethel brings it up, fine. My curiosity is killing me."

"I guess that wouldn't do any harm. But no questions." Lydia tapped Anna smartly on the top of her head.

Lydia and Anna stopped at a liquor store for a bottle of wine. Ten minutes later they were knocking on Ethel's door. There was no answer. Anna tried again. Lydia was positioned in front of the window and realized that the interior was partially visible through the gauzy haze of Ethel's sheer curtains. She could see that Ethel was sitting in a chair with her face in her hands. Her head was bobbing gently on her shoulders.

"Let's go," whispered Lydia. "Now." She pulled on Anna's T shirt and moved her toward the stairs. She put her fingers against her lips to indicate silence.

After Anna had closed the door to her own apartment, she turned to Lydia. "What was that about?"

"I saw Ethel through the curtain. She was crying."

"Oh, crap. She must have heard that Beatrice is here. Did you see Troy?"

Lydia shook her head. "He's probably in bed."

Anna held up the wine. "Do you want to come in for some of this?"

Lydia shook her head. "Not in the mood. I'm going home and to bed."

Sleep did not come easily for Lydia. She tossed and turned for two hours, got up and read for an hour, then laid down and tossed and turned again. When she finally did doze off, she was awakened almost instantly by the malamute next door who felt compelled to bark at phantoms. She was wide awake when Al slipped into bed at 4:30 AM.

The next time Lydia looked at the clock, she was surprised to see it was ten. Al was already up; she could hear him in the kitchen. As she threw her legs over the side of the bed, the phone rang. Al picked up it up the first ring. Lydia dressed and wandered into the kitchen looking for coffee. Al was still on the phone. "So there was no sign of assault," he was saying. The person on the other end spoke for a long time and Al nodded three or four times. "That's sad," he said into the receiver. "And pretty damn strange." Al was quiet again and then said. "I'll wait for the info." When he hung up, he had a perplexed look on his face.

"What's pretty damn strange?" asked Lydia.

"That was Carmichael." Assistant Superintendent Carmichael was Al's boss in Whitehorse. "He was telling me about a retired Anglican priest from Watson Lake. Somebody found his body in an unused village church in a storage room under a stairway. It's clear from the impressions in the dust that he walked into the sanctuary and then was dragged into the storage room. His hands were loosely bound with duct tape but not his feet. There's no sign of injury or trauma. The door wasn't locked. He should have been able pull off the tape and open the door and walk out of the room. But he didn't. It looks like he sat where he had been dumped and died."

"Does Carmichael know his name?"

"It's Maxwell Fleming. He was in his eighties and had been living in Watson Lake for the last thirty years. He hadn't had a congregation for many years. Lived with his sister in an apartment. From all reports, a gentle man. No one knows what he was doing in that church. There hadn't been any services there for a long time."

"Where's the village?"

"That's the other odd thing. It's at least forty miles from Watson Lake."

Lydia frowned. "It's strange that anyone would do that to a priest and doubly strange that he didn't save himself."

"That's the great mystery," said Al. "Whoever dragged Reverend Fleming into that room left a couple of calling cards."

"A book of matches from the Kitkat Club?" said Lydia with a small smile.

Al's face remained serious. "No. Far more subtle. The first was an open bible with a footprint across the passage that reads, "Suffer the little children to come unto me." The second was a bit of window cleaning. The stained glass in the place hadn't been washed in years but someone had wiped the apple in Eve's hand clean."

Lydia took a sharp breath. "An apple. Jesus Christ!"

Al stared at her. "What!"

"An apple. Don't you remember George Jenkins's notes? 'The apple doesn't fall far from the tree.' Maybe the same people targeted this priest and George Jenkins. Maybe this priest taught at an Indian school."

Al pursed his lips and blew out air. "I'll bet you're right." He paused a moment and frowned. "The MO is more or less the same. Frighten the victim but inflict no physical harm."

"Yes," said Lydia softly. "In both cases the physical harm was brought on by the victim's own behavior."

"We're just lucky that one of the elders was having a party at his house and decided to borrow some folding chairs from the church storeroom. Who knows how long Reverend Fleming's body would have laid there undiscovered."

"Was the church locked?"

"No. They leave it open because the old folks in the community like to go in and pray now and then. There's nothing of any real value in the place. Reverend Fleming's assailant even brought his own brand-new pulpit bible. Carmichael's constables are trying to track down the vendor." Al stood up. "I'm gonna call Carmichael and tell him about the apple."

A four page fax arrived from Assistant Superintendent Carmichael at noon the next day. It confirmed Lydia's suspicions. Reverend Maxwell Fleming had taught at an Indian school, one in the very village where his body was found. This school had been called Stony Creek.

According to Carmichael's informants, Stony Creek School had been far better than most. The children were well-fed and well-clothed and real academic courses were provided. Many of its graduates had gone on to college. Among the school's successful alumni were two provincial court judges, one well-known medical researcher, a linguist on the faculty at First Nations University, and the CEO of a major marketing firm in Edmonton. The youngest alumnus was currently making a killing extracting oil and gas from Alberta's tar sands. Reverend Fleming had worked there from 1948 until the school was closed in 1973. In the mid nineteen eighties all the school buildings had been razed but the church was spared.

"George Jenkins's death didn't warrant an investigation at the time but this one sure as hell does. Jenkins and Fleming are certainly linked." Al squeezed his temple between his thumb and middle finger. "We need to get a list of all the children who passed through the doors of those two Indian Schools."

"But, Al, thousands of kids went to those schools. You don't have a name. You don't have any dates."

"We'll start with the years that George Jenkins taught at Salmon River. I'm hoping that Katherine Jenkins will recognize a name."

"Katherine was awfully young. And remember, she didn't even know her father had taught at an Indian school." Lydia paused and frowned. "I wonder if those old school records even exist."

"They exist," said Al. "This was a federal school system. Anglicans and Catholics ran most of the schools but the government paid for them. When the government shells out money, it keeps track."

"Did it keep track of the families torn apart, the self-hatred, the abuse, the ruined lives?" said Lydia softly.

Al's lips tightened and he locked his eyes on hers. "At least my government has publically apologized to the victims of residential Indian schools and offered reparations. That's more than I can say for yours."

Lydia's eyes dropped to the floor. "Touché."

CHAPTER 13

Lydia was packing for the trip to her cabin. She had jammed the last T shirt into her duffle bag when the phone rang. She stopped to answer it and was surprised to hear Anna's voice. It was only 8:00 AM and Anna was not a morning person.

"I need backup," said Anna. She was close to shouting.

"My God, what's wrong?" asked Lydia. Anna was extremely self-sufficient and didn't often ask for help.

"It's about Troy."

Lydia's stomach tightened. "What's happened to him?"

"Nothing's happened to him but his grandmother has disappeared."

"Oh, crap."

"Troy's in my bedroom watching CNN. I need to talk fast."

"CNN?"

Anna sighed. "It has something to do with Wolf Blitzer."

Anna took a deep breath. "I got a phone call from Ethel about seven thirty asking me if I was going to be free all day. I told her yes. Then she asked if I was going to be home for the next hour. I said yes. I was half asleep and it didn't occur to me to ask her what this was about." Anna took another breath. "About twenty minutes later, Troy knocked on my door and handed me a note from Ethel. Let me read it to you." Then Lydia heard paper crackling and Anna was back on the line. She read the note slowly and carefully.

I have an enormous favor to ask of you. Will you please take Troy to his father at the mushroom camp? He knows how to get there. I've had to leave town unexpectedly. I'm very sorry to lay such a heavy burden on you but this is an emergency. I'm not sure how long I'll be gone. Please tell Red I'm sorry that I can't look after Troy right now.

Anna's speech rate accelerated again. "I don't know Red, Lydia. I don't know anybody at the camp. Troy's real upset. He thinks his grandmother has left him just like his mother did."

Lydia groaned. "You want me to come with you, right?" The mushroom camp was forty miles north of Dawson; Lydia's cabin was sixty miles south. She was never going to get home.

"Right," said Anna. "I know it's a lot to ask after Teddy and all that crap with Katherine's father, but I really need your help. Troy's a basket case and he's been asking for you."

Lydia heaved a huge sigh. "Okay. What time do you want to leave?"

"How about if Troy and I meet you at the dock in two hours?"

"Fine," said Lydia. "But we're going up and back in one day, right? I want to get back to my cabin sometime in this decade."

"One day, I promise. We'll take my boat. It's a lot faster than yours."

Lydia left Al a note explaining the situation and told him she'd back at his place in the early evening. With a disgusted moan, she poured herself another cup of coffee.

When Lydia reached Dawson's floating pier, Anna had already loaded her boat with life vests, water bottles, and a small cooler. Lydia could see a water proof duffle bag stuffed under the stern seat, probably Troy's clothes. Troy was sitting on the pier, his legs dangling over the edge. He was motionless and his eyes were fixed on the water. He didn't turn to greet Lydia when she squatted down next to him. She touched his shoulder. "Are you glad to be going back to camp?"

Troy kept his eyes on the roiling current. "I dunno."

"Your dad will be there."

Troy's small face was pinched and his hazel eyes were expressionless. "Grandma went away. She didn't tell me nothin'. She just left." He looked up at Lydia and his eyes filled with tears. "Why did she leave?"

Lydia sat down and threw one arm around the boy. "She had something she had to do. She'll be back."

"You don't know nothin' about it," said Troy, stiffening. "You only met her that one time." His voice was bitter. He knew Lydia was patronizing him even though he didn't know the word. "My mum left and she never came back."

"You're right, Troy. I'm sorry. I don't know anything about it. But at camp you'll have your dad and Karl."

"Teddy ain't never coming back neither."

"That makes me sad, too," said Lydia.

Anna tapped Lydia lightly on the shoulder. "We need to get moving." Lydia hugged Troy, stood, and strapped her Bobo bag to her waist. Then she held her hand out to Troy. He grabbed it hard and hung on until he was in the boat. There were two extra life jackets stowed under the middle seat. A few minutes after they left the pier, Troy hauled them out and made himself a nest on the bottom. He curled up on the vests and pulled his baseball cap over his face. He didn't stir as the boat bounced gently over the waters of the Yukon. Lydia hoped he was sleeping.

There was a surprising amount of traffic on the river. Fishermen in overpowered boats tore past them in the hope of finding a favorite fishing spot unoccupied; families who were spending the summer in downriver fish camps were heading to Dawson to stock up on groceries; heavily laden touring canoes paddled for Eagle or the Dalton Highway or even the Bering Sea. But all of these people were transients. The tourists headed south at the end of summer; the subsistence fishermen went back to their villages before the snow flew. After freeze-up a few hardy souls would return on dog sleds or snow machines to set trap lines. But the river population had steadily dwindled over the years. The old timers maintained that there was only one full-time resident on the river between Dawson and the Alaska border.

Anna's boat was very fast, rendering the beautiful Yukon landscape a textured blur. There was no chance to look for mountain sheep on the rocky ridges or to watch for Arctic foxes hunting rodents in the loose dirt of the cut banks. When she caught sight of a lone caribou walking slowly along a low rise, she motioned to Anna to slow down. The caribou fixed his eyes on the boat as Anna steered into the shallows. The animal's winter fur was long gone, but bits of white hair hung from his belly in patches. He looked thin, bedraggled, and forlorn.

As the engine slowed, Troy awoke. He rubbed his eyes, shoved the life vests under the middle seat, and sat on it. When he saw the caribou, he said his first words of the trip. "That caribou got kicked out of the herd. The old guys wanted all the lady caribous for themselves."

"Yup," said Lydia, turning around in her seat to talk to him. "That's what happens to young bucks sometimes."

"I bet he's lonesome," said Troy.

As Anna's boat approached Fools Gold Creek, Lydia noticed another craft maneuvering around some logs in the confluence."

Troy noticed it, too. "Hey, that's Sam's boat."

Lydia turned and signaled to Anna to slow down as she shaded her eyes and peered at the boat and its operator. He was facing away from them. "Are you sure that's Sam?"

"Sure, I'm sure," said Troy. The insistent thrumming of the engine had been reduced to a hum and shouting was no longer necessary. "Look at the back. It says *High Arctic*. That's the name of his boat." Lydia shaded her eyes but had no hope of reading anything at that distance.

Troy offered Lydia the first smile of the morning as he fixed his eyes on the northern horizon. "Karl told me that the high arctic is at the top of the world. They got polar bears up there and muskoxes and whales. I'm going to see it someday."

"I wonder what Sam's doing at Fools Gold Creek," said Anna.

"I know," said Troy. "His friends live here."

"Friends!" said Lydia.

Troy frowned and thought a moment. "A man and a lady. Their names are from the bible but I can't remember."

"Adam and Eve?" asked Lydia.

Troy nodded. "That's it. How did you know?"

"They're only the most famous couple in the Judeo-Christian religion."

Troy frowned. "What's Jude-Christian?"

"It's a long story," said Lydia as the operator of the *High Arctic* disappeared into the trees.

"Can we get moving?" said Anna. "I'm getting hungry. I want my lunch."

As Anna's boat approached the camp, Lydia was surprised to see a rental boat pulled up on the gravel next to the one remaining agency craft. She was even more surprised to see two men in business suits and brand new hiking boots slipping and sliding their way down the embankment. The men did not acknowledge the presence of the new arrivals. Apparently, traversing the uneven terrain required all their concentration. Both men were bare-headed and the balding pate of the oldest was bright orange from his eyebrows to his to his crown. The other man was fat and Lydia could hear him wheeze as he trudged through the sand. He had a briefcase clutched in his arms.

"Bureaucrats," Lydia whispered to Anna.

Troy squinted up at Lydia and wrinkled his nose. "*Bureau cats*? Cats that live in a dresser? That doesn't make any sense."

"Bureaucrats never make any sense," responded Anna.

It soon became clear that the bureaucrats were not boat savvy individuals. The fat man untied the boat while the sunburned man climbed in. The fat man gave the boat a mighty push but couldn't move the bow off the gravel. As Lydia and Anna headed in his direction to help, he gave one more heave, slipped, cracked his forehead on the bow, and sat down hard in a muddy pool with his legs straddling the V. "Fuck," he yelled.

Troy, who was at Lydia's heels, whispered, "He said the *f*-word. Did you hear him?"

"The whole camp heard him, Troy."

The bureaucrat pulled himself up and looked down at his dripping pant legs. He put his hands on his buttocks and tried to scrape off the sticky Yukon River mud, further grinding it into the fabric. He put his muddy fingers to his forehead and ground dirt in the small cut put there by the bow. "Fuck," he yelled again. Troy grinned.

As Anna strolled toward the boat, she raised her hand in a placating gesture. "Relax. We'll give you a hand."

"We don't need any help, miss, but thank you," said the sunburned bureaucrat, who was sitting in the stern.

"Bullshit," said the fat guy, spraying spit into the Yukon River. "We can use all the help we can get."

"You certainly can," said Anna as she pointed to boat's outboard. "You didn't raise the prop when you landed. No wonder you're stuck."

Anna issued orders until the five of them had managed to push the boat off the gravel. When it was afloat, Lydia took the line and the sunburned bureaucrat clambered in. The fat bureaucrat got hung up on the gunwale with one leg in the boat and the other wedged against the outside. Out of the corner of her eye, Lydia could see Troy pressing his lips together to suppress a giggle. She winked at him as she put her hands under the man's butt and heaved. Troy laughed out loud when the man landed in the bottom with a great metallic thud and another "Fuck!"

Anna shook her head. "You could use some vocabulary enrichment," she said.

"Fuck you," yelled the man, his voice bouncing off the aluminum bottom.

"See," said Anna.

Their good deed done but unappreciated, Anna, Lydia, and Troy trudged up the embankment toward camp. They could hear the *arrrr, arrrr, arrrr* of the starter motor. "They choked it too much and now it's flooded," said Lydia. "Shall we go back and help them."

"Fuck 'em," said Anna. Troy doubled over.

When they reached camp, they found Karl sleeping in one of the deck chairs. Troy hurled himself into his lap and capsized the chair. The two lay on the ground in a heap. "Hey, man, these are my only clean pants," groused Karl as he gently pushed Troy off his torso and stood up. He reached down, pulled the boy up, and gave him a hug. "What're you doing back so soon? I thought you were going to be at Grandma's for two weeks." Troy buried his face in Karl's shirt and said nothing. Karl raised his eyebrows and looked at Lydia. "What's up?"

"This is my friend Anna Fain. Anna, Karl Kovacs. Anna lives above Troy's grandmother. Show him the note." Anna pulled a crumpled piece of paper from her shirt pocket and handed it to Karl. Karl read it, grimaced, and shook his head. He silently mouthed the word *damn.*

"Who were those sunburned guys?" asked Lydia. "They certainly weren't dressed for success in the wilderness."

Karl rolled his eyes. "No kidding. They never should have been let loose in the woods. They're administrators with the salmon project."

"Why are they here?"

"Routine check-up."

When Troy ran off to put his things in the tent, Anna said, "Where's Red? I need to show him the note."

"He's out picking," said Karl. "He should be back for lunch."

Gretchen and Bob Dunlap were in the kitchen tent making sandwiches when Karl opened the screen door. Bob's long grey ponytail swayed as he diced onions with a cleaver. Gretchen was slicing tomatoes with the blade of a fancy Leatherman tool. She greeted Lydia by waving the dripping knife blade in her direction.

Bob grabbed Gretchen's arm and lowered her hand. "Jesus Christ, you almost sliced my nose off."

Gretchen grimaced at Bob. "Sorry." She looked tired and tense. Apparently the bureaucrats had taken a lot out of her. She turned back to Lydia. "What brings you up here?"

"We brought Troy back to camp. He needed a ride." Just then Troy burst through the tent door.

Gretchen frowned as she glanced at him. "I thought he was staying in Dawson awhile." Karl put his index finger to his lips. Gretchen nodded. She put down her Leatherman and reached for two more tomatoes. Lydia picked the knife up and inspected the blade. It was long and strong, the perfect camping tool. Lydia's Swiss Army knife sported a number of clever gadgets but it wasn't hefty enough for use in the bush.

"I like this," said Lydia.

Gretchen nodded. "It's great. It cost a bundle though." She turned toward the table. "Hey, you guys want lunch? We're making tuna salad with tomatoes for dessert."

Anna shook her head and held up a deli bag. "We brought our own."

"How about a cup of coffee?"

Everyone nodded including Troy. "He drinks coffee?" said Anna. "Doesn't that stunt a kid's growth or something?"

"Don't worry. His is ninety percent milk. It won't hurt him," said Gretchen. "I let my own boy drink it like that."

"How old is your son?" asked Lydia.

Gretchen pressed her lips together before she said, "Actually, I have two. They're fifteen-year-old fraternal twins. Tommy and Tim." She gave a small sigh. "Tommy is severely autistic. He doesn't speak and he has behavior problems. He's gotten too big for me to handle so he's in a special school in Regina."

"That must be tough," said Lydia.

"Yes," said Gretchen. "I'm from Whitehorse and I hate having him so far away, but it's a wonderful school. It's done Tommy a world of good even though my asshole ex-husband thinks it's a waste of money. I'm working my tail off to keep Tommy there, and he refuses to help me pay for it. He'd pull Tommy out instantly if it was up to him. Half the time, he doesn't even pay child-support. When I complain, he threatens to sue for custody."

"Where does Tim stay when you're working in the bush?" Lydia asked gently.

"With my sister Suzanne. She's wonderful. Tim loves her. I don't know what Tim would do if he had to live with his dad." She clenched both fists. "Yes, I do. He'd run away. He hates his father." Lydia saw Troy flinch at her words.

"You've got a lot to contend with," said Lydia.

Gretchen nodded and threw Lydia a grateful look. "It's nice to have that acknowledged. Thanks."

Anna was sitting at the table eyeing the deli bag. "Hey, would you all mind if we eat? I'm starved."

"Not at all. I'm almost done with our sandwiches anyway," said Bob.

The four of them sat down at one of the tables while Bob finished his creations. Anna pulled three well wrapped packages from the bag and handed one to Lydia and one to Troy. Lydia unveiled her sandwich first. It took two hands to remove it from the butcher paper. When she took her first bite, oil dripped down her chin.

"The health food special, I take it," said Bob as he carried a plate stacked with tuna sandwiches to the table. He surreptitiously removed a long white hair from the top sandwich before he handed the plate to Gretchen.

"You bet," said Lydia through a mouthful of salami, cheese, onion, tomato, and hot peppers. Troy unwrapped an unadorned roast beef which he immediately doused in ketchup. Anna had opted for corned beef with mustard on rye.

Lloyd walked in, sat down between Anna and Bob, and grabbed a sandwich. Lydia introduced him to Anna and then watched with amusement as he trained a dazzling smile on her friend and began running a line of flirtatious blarney.

"We ran into some frighteningly incompetent boaters down by the river," said Lydia. "Who are they?"

Gretchen hesitated. "Oh, they were from Alaska Fish and Game. There's usually at least one site visit over the summer. No big deal."

Lloyd pulled his gaze from Anna's face. "The U.S. Canada salmon treaty expires next year and tensions are running high. It's important the count be as accurate as possible." He grinned. "We're the peacekeeping force. If we fail, the salmon wars resume."

"What do you mean?" asked Anna.

"Canadian fishermen have always believed that the Alaskans catch too many fish before they come up the rivers to spawn. But there's factors besides over-fishing that can lower a salmon count. The major spawning grounds are on the Canadian side of the border. When the numbers of spawning fish are low, it depletes the salmon stock for years to come and that hurts everybody on both sides.

"Last year's King salmon run on the Yukon River was the worst in thirty years and it was almost as bad the year before that. Some Kings spawn in Alaska but most lay their eggs on the Yukon side. You probably know that salmon have this weird genealogical memory based on smell. The offspring come back to the very same gravel beds where they were spawned and so on and so on." Anna nodded. "Last year the King salmon population was so low on the Yukon that subsistence fishing of Kings in Alaska was suspended so that all fish could reach their spawning grounds. There were lots of pissed off Alaskans, let me tell you."

"Screw'em," said Sam. "Who cares about Alaskans."

Lloyd sighed. "And the wars continue."

At that moment the screen door to the kitchen banged. Lydia was facing in the other direction and didn't see who had entered.

She didn't turn around until a deep voice said, "What in the hell's going on? The professor's back and so is my kid."

Troy leapt up and ran to his father. He grabbed him around the waist and buried his face in Red's shirt. Lydia could hear his muffled, "Grandma left, Dad. She left. I don't know why."

Red pulled the child close and looked at Lydia. "What do

you know about this?" His voice was gruff.

"I'm the one who knows about it," said Anna. She explained as she extracted Ethel's note from her shirt pocket.

Red read it twice. At first he looked angry and then he looked scared. He pulled an empty chair over to the table and sat down. He pulled Troy into his lap. "You got no idea where she went?" he asked Anna.

"None whatsoever."

"Jesus Christ," Red said softly. He laid his chin on top of Troy's head and was silent for a long time.

Finally Anna broke the silence. "Look," she said. "If you need to leave Troy in town, he can stay with me until Ethel comes back. I'll just take him to work with me." Lydia's jaw dropped.

"*If* Ethel comes back," said Red bitterly.

Troy's body stiffened. "You mean she's not coming back. Not ever?" He began to sob.

Red grimaced and pulled the boy close. "She'll be back, son. I was just being ...." He groped for words. "A worry wart." Red took a moment to compose himself and then clapped Troy on the shoulder. "Hey, everything's fine. We got each other and I could use a good right-hand-man today. You wanna go picking with me?"

Red's uncharacteristic heartiness saddened Lydia, but Troy brightened immediately. He wiped his eyes with his fists. "Sure, I do. Can I carry a crate?"

"You betcha," said Red. He lifted Troy off his lap and turned to Anna. "Can I have your phone number? That way I could call you from Eagle in a few days and you could tell me if you've heard from Ethel. And I do appreciate your offer, but I'll keep Troy here for now. He needs to be with me."

Bob offered Anna a scrap of paper and a pen. She scribbled for a moment and handed the paper to Red.

"Thanks," said Red. "I really appreciate this." All trace of gruffness had disappeared. He turned to Lydia. "Can I talk to you for a couple of minutes when you're done eating?"

"Sure," said Lydia. She finished off the last bites of her sandwich and wiped her mouth. "Okay, I'm done."

"In private," said Red. He beckoned with an index finger and Lydia followed him outside and out of earshot of the others. "I need to ask you something."

"Okay," said Lydia.

"I heard you were at that meeting about the mine."

"Yes, I was."

"I heard my wife was there. Did you see her?"

"Maybe. Ethel showed Anna an old picture of Beatrice once and there was a woman there who resembled that photo."

"Somebody said she left with that professor guy, the archeologist." Lydia shrugged. She had gone as far as she was willing to go.

"You know that professor, right?" said Red.

"Sort of. He helped Karl and me look for Teddy and then he gave us coffee. That and the meeting are the only times I've seen him."

"Some people tell me he's First Nation; other people say he's not. What do you think?" asked Red.

"He might have some amount of Indian blood, but he looks white."

"So why is Beatrice with him? She doesn't like white people anymore."

"I have no idea, Red. Really. And I don't know for sure that the woman I saw at the meeting *was* Beatrice. I don't know that Marsh isn't part First Nation and I don't know that those two are a couple."

Red ignored Lydia's caveats. "I'd sure like to talk to that guy Marsh. Find out what's going on."

"What would be the point?" asked Lydia.

"I know Beatrice isn't coming back to me, but I do wonder if she left me for another man or for a cockeyed cause."

Lydia looked hard at Red. "And which explanation would you prefer?"

Red was silent for a moment. He scowled; then he gave her a small smile. "Damned if I know," he said. "Damned if I know." He paused and narrowed his eyes. "You remind me of Teddy. You both got a way of cutting through the bullshit."

"Can I ask you something now? It's personal and you don't have to answer." Red nodded. "Troy's getting older and he's smart. Do you think home schooling him is adequate at this point?"

Red's lips tightened. He was silent for a moment and then he spoke softly. "I know it's not enough, but I don't have a lot of choices. I can't ask Ethel to take him for nine months. He would wear her out. My sister has five kids already. I got no money to send Troy to boarding school. Hey, I graduated from high school and even did a year of college. I know the value of education but I also know it can screw you up."

"What you mean?"

"Look at Beatrice. She took some stupid course at the community college and got a bunch of crazy ideas."

"What course was that?"

"Something about Indian history and how the white man destroyed the culture of the Indians. That's true enough, but Beatrice took it as an excuse to drum all the white people out of her life. Me included." He bit his lip. "She left Troy, too. I'll never understand that." He shook his head.

In an effort to lighten Red's mood, Lydia asked, "How did you come by the nickname *Red*. Did you have red hair as a kid?"

Red shook his head. "No. My actual name is Redmon. It was my mother's maiden name." The edge returned to his voice. "Ironic, isn't it? I'm Redmon but not a red man, so Beatrice left me." So much for lightening the mood.

Red looked toward the kitchen tent. "I gotta go. Troy's waiting." He turned and walked toward the boy, who was sitting expectantly beside the crates.

At that moment Karl and Anna walked up. "We'd better get going," said Anna.

"I'll walk you to the boat," said Karl.

As the three strolled slowly toward the river bank, Lydia asked, "Karl, what do you think of Red?"

"Red's okay. I think his gruffness is just a way to keep people at arm's length. Not only does he dote on Troy, he's very generous with the other pickers. He loans them money and helps them pick when they're sick. Sam and Red go way back and I know he's bailed Sam out of jail more than once."

"Jail!" said Lydia. "For what?"

"Drunk and disorderly mostly. Once he got busted for selling pot. He actually did a little time for that."

"That's interesting," said Lydia. She flashed on the day Sam went into the alley during the sour toe contest. Then she thought of something else. "We saw him going into Fools Gold Creek this morning. Is it true that he's friends with those miners up there? Troy said he was."

"Could be," said Karl. "I don't know. He was supposed to be on his way to Dawson."

"Maybe he just stopped in for coffee. I hear they make dynamite coffee," said Anna.

CHAPTER 14

Lydia checked her watch as Anna steered her boat into the current. She smiled when she realized she'd be home in time for dinner with Al. He had promised chicken and biscuits.

Shortly after they passed Fools Gold Creek, Lydia saw another boat ahead of them. As they got closer, Lydia realized that they were coming upon *High Arctic*. She also realized that there were now three people in the craft, Sam and two others. Once again Lydia signaled Anna to slow down. "Pass that boat slowly and take a good look at the passengers. I've got to keep my head down. I don't want to be recognized."

Anna nodded, gave her boat more gas, and passed *High Arctic* on the left. She smiled and waved as Lydia rummaged around on the bottom of the boat as if looking for something. Then Anna gunned the engine, took the next bend, and slowed down. "The passenger in the bow is a woman, heavy-set, her hair in braids. There's tall, skinny guy in the middle seat. The guy at the throttle has curly dark hair."

"Okay," said Lydia. "Go slow and let that boat pass us." She pulled her hat down to obscure her face. A few minutes later she heard the sound of an outboard. It got louder then softer as it proceeded upstream.

"Give them another few minutes, then we're going back to Fools Gold Creek," said Lydia.

"You're shittin' me," said Anna. "Why would we do that?"

"Sam's passengers are Adam and Eve Bullock. I want to go back up to their place and see what's going on up there. I prefer to do that when they're not home."

"Oh, for God sake. Last time you went up there somebody shot at you."

"That, dear friend, is why I want to go when nobody's home. There's something weird going on up there. Those miners are excessively hostile to visitors, but they're friends with Sam. Sam's been busted for dealing pot. Sam's boat is called *High Arctic*. Gold mining hasn't been lucrative. Maybe the three of them have embarked on a new enterprise."

"Okay, so they're growing pot. What do you care?"

"I *don't* care. But what if Teddy found it?"

"You think the Bullocks killed Teddy because they're growing weed!"

Lydia looked down at her boots. "Actually, I know that they *didn't* kill Teddy. They have a strong alibi. But they ran her off and they ran me off and I want to know why. It's all connected somehow."

"You drive me nuts," said Anna. But she made a wide U turn and headed back downstream. They were at the confluence of Fools Gold Creek and the Yukon in a few minutes.

"Go as far upstream as you can," said Lydia as Anna steered the boat into the creek.

They passed Jack Marsh's elegant craft and two rental canoes piled high with dry bags, bear canisters, and a Coleman stove. None of it was strapped in. "Idiots," muttered Lydia.

The battered skiff with the tiny outboard that Lydia had seen on her last visit was tucked between two fallen logs. "That must be the Bullocks' boat."

"Wow. It must take them forever to get to Dawson in that thing," said Anna. "It's worse than yours."

She skillfully maneuvered her own boat through the floating alder limbs and knots of brush. About two hundred yards upstream from Marsh's boat, a large spruce had toppled across the river, blocking passage beyond that point. Anna steered the boat into a natural cove created by small grove of alders on a small gravel bar.

After tying off, Anna stood and looked down the trail. "I want to see where Teddy died," she said softly.

"Are you sure?" Anna nodded.

Lydia took her hand and they headed toward the village. Little brown song birds flitted among the alders and a crow scolded from a low cottonwood branch. Clouds of mosquitoes appeared and then evaporated in the breeze.

As the women approached the dancehall, they heard bursts of shouting and raucous laughter but no one was in sight. The noise got louder and it sounded as if were coming from the trees. Lydia looked up and saw two guys and two young women hanging out of the paneless windows on the second floor of the dancehall. "Come on up," one yelled. "There's a great view of the river." Lydia wondered how they had managed to reach the second floor until she saw Marsh's ladder leaning against the building. He had never put it away.

"Never mind," said Anna.

The trail up to the Bullocks' had improved immeasurably since Lydia's last trek. It was sunny day and, except for a few patches of moss on shaded rock, the path was dry and the footing acceptable. Anna, however, did not appreciate these improved conditions and grew ever testier as she fended off the branches that reached over the trail to snag her shirt and knock her hat off.

"Why do I listen to you? This sucks. Let's turn around."

"Come on. We're almost there."

"Okay. Another ten minutes. If I don't see a field of pot, or a pot of gold, or a gold mine within ten minutes, I'm going back. You can walk to Dawson."

"Jesus. You sound just like Katherine Jenkins."

Seven minutes later, Lydia put her arm out and the two women halted just before the clearing in which Adam and Eve Bullock had pitched their army tent. The front flaps on the tent were down and tied shut. Anna and Lydia stood in the trees and watched for almost five minutes. There was no movement anywhere in the vicinity.

"See," said Lydia as she stepped out of the trees. "Nobody's home. Perfectly safe. Let's see what the Bullocks are up to."

"The place looks like a junkyard," said Anna as she surveyed the piles of metal and PVC pipe and the rusty buckets.

"Exactly." Lydia knelt and picked up a hose clamp, the bolt of which had rusted within its sleeve. "I rest my case."

"What case!"

"My case that the Bullocks aren't mining anymore. Let's see if we can find the mine site."

Anna groaned. "Damn it, I don't want to crawl around in these woods for the rest of my life."

Lydia turned slowly and checked out the perimeter of the clearing. She pointed at two well-worn paths leading into the woods. "Those have to go somewhere."

The first dead-ended at a ramshackle privy. The door was open and a large coffee can sat just inside the doorframe. Anna reached in and grabbed it. "Do you think they toke up while they're on the potty?" she said with a grin. She was visibly disappointment when she opened the can and pulled out a roll of toilet paper.

They returned to the clearing and took a second path that culminated in a large pile of cans, some rusty, some relatively new. Then Lydia noticed that a narrow trail continued into the trees. She motioned Anna forward. Weeds tickled their arms and burrs stuck to their pant legs as they walked deeper into the woods. A Redpoll greeted them from the highest branch of a dwarf willow, his song a drawn out *sweeeeet,* punctuated with twittering and trills. With his red cap and chest feathers and a black patch under the chin, he looked like a tiny Catholic cardinal.

This trail was used by both humans and game. Lydia spotted old moose prints in the dried mud and the faint imprint of lynx paws in a patch of sand. Something had dug the rotten heartwood out of a spruce log and scattered chunks of it across the path. A small rubber band lay in the dirt, along with a disintegrating paper bag. A candy wrapper had been caught by the spines of a devil's club plant.

The spruce forest ended abruptly and Lydia and Anna found themselves looking down at a small, fast creek. The bank was littered with lengths of rusty angle iron. A long, wooden sluice box lay partially submerged in the water. It was weathered and grey. A long, rusty piece of grating lay next to it, along with a piece of tattered astro-turf. Piles of rock dotted the edge of the creek.

"The placer mine, I assume," said Anna. "It sure doesn't look operational."

"Nope," said Lydia as she turned her head to look upstream. She squinted hard and then grabbed Anna's arm. "What's that?"

Anna peered in the direction Lydia was pointing. "It looks like a hose."

It was, in fact, two hoses. A short one was held under water by a piece of metal strapping which was secured in place by long metal spikes driven deep into the gravel. The long one ran up the ridge where it was kept from wandering by a series of staggered wooden stakes. Both were attached to a small gasoline pump which sat on the creek bank. The pump was relatively new.

Anna and Lydia followed the hose up a squat hill and into a sunny clearing. It was filled with marijuana plants, each of them about four feet tall. "Wow," said Anna.

Lydia turned to her with a self-satisfied grin on her face. "See. I was right."

"It happens occasionally," said Anna as she picked some of the cannabis flowers and rubbed them between her hands. She waggled her fingers at Lydia. They were stained with resin. "This is quality weed."

Lydia looked at Anna with surprise. "When did you become an aficionado?"

"Hey, you have your areas of expertise and I have mine." She grinned. "Actually, Drew was the aficionado." Drew had been Anna's last boyfriend. He had grown up on a ranch in Saskatchewan. They had broken up over literary differences.

Drew loved cowboy poets; Anna hated them.

"It certainly explains why the Bullocks gave Teddy and me such a hostile reception." Lydia took a deep breath and blew out between pursed lips. "I know the Bullock's didn't kill Teddy but what if Sam Avakian did. What if Teddy found the plot and Sam knew she found it and decided to get her out of the way?"

Anna scowled and shook her head. "Oh, come on. A pot crop this size is hardly worth murder. Besides, the government is going to legalize it in a year."

"Yeah," said Lydia, "but only four plants per household. Beyond that you need a grow license, something these bozos could ever afford. And no one with a criminal record can get one. That eliminates Sam."

Lydia sat on a log and put her head in her hands. She was quiet for a long time. Finally, she looked up at Anna. "You're right. Sam didn't kill Teddy. Whoever killed her planned it carefully. Her body could have lain undiscovered in that cellar a very long time. I'll bet that whoever did it planned on sinking her boat, so it would look like she capsized."

"But the Yukon Queen got it first," said Anna.

Lydia nodded. "Even if Sam had a reason, I can't see him pulling it off. Too complicated." She offered Anna a wan smile. "Besides, stoners aren't known for their violence."

Lydia and Anna trudged back to the Bullocks' tent in silence. When they reached the privy Lydia stopped. "I gotta pee and they've got toilet paper."

"So go."

The door creaked and groaned as Lydia closed it behind her. The place was clean and the pit had been well treated with lye, so there was very little smell. Light came in from gaps in the walls and through screened openings below the roof. The facilities were nothing more than a bench with a round whole cut in it; a lidded, wooden toilet seat had been bolted over the hole. Lydia checked for spiders and dropped her pants. As she wriggled onto the seat, she noted that it could have used a good sanding and a coat of epoxy paint.

There was a pile of magazines next to her on the bench. She picked up the top one, a recent copy of *Mother Earth News*. That's when she realized that the cover had been defaced. Random letters had been cut from text and one entire word had been excised from a headline. It now read *Recipe for ___Chili*. What was missing? *Hot* chili? *Mexican* chili? Suddenly it came to her. *Vegetarian* chili! *Vagetarian*. That's when she noticed that three *a*'s and a *g* had been cut from what might have been the word *asparagus*.

"*Vagitarian* and *hag fag*," she said out loud.

"What are you babbling about?" said Anna.

When Lydia exited the privy, she had the *Mother Earth News* in her hand. She waved it in the air. "The Bullocks wrote those hate notes Teddy found in her tent. Look at this. It was *them*!" She showed Anna the defaced cover.

Anna nodded. "I guess it makes sense. They wanted to scare her away from their little plantation. They certainly misjudged Teddy if they thought *that* would work."

Lydia nodded. "No kidding." She frowned. "I wonder if they stole her journal, too. They seem to be excessively paranoid." She took a deep breath. "I have to know." She looked over at the Bullock's tent.

"No," said Anna, stamping her foot. "Absolutely not. Hiking around is one thing, but entering that tent is truly trespassing."

Lydia pressed her lips together and squared her shoulders. "Look, I know I'm obsessed, but the Bullock's have a connection with Teddy, and I have to know how far it goes."

Anna's lips were set in a firm line, but then, suddenly, she began to smile. Soon she was laughing out loud. "Do you realize what's going on here? I'm trying to talk *you* out of doing something stupid, instead of the other way around."

"We don't have time for irony. You can act as lookout. Make an owl noise if you hear anyone coming."

"Oh, crap. I can't do bird calls."

"Anybody can do an owl. Go hide in the trees. Take the magazine with you."

"Al's going to be so pissed," said Anna. She was still shaking her head when she reached the woods.

Lydia untied the tent flaps and, leaving them hanging, opened the screen door. The interior of the tent was clean and tidy, just as before. The table was scrubbed, the plank floor swept, the bed was made, and everything was neatly put away on shelves.

The search wouldn't take long. The Bullock's didn't have much furniture. Lydia checked the dresser top and both bedside tables. No notebook. The dresser contained nothing but Ms. Bullock's clothes—underwear, socks, two long skirts, two pair of pants, two peasant-style blouses, and three T shirts. Lydia checked all the shelves in the kitchen area. No notebook. She stood on a chair and ran her hand over the top shelf of the wardrobe. When she turned to the bookcase, she noticed a gap between *Murder on the Orient Express* and the *Whole Earth Catalog*. She stuck her thumb and index finger into the hole and pulled out a small volume which had been jammed toward the back of the shelf. The cover read *Notes on the Yukon* followed by the year and Teddy's full name.

Lydia opened the journal and quickly scanned a few pages. The entries were dated. They seemed to be a random collection of observations—detailed catalogs of Fools Gold artifacts, descriptions of the plants and trees some with their Latin names, notes about the weather, and short, often humorous, anecdotes about the denizens of the mushroom camp. Lydia was about to sit down and peruse the little book more closely when she became aware of a soft *hoo hoo hoooo* in the distance. It came again. Then the hooting grew frantic.

Lydia's heart began to pound. She ran to the screen door and opened it until her fingers could peel back an inch of canvas flap. She could see the trail clearly. She sucked in air as she watched Adam and Eve Bullock stride out of the woods. Adam was carrying a Coleman stove in one hand and a can of fuel in the other. Lydia's hands shook as she lowered the flap. She jammed the notebook into her pants pocket.

"Oh, shit," she whispered as she looked frantically around the tent. There was no place to hide. The bed was on a platform, there were no closets or curtains, and most of the furniture was too small to hide behind. The only possibility was the old fashioned wardrobe. Lydia pushed aside the clothes and slipped in. When she closed the door, she almost gagged at the smell. Some of the boards in the wardrobe had separated and she could see that the rod was full of men's shirts and pants, clothes that had not been washed in weeks if not months. The overwhelming odor of sour sweat didn't quite mask the other smells—kerosene, engine oil, and worst of all moth balls. Lydia had some sympathy for Adam Bullock. Hygiene was hard to maintain in the wilderness and since wool doesn't wash well under any circumstances, most bush types simply let the patina build and the odor grow.

The clothes rod prevented Lydia from standing upright. She squatted, knees bent, arms plastered to her sides. The notebook dug into her thigh. It was the worst possible position for a fast getaway but it did place her below the smell of Adam's armpits.

Lydia heard footsteps and then fumbling at the tent door. "Hey, you forgot to tie the flaps," said Eve. "It's lucky a wind didn't come up."

"That's strange," said Adam. "I thought I did." Lydia's throat tightened. Then Adam chuckled. "Just another senior moment, I guess." Lydia fervently hoped that they hadn't heard her sigh of relief.

The screen door creaked as someone opened it. Two sets of boots thumped around on the plank floor. She heard two softer thumps as Adam put down the stove and the fuel can. There was rummaging, the sound of metal on metal, the hiss of air being released, and then a soft gurgle. Somebody was filling the camp stove.

"Look," said Eve. "I'm glad Sam had a friend with a stove we could borrow, but we've gotta get the wood stove fixed before AJ and the kids come up. I wanna to be able bake for them."

"I'll fix the carburetor on the boat tomorrow. I promise. You'll have a new stovepipe by Saturday."

"Good," said Eve. Lydia could hear clanking as if someone were moving pots around. "It's important that everything be just right."

"It will be, honey," said Adam. "We'll show them a great time."

Adam and Eve proceeded to chat about inconsequential things. Did they need for a bag of lye for the privy, should they smoke some salmon for the family, whose turn was it to chop wood?

Lydia was beginning to wonder if she was going to be stuffed in the wardrobe forever. There was little ventilation and her legs were cramping. She used the sleeve of one of Adam's shirts to wipe the sweat from her face and her neck. Her own body odor was becoming part of the toxic mix.

Then she heard Eve heave a long sigh. When she spoke, her voice was soft. "I hope Sam can get himself some sleeping pills. If he doesn't, he's gonna get sick. I've told him over and over that it wasn't his fault but he feels so responsible."

"Sheeesh," said Adam, "if it was anyone's fault, it was ours."

"I know but Sam doesn't believe it. It's like he's full up with guilt. It's ridiculous."

Suddenly the screen door rattled in its frame as if someone were trying to knock on it through the tent flap. "Who the fuck could that be?" said Adam softly. Lydia heard footsteps and then heard someone open the door.

"Hi," said a cheery voice. "Can you guys give me a hand? I have a situation." Lydia couldn't decide whether to be furious at Anna for cutting short the Bullock's conversation or relieved that rescue was at hand. She decided to be both.

"Jesus, girl," said Adam, "you're covered with mud."

"That's what I need a hand with. I was hiking along the creek with my boyfriend and he got mired in quick mud. He's in up to his hips. I don't know what to do." Lydia had to suppress a giggle at Anna's breathless, girlish delivery.

Lydia heard Eve clomping toward the door. "You just left him there?" She sounded aghast. "How long have you been gone?"

"About half an hour."

"He could be up to his neck by now," said Eve.

"Well, I couldn't stay with him and get help at the same time, now could I," said Anna testily. She caught herself and the girlish persona returned. "I think he's okay. He stopped sinking a while ago. I think he hit bottom." She giggled.

"Shit," said Eve. "I didn't know there was any quick mud in the area. We'll have to keep a close eye on Stevie and Caroline."

"Times a-wasting," said Adam. "I've got some two by fours we can use. How big is this guy?"

"Oh, he's big" said Anna. "It'll take all three of us. Once we get Hank out, I'll take him down to Fools Gold Village. He told me that the archeologist down there has a satellite phone, so we can get help if he's hurt."

"That bastard's been holding out on us," said Eve. "He never told us he had a phone."

"We never asked," said Adam. "Come on. Let's go." There was a touch of urgency in his voice.

The screen door slammed and Lydia could hear the Bullocks moving lumber behind the tent. Finally, she heard Anna say a little too loudly, "He's up the creek a little more than a kilometer. It won't take long."

The voices faded and Lydia reached over and pushed the wardrobe door open. She took a deep breath of cool, clean air, unkinked her body, stood and stepped out. She had no idea how Anna was going to pull this off, but she had great confidence in her friend's dramatic talents. She quietly opened the tent door.

Lydia hurried down the trail as quickly as conditions would allow. Periodically, she stepped into the trees to rest and to assure herself that neither of the Bullocks was coming up behind her. During one of these breaks, she saw a brief flash of red in the woods. The hue was in contrast to the deep green, brown, and grey of the forest flora.

Lydia squatted behind a dense alder bush and waited for a few minutes. She saw nothing suspicious and heard only the call of a redpoll. The woods was thick with them this time of year. She stood up and listened again. Another redpoll responded. This one was close. She turned and saw it perched on a branch over her head. He thrust his red chest forward, chortled with gusto, and then, with uncanny accuracy, dropped a viscous white blob on Lydia's shoulder. With a sigh, she regained the trail and trotted the rest of way back to Fools Gold Village. When she reached the boat, she found a wide log on the creek bank that was bent into a nice chaise lounge. She stretched out and closed her eyes.

CHAPTER 15

Lydia had no idea how long she'd been dozing when she felt a tap on her shoulder. She turned to find Anna standing next to her. She was covered from chest to feet with mud and grinning from ear to ear.

Lydia grinned back. "Hey, it's Sarah Bernhardt. So how did your little drama play out?"

"They bought it hook, line, and sinker. But I did a good job of setting the scene. I found a nice big patch of regular mud and tromped around and churned it up. I even laid down in it. Then I threw a couple of thick branches into it so it looked like I'd tried to get my boyfriend out. After that I muddied my bandana and tied it to a tree."

"Why'd you do that?"

"I had to have some explanation as to why my boyfriend had disappeared. The situation was obvious. He had managed to extricate himself and he left me his bandana as a sign. I told the Bullocks that he had undoubtedly headed back to our boat. My biggest problem was keeping Adam Bullock from walking back here with me. Mrs. Bullock put the kibosh on that though. I think she was teeniest bit threatened by my girlish charm." Anna grinned again.

Then Anna lowered her eyes to the ground and the smile evaporated. "I have a confession." She kicked at a stick. "The magazine fell in a big puddle when I was stomping around in the mud. It completely disintegrated. It was nothing but pulp. I hid it under some leaves."

Lydia sighed. "Well, we both saw it and that's worth something."

"So did you find Teddy's journal in the tent?" Anna's tone was skeptical.

Anna's eyes widened, when Lydia said. "I did." She pulled the book from her pocket and handed it to Anna.

"Wow," said Ann as she flipped through the pages. "They're thieves as well as purveyors of hate notes."

"Yes, th …. No, wait. I'm sure they've never been to the mushroom camp. Karl didn't know anything about them when Marsh mentioned them. Sam must have delivered the notes. He probably took the notebook, too, in case there was anything incriminating in it."

Anna continued to flip through the notebook. Suddenly, her eyes widened and her mouth opened. She pointed to a page in the little book. "And there is" she said breathlessly

Lydia took the book. In an entry dated early in her stay at the mushroom camp, Teddy had written,

I just saw Sam pass two rolled baggies to a fisherman friend of his in exchange for money. Troy was standing five feet away. Sam Avakian is a frigging idiot.

"She wrote this before she visited you," said Anna. "I wonder why she didn't mention it."

"She probably didn't think it was a big deal. She wouldn't care about Sam selling pot, only that he did it in front of Troy. This entry might have scared Sam. He's clearly upset about something."

"How do you know?"

"When I was crammed in that wardrobe, I overheard a weird conversation between and Adam and Eve. Adam said something like, 'Sam thinks it was his fault but if it's anybody's fault, it's ours.'"

"*What* was Sam's fault?"

"I don't know. You pounded on the door at the critical moment."

"It can't be the murder. *Fault* is such a weak word for such a horrible act."

Lydia nodded. "It's hard to imagine Macbeth saying, 'It wasn't my fault, it was my wife's.' Lydia paused. "What a minute! When everyone at camp was speculating about how Teddy died, Sam said, 'I think she jumped.' Maybe he feels guilty because he delivered the notes and he thinks Teddy committed suicide because of them."

"Good grief. That's ridiculous."

"I don't think Sam reads people very well."

Anna closed the journal and handed it to Lydia. "We'd better not lose this. It's all we've got left for our heroic efforts."

Lydia grimaced. "I doubt that Al will see it that way." She shoved the journal into a zipped compartment in her daypack."

Suddenly a cold blast of wind whistled up the creek. Anna shivered and hugged her chest with her arms. She turned her eyes to the sky. Dark clouds were piling up in the west. The wind was picking up and cottonwood fluff filled the air. "We need to get on the river. I don't want to get caught in a storm." She pulled a bright yellow rain suit out of her day pack. When she sat down on a log to put the pants on, she peered down at her legs and torso. "Goddam it," she groaned. "Every inch of me is covered in mud and this suit is brand new. Cost me over two hundred bucks. Damn. Damn. Damn."

"Come on," said Lydia who was donning her own waterproof outfit. "It's like getting the first scratch on a new car."

"I've never had a new car so that analogy is lost on me." She grimaced as she gingerly inserted one muddy boot into pristine yellow Gortex.

When Anna donned the yellow jacket and cinched the yellow hood, Lydia hooted. "Hey, it's Big Bird's big sister."

"Very witty," said Anna, casting Lydia a sour look. They donned their life jackets and snapped their Bobo bags around their waists. As they pushed off, intermittent drops of rain drilled tiny craters in the surface of the creek. Soon they were engulfed in a symphony of noise. Thunder rolled in uneven waves down distant canyons. The slapping of waves on the aluminum boat hull was sharp and rhythmic. Large alder branches creaked as they rubbed against one another while the small branches squealed. Lydia's rain suit snapped in the wind. When the boat reached the Yukon, the noise of the engine drowned out everything but the thunder.

Conditions were worse on the river. As they traveled upstream, the sky steadily darkened until it was the color of pewter. Rolling thunder had been replaced by brittle cracks and rain pounded the boat and its passengers. Sharp gusts were curling the waters of the river into standing waves. When the wind caught the edge of Lydia's rain suit hood and pulled it off her head, cold water trickled under the collar of her jacket and down her back. Soon the rain was blowing sideways. Lydia turned around and threw Anna look of alarm.

"Yeah, I know," yelled Anna. "I'm heading back to the village."

As Anna began a slow 180 degree turn, Lydia heard a crack which blossomed into an echo as it spread across the water. Then there were two more cracks in rapid succession. There was no mistaking that sound. Gunfire. The noise of the storm made it impossible to tell from which direction the shots had come. Maybe a hunter had tracked a moose to the river's edge. Then there was a boom and a fountain of water erupted just ahead of the boat. Lydia emitted a yelp.

Lydia bent low in the bow and turned to yell at Anna. That's when she saw something bright red behind them. The swatch of red was attached to a boat and the boat was probably 150 yards away and coming toward them fast. "Gun it!" screamed Lydia. "They're shooting at *us*." Anna twisted the throttle hard. Lydia had to grab the gunwale to avoid being thrown backward. As the boat sped forward, her butt pounded on the seat. She felt as if her face were being pelted by tiny ball bearings.

Realizing that Anna could see virtually nothing from the stern, Lydia crawled into the bow to watch for river debris. Her own visibility was impaired by the wall of rain and the sheet of water that had spread over her glasses. Her knees bounced on the aluminum hull as the boat pitched in the wind and three foot waves. She held on tight and leaned out over the point. Out of the corner of her eye, she watched as the other boat narrowed the gap. Now there was less than thirty yards between them. The splotch of red quickly morphed into a person, someone wearing a red, hooded sweatshirt. Two red arms were struggling to hold a long gun horizontal. Lydia knew that boat and she knew that sweatshirt. Both belonged to Sam Avakian.

Just then Lydia heard a deafening blast and felt the boat lurch sideways. She turned around and looked with horror at a jagged hole in the aluminum, about five inches above the water line and just a few inches behind her seat. She twisted the other way and saw that the bullet had passed through her day pack and the cooler before it lodged in the other side of the boat. When Lydia turned back to watch the river, it was too late. The boat was barreling toward a submerged cottonwood tree. It hit the trunk head on. The bow leaped skyward and then torqued sideways. To Lydia it felt like a banked curve on a fast roller coaster. She reached for something, anything, but clutched only rain. As she was launched over the side, she sucked in all the air her lungs would hold.

Lydia hit the river hard, face first. She felt herself go under and almost gasped at the iciness of the water. She felt an awful stabbing pain behind her eyes. She kept her mouth and eyes closed, tried to relax, and waited for her life vest to lift her back to the surface.

But it didn't. Lydia remained suspended under the churning, swirling, brown current. Her body was slammed back and forth by powerful waves. Branches scratched her neck and pulled the braid out of her hair. Heavy limbs smacked her torso. Lydia could taste the river's tannin on her lips; silt scoured her exposed skin.

She could hear a ragged *rahr rahr rahr* as the boat's engine took on water somewhere downstream. It was a strange sound, deep and full and at the same time diffuse and directionless.

Lydia pushed water down with her hands and arms and tried to kick. That was when she realized that her left boot had been captured by the root ball of the waterlogged cottonwood. She felt panic rise in her chest. A dozen terrifying scenarios flitted through her consciousness. She squeezed her eyes tight and tried to focus on the act of freeing herself. The effort calmed her.

Lydia opened her eyes and tried to determine how badly the boot was wedged, but it was impossible to see anything through the suspended silt and whirling debris. She yanked her left leg and twisted her foot in an attempt to remove the captive boot. Unfortunately, she had used a surgeon's knot and the lace refused to budge. She grabbed her pant leg and slowly pulled herself hand over hand toward her left ankle. Her extremities were growing numb and she could barely feel the fabric.

Every inch of progress reduced Lydia's oxygen reserve. Her lungs were burning and her arm muscles were growing flaccid. There was a strange acid taste in her mouth. The river was at the same time her ally and her foe; the downstream current pushed her toward her goal; whirlpools pulled her back. She wanted desperately to take a deep breath; she wanted even more desperately not to. Her heart sounded like a timpani in her ears and she was growing nauseous.

Lydia's cramped and frozen fingers finally located the top of her ankle but couldn't reach her boot laces. I'm going to die in this river, she thought. Just like my father did. There was a certain symmetry in that.

For a brief moment Lydia felt resignation. Her muscles began to relax. Then another voice in her head screamed, No! She renewed her grip on her left ankle and jammed her right hand beneath her rain pants. With great concentration she ripped the Velcro tab on her sheath and forced her fingers around the handle of her Swiss Army knife. She could barely feel it in her hand. She pulled the knife out of its sheath and somehow got the blade open. She laid it against her cheek to locate its cutting edge. Then she pulled her torso forward with her left hand at the same time she extended the knife toward her captive boot and slashed upwards. The blade sliced water and Lydia nearly dropped it. She willed her fingers to tighten and slashed again. This time she met resistance and then lost her grip. She had to fight the desire to scream as the knife dropped. With little hope of success, she put her right toe onto the back of her left boot and pushed. The lace gave way and her foot was free.

Lydia kicked hard, or thought she did. But her legs barely moved. Hypothermic, lungs starved for oxygen, her body had nothing left to give. Lydia knew she couldn't hold her breath much longer. The noise in her ears was deafening. The pressure on her sternum was excruciating. Every muscle in her body was on fire. She opened her eyes wide realized that her underwater world was growing darker, as if the Yukon Territory were experiencing a precipitous and unexpected nightfall. She could feel her eyes bulging and her cheeks pushing out. Her lips were about to explode open. Lydia was going to die just inches below the river's surface and life giving air. As her mouth formed a wide O and her diaphragm relaxed, she was aware of a sudden brightness and a strange chill.

CHAPTER 16

When Lydia opened her eyes, the first thing she saw was a strange yellow apparition coming toward her. The apparition appeared to be dancing on water. Lydia wasn't dancing; she was undulating, up and down, up and down. Then something hit her bare left foot and scraped her toes. Her knees began dragging on a rough surface, back and forth, back and forth. She tried desperately to focus on what was happening. She couldn't fathom it.

The yellow apparition reached her side and yelled into her ear. "You're alive."

Lydia looked up and blinked. I am, she thought. She pushed her top teeth into her bottom lip. It hurt. "Ah, ah ...," she croaked. She didn't have enough breath for words. She tried to fill her lungs with air but all she could manage were tiny gasps.

The figure in yellow grabbed Lydia under the arms and dragged her through shallow water and then over solid ground. Every now and then something sharp caught the heel of her shoeless foot. She wanted to cry out, to protest, but it was too much trouble. It seemed to take an eternity to get wherever it was they were going. But even with a sore and battered heel, Lydia didn't care. Her eyes were closed; she was relaxed and sleepy. Someone else was doing all the work and it wasn't raining anymore.

Then Lydia began to shiver. At first it felt like the chills that accompany high fever. She could feel goose bumps rising on her skin. Her shoulders began to jerk and her breath grew labored.

Suddenly violent spasms seized her back muscles. Incredible pain. Soon her body was jerking in every direction. She tried to free her arms so she could hug herself and stop this teeth-rattling motion, but the yellow phantom wouldn't release her. Just when Lydia thought she would be shaken apart, she felt warmth. Her rescuer gently laid her on the ground. Lydia opened one eye and saw another dancing apparition. This one was yellow, too, yellow and orange. Lydia reached for it. Someone grabbed her hand. "No," said a voice. "You'll burn yourself." Lydia passed out again.

When she finally awoke, she saw that she was lying in front of a small driftwood fire. It took her a moment to realize that the tremors had stopped and there was warmth. With great effort she raised her arm and laid her hand on her chest. It rose and fell in a steady rhythm. Then her hands went to her face. Astonishingly, her glasses were still there, the wire temples wrapped securely around her ears.

When Lydia dropped her arm, the fabric around it made a strange crinkling noise. She moved a leg and the same thing happened. With great effort, she pushed herself up on one elbow and inspected her body. It was engulfed in something shiny, something which clung to her skin outlining the curve of her breasts, the swelling of her hips, and the mounds of her knees. Anna was sitting next to her in an identical shroud. Lydia looked up and saw her own clothes and Anna's draped over a tall tangle of branches that had been assembled near the fire.

Anna reached over and gently touched Lydia's face. "You're gonna be fine," she said. "You owe your life to Bobo and you look exquisite in your space blanket." Then Anna shook her head as she pointed to the clothing draped over a tangle of branches. "Cotton. Every stitch of it cotton. What idiots we are."

Lydia frowned as she tried to parse Anna's words. Then it came to her. *Cotton kills.* Wet cotton sucks the warmth right out of a body. Lydia patted her Mylar gown. "Thank God for Bobo," she muttered. Moving and speaking those words wore her out. She dropped back to the ground.

Not quite asleep but not awake either, she heard Anna say, "I tied your red bandana to a log. Maybe somebody will recognize it as a distress signal and stop to help us." Red. There was something important about red. Lydia screwed up her face and tried to remember but she couldn't.

She didn't know how long she had been dozing when she felt Anna stand up. "I hear a boat," Anna said. "I'm going to flag it down." Lydia turned her head just in time to see Anna loping over the sand, her space blanket flapping behind her.

Lydia pushed herself up into a sitting position. She took stock and concluded that she was feeling much stronger. She got on her hands and knees and then slowly stood. A wave of dizziness hit her. She grabbed a driftwood branch and steadied herself. Her head began to clear. She took a deep breath and turned around slowly, taking in her environment. The Mylar swished around her ankles.

Lydia found herself standing on a dry spot in the middle of a small wet island. It was a desolate, colorless patch of sand. The segmented reeds that grew at the island's edge were grey and brittle. The cotton grass stalks at her feet were headless and bent. Muddy rivulets meandered in long S curves before they disappeared into muddy pools at the river's edge. The only trees on the island were the scraggly alders behind which Anna had made Lydia's bed. Fortunately, the upstream end of the island had captured a jungle of dead branches and small tree trunks, fuel for Anna's fire.

Lydia looked up at the sky. The worst of the storm had passed but there was still heavy cloud cover. The breeze was stiff and she was beginning to feel chilled again. She sat down and moved as close to the fire as she dared. Shivers began to crawl up her backbone. She drew her shoulders up to her ears and grabbed her elbows. The spasms returned.

Lydia heard voices but she was too miserable to turn around. Suddenly a stranger was standing next to her, pulling off a jacket. The woman kneeled down and threaded Lydia's arms through the sleeves. Then she zipped it up over Lydia's space blanket. The jacket was tan. Tan with red trim. Lydia breathed in sharply. "It was Sam," she whispered. "It was Sam in the other boat."

Anna stared at her. "You saw him?"

"I saw his sweatshirt, his red hoodie."

"Look," their rescuer said to Anna, "she'll be in serious trouble if we don't get her warm soon. There's a cabin nearby. I'll take you there."

"Fools Gold Creek?" asked Anna.

"Yes," the woman said. "It's only a few minutes away. I've got a tarp in the boat. You can both cover up with that. I've also got a thermos of warm tea."

The woman took one of Lydia's arms and Anna took the other and they pulled her to her feet. The stranger held on to Lydia while Anna inspected the soggy pile of clothes draped over the wood pile. She waved her hand over it in disgust. "I can't cope with these now." She picked up the two Bobo bags and grabbed Lydia's other elbow. Arms locked together, the three women walked slowly to the river. Their rescuer seated Lydia and Anna together on the center seat and drew a blue tarp around them. She threaded a thin piece of cord through the grommets and pulled the tarp closed. "We must look like a teepee," said Anna as she put her arms around Lydia to share her body heat.

The woman disappeared behind Lydia and Anna for a moment and then returned with a thermos top filled with warm liquid. She held it to Lydia's lips. "Drink slow," she said. Lydia sipped the tea. It felt like a river of warm honey spreading inside her chest.

When Jack Marsh opened his cabin door ten minutes later, his mouth dropped in astonishment. "What in the hell happened to them?" he asked the rescuer, who had one arm around Anna and the other around Lydia.

They need to get warm. Their boat capsized." She squeezed Lydia's shoulder. "This one's hypothermic."

Marsh frowned and stared at Lydia. "Hey, I know you."

"Let us in," snapped Anna. "You can renew your acquaintanceship later."

"Of course," said Jack.

Anna helped Lydia off with the jacket and returned it to their rescuer. She took the woman's hand. "Thank you so much. Without you I don't know what would have happened."

"It's what we do for each other on the river," said the woman. "I'll be on my way now. Take care." Anna nodded and led Lydia into the cabin.

"Let me get you both some dry clothes and you can tuck her into my bed," said Marsh. He rummaged around at the back of the room and reemerged holding two pair of sweat pants, two sweatshirts, socks, and a down sleeping bag. "You'll swim in these track pants but they're the best I can do. I'll step outside for a few minutes."

As soon as the door closed behind Jack Marsh, Lydia grabbed Anna's arm. "It was Sam Avakian who was shooting at us. He's insane!"

"And you said stoners weren't prone to violence," said Anna. "But we don't have time to psychoanalyze Avakian. We have to get you warm. Then I'll call the Mounties." She stripped off Lydia's space blanket. The shivering had passed and Lydia's mind was clearing. She was startled by the appearance of her own body. Any spot not protected by her life vest was scratched and abraded. Massive bruises were starting to materialize on her upper arms and her hips. Her left foot was gouged and bloody.

"I guess I took a beating in the river," she said, tracing a deep scratch on her thigh with her finger.

"This is no time to admire your injuries," said Anna. She yanked the sweatshirt over Lydia's head. Lydia gently pushed her away and finished the job herself. Then, holding on to a chair, she managed to get into Jack's sweatpants and cinch the string. She let Anna put a sock on her uninjured foot.

"To bed with you. If you don't start to warm up in a few minutes, I'm climbing in there naked."

Lydia crawled in. Anna drew the blankets to Lydia's chin and then spread a down sleeping bag over her. Lydia knew it would take a while for her body temperature to return to normal, but she also knew that she was out of danger. She snuggled down into the blankets and bag and savored the warmth.

By the time Marsh reentered the cabin, Anna had also donned dry clothes and was trying to roll up the cuffs on the sweat pants. Finally she resigned herself to treading on a puddle of grey jersey every time she took a step. "Lydia told me you have a satellite phone. Can I use it?"

"Of course," said Marsh. He leaned under the bed and pulled out a large storage box. Lydia pushed herself up on an elbow and watched him as he pulled the top off and began rummaging around. Finally he extracted a small black box. But it wasn't the black box that caught Lydia's attention. It was a Canon digital camera nestled between a pair of binoculars and a boat compass. Lydia tapped Marsh's shoulder.

"That camera. Where did you get it?" Her voice was sharp.

Marsh stood up before he answered. He looked down at her and frowned. "I found it under a log near the creek. It looked like somebody had a picnic there and forgot it."

"When?"

Jack wrinkled his brow as if he were thinking hard. It wasn't a convincing performance. "I'm not sure. I guess it was about a week and a half ago. I thought the owner might come back for it but so far nobody's claimed it."

"That's because this camera belongs to Teddy Gianopoulous." She pointed to the tiny red carabiners which attached the strap to the body. "She put those on."

"Gianopoulous," Marsh said as if he were trying the word out on his tongue. Then his eyes grew large and his mouth opened. "That's the gal we found in the dance hall, isn't it?" he said finally.

"Yes, it is," said Lydia.

"Oh, man, that never occurred to me. Do you think it's a clue?" Lydia shrugged. "There aren't any pictures on it. I checked."

"That's too bad," said Lydia. "Even so, I think it should be turned over to the Mounties."

"I'll do that," said Marsh.

"You can do it tonight," said Anna. "It's the Mounties I need to call."

"Just because your boat capsized? That seems extreme. I can take you back to Dawson."

"Our boat capsized because somebody was shooting at it," said Lydia.

Marsh gave a low whistle. "Who would do a thing like that? And why?"

"We've got no clue," said Lydia quickly.

"Wow," said Marsh shaking his head. He turned to a shelf and took down a waterproof bag. He slipped the camera into it. "Now it won't get wet if the weather gets bad on the way to Dawson." He laid the bag on the floor next to the bed.

"Thanks," said Lydia.

Anna put her hand out. "Times a-wastin'. The phone, please."

Marsh handed her the box. "I'll go outside with you and show you the best spot to make the call."

While Marsh was gone, Lydia leaned over the bed and reached into the drybag. She extracted the Canon and turned it on. The batteries still worked but there were no pictures stored in the camera. "Shit," she said. She replaced it and was plumping her pillow when Marsh pushed open the cabin door.

"Can I get you anything? How about something warm to drink?"

Lydia gave him a sheepish smile. "You know what I really want? Coffee."

Marsh shook his finger. "You know that's bad for hypothermia victims." Lydia rolled her eyes. Marsh grinned, picked up a bag of beans, and dumped some in a hand coffee grinder. Lydia breathed in deeply. The smell of the freshly ground coffee was intoxicating.

Anna was back within a few minutes. "The boat should be here in less than two hours."

"Since we're going to have the pleasure of each other's company for a while, I think introductions are in order," said Marsh, casting a flirtatious smile in Anna's direction. "I know she's Linda, but who are you?"

Anna gave a small snort. "Well, you know wrong. She's Lydia. And I'm her faithful companion, Anna."

"Are you faithful to anyone other than Lydia?"

"Not at present," said Anna. Even in sweats five sizes too large and curls stiff with silt, Anna was irresistible. Sometimes it got on Lydia's nerves.

"Maybe you'd have dinner with me in Dawson sometime," said Marsh.

Anna's voice was neutral. "We'll see."

Lydia was not in the mood for the dating game and the gurgling in the blue enamel pot had stopped. She sat up in bed. "Coffee's done," she announced as she threw back the covers and swung her legs over the side. "I take it black."

CHAPTER 17

It was midnight when the RCMP jet boat docked in Dawson. Anna checked her watch and grinned at Lydia. "I told you we'd be up and back in one day."

Al Cerwinski was pacing the length of the pier. His hair was uncombed, his shirt was half out of his pants, and his face was grey with worry. As soon as Lydia stepped off the boat, he pulled her into his arms and held her. "Thank God you're all right." Then he gently pushed her away and looked into her eyes. "You attract gunfire like sugar attracts ants. You have a special and perverse gift." Then Al hugged Anna, too. "And you—you keep going along for the ride."

Anna grinned. "Yeah, but I hate being bored. Lydia is the ultimate antidote to boredom."

"That she is, to the peril of us all," said Al. "We've got a boat out looking for Avakian. Wilbur will take your statements tomorrow."

Al bundled the two women into the police cruiser. He dropped Anna off at her place and took Lydia to Dawson's small Nursing Station. A nurse cleaned Lydia's wounds, stitched her left foot in two places, and her right thigh in one. He also gave her a tetanus shot and a pair of crutches. We they got home, Al dropped the little bag he was carrying on the hall table and tried to lead her into the bedroom, Lydia said, "No. Make me a cup of coffee. We have to talk. There are some things you need to know before I make my official statement."

Al's eyebrows went up. "Uh, oh," he said. He sighed as he

walked into the kitchen. Lydia hobbled into the living room and collapsed on the couch. A few moments later, Lydia heard the ding of the microwave and then Al reemerged with a plain white mug. No Mountie Python. The fact that he was offering her reheated coffee did not bode well either.

Lydia clutched the cup in both hands and stared at it as she considered how to tell Al her story. There was no getting around the fact that he would be angry, but she had no choice but to plunge ahead. "Here I go," she said more to herself than to him. "I did something today that could have precipitated a negative reaction from Sam Avakian." Al groaned and Lydia raised her hand, palm out. "Let me tell the whole story before you get worked up. I'm exhausted and sore and I just want to get through this." Al's shoulders sagged but he nodded.

His face remained expressionless as Lydia gave him an abbreviated account of the trips to and from the mushroom camp, including the sighting of *High Arctic*. When she described wandering around the Bullock's clearing, his eyes narrowed. When she told him how she and Anna had followed the trail to the placer mine, he bit his lip. When she described how the hose had led them to the marijuana crop, he put his head in his hands. When she described finding the magazine in the privy and entering the Bullock's tent, his nostrils flared and his breathing quickened. She tried to ignore these signs of an imminent explosion.

Lydia told Al about finding Teddy's missing journal, about hiding in the toxic wardrobe, about Anna's inventive story. She told him that both the magazine and the journal had been lost to water. Then she put her hand on Al's knee. "I know the Bullock's didn't see me, Al, but I think Sam Avakian did. I saw a bit of red in the woods. It was probably his sweatshirt. I'm sure the Bullocks wrote those notes and Sam Avakian delivered them. He must have stolen the notebook too."

Al's face was rigid and he was silent for a very long time. Lydia kept her eyes on his and refused to look away. When he finally spoke to her, his voice was low and tight. "You keep trying to do my job for me, don't you, Lydia? You love to play cop. How am I going to explain to the Assistant Superintendent that my girlfriend trespassed on private property and, in the process, discovered illegal activity, the source of some nasty notes, and a stolen journal, which no longer exists in readable form? We can't use any of this information and, frankly, I'm not sure I have the balls to tell him about it."

Lydia bristled. "I could've found the pot when I was hiking around. That's not exactly trespassing."

"It's not going to fly."

"But, Al, the magazine proved that the Bullock's wrote those notes."

Al's voice did not reflect sympathy. "It doesn't matter. You don't have the magazine and writing notes isn't illegal anyway."

"But they were hate notes. That has to be against the law."

"Canadian laws on hate speech are different than U.S. laws. Here it's about spreading hateful views publically. The notes to Teddy were private, directed only to her. Besides, Teddy wasn't intimidated. She laughed about it."

"Well, they should be illegal, goddam it." Lydia was in no mood to be rational. "It's crappy and mean to do something like that."

"Yes, indeed. Crappy and mean," said Al with a sarcastic lilt. His voice deepened. "Fortunately, Teddy wasn't bothered by crappy and mean."

Lydia wasn't giving in. "Even if Teddy wasn't intimidated, don't you think that's what the Bullocks were attempting to do, scare her away from their crop? Anna says it's good stuff. What if Sam killed her to keep her away?" Lydia knew this wasn't true, but the words tumbled out of her mouth.

"Sam Avakian was picking mushrooms the morning of the murder. He has two witnesses including your friend Karl. Neither he nor the Bullocks killed Teddy Gianopoulous."

Lydia looked down at the floor. "I know," she said. Then,

very abruptly, she stood up and hobbled into the hall on one crutch. Al sighed and shook his head.

When Lydia returned to the living room, she did not look the least bit contrite. Nor did she look upset. In fact, she was smiling. She held a camera in one hand at waved it Al.

"It's a camera," he snapped.

"It's Teddy's camera."

Al traces of irritation vanished from Al's face. His eyes widened. "How in the hell did you get hold of that?"

Lydia told him. "I meant to give it to Rogers, but I was so wiped out, I forgot." She clicked the snap, unrolled the top of the bag, and removed the Canon.

"Did Marsh say how he got it?"

"Yeah. He says he found it next to the creek."

"Are there any pictures on it?"

"No," said Lydia and she handed the camera to Al. He turned it on, clicked the review button, shrugged at the blank screen, and put the camera on the dining room table.

Lydia picked it up again. "But there *were* pictures. Teddy took some at the BBQ. Remember? And Gretchen said she carried it with her all the time."

Al nodded. "Maybe that's a new memory card."

"Did you find another memory card in her tent?" Al shook his head. "Then maybe somebody deleted those pictures."

Al nodded. "You might be right."

Lydia frowned. "I wonder if there's any way to retrieve deleted pictures from a camera. I know you can bring back deleted computer files."

"I don't know," said Al, "but I can find out." He went into the kitchen and picked up the phone.

Al was back in five minutes. He was grinning. "Bingo," he said. "I got our tech guy out of bed. He can do it. He'll be over first thing in the morning."

"I hope there's a picture of Teddy in there," said Lydia softly. "A close-up that shows her goofy smile and her freckles." She bit her lip. "I need something to erase the image of her in that body bag."

"I hope there's a picture of her murderer," said Al.

Lydia stood. "I feel like I've been hit by a cement truck. I'm going to take a bath, soak my battered body," she paused and gave Al a sidelong look, "and remove the stink of high crimes and misdemeanors."

Al leaned toward her and sniffed. "All I can smell is ..." he stuck his nose in her tangled hair, "Mr. Bullock's armpits."

Despite the fact that Lydia was gouged, scraped, bruised and contused, she slept hard and long that night. She got up when the computer tech rang the bell at 6:00 AM, had breakfast, and went back to bed.

The doorbell peeled again at ten. Al opened the bedroom door and peeked in just as she was gingerly pulling loose cotton pants over her battered legs. He smiled and waved a thumb drive in her direction. "We've got pictures," he said. "Lots of them." He withdrew and Lydia finished dressing. Her left foot was too sore for shoes, but Al's misshapen old slipper socks felt fine.

Al was standing in the living room, nervously rocking back and forth on his heels, a thumb drive clutched between his index finger and thumb. "Come on," he said. "Let's see what we have." Lydia grabbed her crutches and followed Al to his study. She dragged a straight chair up to the computer while he settled back into his adjustable desk chair. As usual, it groaned and squealed to protest his 215 pounds.

Al slipped the little drive into a USB port on his machine and brought up a photo management program. Thirty postage stamp size images popped onto the screen. He clicked on the first and it enlarged instantly. It was a picture of Troy standing in a narrow creek. His hair was in tangles and his shoes and pants were soaking wet. He held a stringer of grayling in one hand and a rod and reel in the other. He was smiling broadly for the camera.

The next four pictures had been taken around the mushroom

camp. There was a nice portrait of Sam Avakian, his face serious as he stared off into the distance. He was a very handsome man. There was a photo of Liz and Gretchen, arms around each other, mugging for the camera. The next picture caught Red and Bob Dunlap raising beer cans high in a mutual toast. Lydia realized that this was the first time she had seen Red smile. The last camp photo was of Troy again. He had fallen asleep leaning against a tree. Teddy had focused on the child's face. His hair was windblown and his cheeks were streaked with dirt. A milk stain outlined his lips and long dark eyelashes brushed his tawny cheeks.

Next came pictures of Lake Laberge, the BBQ, and a magnificent golden eagle perched in a dead spruce. The eagle had been photographed from the side but his head was turned in the photographer's direction. The creature's bearing was regal, his yellow eyes cold and haughty. A cloak of golden feathers swept around his shoulders and down his neck. His powerful wings were tucked in close to his body. The only imperfection on this powerful, streamlined form was a single tail feather which bent upward at a jaunty forty-five-degree angle.

Lydia was surprised by the next photo. She leaned back and stared. It featured a grid laid out with stakes and string. All of the squares were large and most had been dug out to depth of about two feet. Sifting screens were propped against a large rock.

The picture had been taken from some distance. Lydia could see a single human shadow on the ground but its owner was invisible to the camera.

"Marsh's archeological dig, I assume," said Al.

Lydia nodded. "Must be."

Al clicked on the next thumbnail. It showed Jack Marsh kneeling in a grid that was only partially dug out. He had a trowel in his hand. The other was poised above a large pile of dirt. Except for slight changes in Marsh's posture and the position of the trowel, the next seven pictures varied very little in composition.

"Maybe Teddy didn't take these photos. Maybe one of the

grad students took them after Marsh found Teddy's camera," said Al. He scowled. "But why delete them then?"

"Maybe somebody had already downloaded them to a computer," said Lydia.

Al stroked his chin. "We're missing something in these photos. Something crucial."

"A motive for murder?" asked Lydia.

"I wish I knew," said Al.

CHAPTER 18

Lydia hurt too much to contemplate motives for murder. Her strained muscles were burning and the cut on her thigh was throbbing. Her bruises protested whenever she sat down or lay down and her mangled foot screamed whenever she stood. "I'm going to go and nurse my wounds," she announced as she pulled herself out of the chair with a groan and limped on one crutch toward the study door.

"The solution to your ills is alimentary, my dear Lydia. I shall bring you a butter tart."

Lydia shook her head. "No thanks. What I need is aspirin, water, and ice packs."

Lydia hobbled toward the living room and Al headed for the bathroom and then the kitchen. She curled up on the couch and cycled through the TV remote until she found the Coen brothers' classic movie *Fargo*. Al returned with an aspirin bottle, a glass of water, and three ice packs wrapped in towels; he placed one of the packs on each of Lydia's shoulders and one on her left thigh. Five minutes later, Lydia picked up the remote and changed the movie to *Body Heat*.

A cop was in the midst of warning Kathleen Turner's besotted lover that, "She's trouble, Ned. Real big-time major-league trouble," when the phone rang. Al got it in the kitchen. Lydia could his voice rising and falling when suddenly there was a loud whoop. He stuck his head through the pass through and flashed her two thumbs up. Then he laughed long and loud. When he finally came into the living room, he was bouncing on his toes with excitement.

"What happened? Did you win the lottery?"

"Better than that. We got Samuel Avakian."

Lydia sat upright. Her back protested the sudden movement. She groaned softly before she said, "You're kidding me! Where'd they find him?"

"At the mushroom camp. In his tent. Asleep."

"You're not serious."

"I *am* serious. After shooting at you, he went home and went to bed."

"How dumb can you be!"

"Not dumb. Stoned. Stoned out of his mind. The first thing Snowshoe and Rogers see when they get to the camp is Avakian's boat bobbing around in an eddy. Apparently, he'd neglected to tie it off. His rifle was in it. It had been fired recently and the magazine was empty. Then they found one of his boots stuck in the mud. The other one is missing altogether. Avakian was lying half in and half out of his tent, stark naked and covered with mosquito bites. He was using the red sweatshirt as a pillow."

"Did he admit shooting at us?"

"No and yes."

"What in the hell does that mean?"

"At first he stone-walled." Al grinned. "*Stone*-walled. Get it?"

Lydia offered no hint of a smile. "Go on," she said.

"After Snowshoe found seven baggies of pot in his tent, he became more cooperative. Avakian admitted shooting in the general direction of Anna's boat but said he only wanted to scare you. Keep you away from Fools Gold Creek. He was terrified that you'd find the pot plantation. He didn't know you already had. He insisted he had no intention of hitting the boat or you."

"Oh, sure. That's why there's a bullet hole in the aluminum, right where my left side should have been."

"Avakian seemed genuinely shocked to learn that one of his bullets penetrated the hull. He insisted that the weather was so bad and he was so zonked, he couldn't have hit you even if he'd wanted to."

"Let me get this straight," said Lydia. "Sam didn't intend to hit the boat. If he'd been straight, his aim wouldn't have been. But stoned, he was Buffalo Bill. What kind of screwed up karma is that?"

"He was worried about the pot but mostly angry at you. The Bullocks are good friends. He saw you coming out of their tent. He said you are a nosy bitch and a trespasser and you need to be taught some manners."

"He's right about that. Will you be able to hold him?"

"Oh, yeah," said Al. "We've got evidence that he was dealing and I hope that when we raise Anna's boat, we'll have the ballistics to prove assault."

"Did Snowshoe ask him about the journal and the notes?"

Al nodded. "He told her about the notes very reluctantly. He wanted to protect the Bullocks. They were all afraid that Teddy knew about the pot and that they would lose their land if she went to the Mounties. Apparently, they had sunk their very last loonie into that property and they had to get something out of it. When the mine proved to be a bust, cannabis seemed like a good solution. The notes were meant to make Teddy believe some of her campmates were bigots. They hoped she'd get pissed off and quit the project. They abandoned the notes early on when Sam realized that Teddy was well-liked and wasn't taking the notes seriously anyway. He took the journal later in the hopes he could find out what she knew."

A wave of melancholy washed over Lydia. "Do you think we'll ever find the killer, Al?"

He gave her a bemused smile. "What's this *we* stuff. He picked up her hand and looked into her eyes. "This murder wasn't a drive-by or a ghost from Teddy's past. We'll figure it out. That's *we* the Mounties, my love. Not you and me."

Lydia put out her hand and pulled Al down on the couch. She stretched out with her head in his lap. He stroked her cheeks and gently massaged her head. His eyes turned from grey to blue as he gazed into hers. It was only then that Lydia told him how close she had come to drowning. She described her futile attempts to surface, her frantic fumbling to find her knife, her panic when it disappeared beneath the whirling current. Al's breathing quickened and his jaw clenched. When she stopped talking, he looked straight ahead and was silent for a long time. Then his arms tightened around her until she yelped. "Bruises, remember?"

His voice was almost a whisper. "I could have lost you in that river. You were trying to help me do my job and you almost died. And I've been chewing you out. Jesus Christ." His face collapsed. He grabbed Lydia's hands and held them for a long time. Then he gave her a small smile. "Thank God you have the lungs of a blue whale and the will of a grizzly bear."

CHAPTER 19

Al and Lydia had fallen asleep on the couch when the phone rang yet again. This time it was Al's cell. "Stop that infernal noise," muttered Lydia.

Al gently untangled himself and pulled the phone from his pocket. After a perfunctory "hello," he was quiet for a long time. The next thing he said was, "We'll be right over."

Lydia groaned out loud. She glared at Al. "Right over where?"

"That was Anna." Lydia's eyebrows shot up. Anna never called to talk exclusively to Al. "Her neighbor, the grandmother of that little boy, is back."

"Ethel Haugen."

"Yes, Mrs. Haugen. She wants to talk to us."

"To us! Why?"

"She told Anna a story—a story involving a priest who used to teach at an Indian school."

Lydia's eyes grew wide. "It's that priest from Watson Lake, isn't it? The one who was dragged into the closet."

"Yes. The story reminded Anna of George Jenkins and she suggested that Mrs. Haugen talk to the Mounties. The woman was hesitant until Anna explained that I was your boyfriend as well as a good friend of hers. Mrs. Haugen agreed. She wants you there, too. Apparently, she thinks your presence will keep me from engaging in police brutality."

"Oh, God, I don't feel like moving. Everything hurts."

"We have to go," said Al. "We'll drive."

Ten minutes later Al and Lydia were standing at Ethel

Haugen's front door. Anna opened it before they had a chance to knock. Ethel was sitting on an old fashioned, overstuffed couch. This woman was not the immaculate, well coifed person Lydia had met five days ago. Her clothes were wrinkled, her hair needed washing and her face was drawn and grey. She kept picking at something invisible on the arm of the couch. She gave Lydia a half smile, the kind of smile that never reaches the eyes.

Anna waved Lydia and Al into chairs and she seated herself on the couch next to Ethel. "This is Sergeant Cerwinski, Ethel. Tell him what you just told me."

Mrs. Haugen blinked and for a moment Lydia thought she was going to cry. But she didn't. She clasped her hands tightly in her lap and began. "A few nights ago I received word that my foster father had died, a retired priest named Maxwell Fleming. I flew down to Watson Lake yesterday to be with his sister. That's when I found out that Max hadn't died of natural causes. He had been dragged into a room in an old church and left to die." Ethel's voice caught and her eyes filled with tears. She pulled a tissue from her pants pocket wiped them. Then she clenched her teeth, moved to the edge of her seat, and began to speak again. Her body was rigid; her voice was low and halting. "I came back right away because I know ... I know who did it."

Lydia could hear Al's intake of breath. "Who was it?" he said softly.

Mrs. Haugen took a deep breath. "I don't which person did it but I know it was done by a group called Northern Fire."

"How do you know this?" asked Al.

"Because my daughter is in this group, Sergeant." Lydia's jaw dropped.

"Did she tell you that they did it?" asked Al.

"No, but I know. I heard about the apple in the stained glass window being wiped clean. The apple is Northern Fire's symbol for assimilation. They target teachers from the residential Indian schools and Max taught at Stony Creek for almost fifteen years."

"Do you think your daughter did it?" asked Al.

Ethel shook her head vigorously. "No. Beatrice didn't do it. She's got some strange ideas but she wouldn't do a thing like that. She loved Max. He was like a grandfather to her. She would never hurt him."

"Did you attend Stony Creek School, Mrs. Haugen?" Al asked.

She nodded. "My parents died in a car wreck when I was young and I had no other family in the Yukon. Max and the school were my salvation. I know that most Indian Schools were terrible but Stony Creek wasn't like that. They took good care of us and gave us a good education—good enough that I was able to earn a full scholarship to the University of Alberta." She paused and her eyes filled with tears again. Her chest began to heave and she broke down completely. Anna put her arms around her.

She held Ethel Haugen for a long time. The two sat beneath a framed print of Manet's *Le Repos*. The beautiful well-coifed girl lounging on that couch was a stark contrast to the distraught and disheveled woman in Anna's arms.

Finally Ethel pulled away and composed herself. She turned to Al again. "I'm sorry but this is terrible for me. Until I married Eric, Max was the only family I had. Max was a good man and he didn't deserve to die like that." She clenched her teeth and then her fist which she dug into her own thigh.

Al waited a few moments before saying, "Mrs. Haugen, Reverend Fleming wasn't left to die. At least not deliberately. His hands were loosely bound and the door wasn't locked. It doesn't appear that he had a heart attack or anything like that. He could have walked out of that room. Do have any idea why he didn't?"

Ethel put her hand to her mouth. She gave a small groan. "No. I can't imagine why. Maybe he was unconscious."

"Not according to the coroner," said Al. "And there were signs in the dust on the floor that he repositioned himself many times."

Ethel fixed her eyes on Al's and in a very small voice she asked, "What did Max die of Sergeant?"

Al coughed and cleared his throat. "Dehydration."

Ethel put her hands over her face and sat immobile for a long time. Finally she lowered them. "Was that a painful death?"

"I don't think so. He probably just went to sleep."

Ethel nodded. "I hope so."

"Mrs. Haugen, has your daughter told you anything about her activities in Northern Fire?" asked Al.

Lydia watched Ethel closely as her face tightened and her eyes narrowed. "My daughter hasn't talked to me in five years, Sergeant. That's when she abandoned me, her husband, and her child."

"What do you know about the organization?"

"I know that it's a radical anti-assimilation group. They feel that the First Nations of Canada have been destroyed by assimilationist policies on the part of the government and by inter-marriage. Beatrice used to be proud of me, proud of all that I had accomplished. But when she got mixed up with Northern Fire, she learned to despise me. She despises me for marrying Eric and making her a half breed. That's what she calls herself, a half breed. She won't even say *Metis*." Lydia knew that Metis was the Canadian term for someone of mixed First Nation and European blood.

Ethel paused to catch her breath and then continued. "And Bea despises herself for marrying Red and making Troy even whiter."

"Do you know anyone else in the organization?" asked Al.

"A friend of Beatrice's joined the group at the same time she did. This girl and Bea met at Yukon College taking night courses. Emily, that's the other girl, she left the organization after a year. She told me she found it cult-like and it scared her. She said it's a very small group, maybe fifteen people but they make up in intensity what they lack in numbers."

"Do you know where the group is based?" asked Al.

"There was a commune somewhere near Johnson's Crossing. Emily and Beatrice lived there but that was three years ago. Bea could be anywhere by now."

"Can you give me Emily's full name and address?" asked Al.

"Her last name is Amos. Someone told me she moved to Whitehorse recently but I don't have an address."

Al stood up. "Mrs. Haugen, you have been a tremendous help. If you hear from your daughter, please contact me immediately." He held out his card.

"I won't hear from her," said Ethel as she took the card and laid it on the coffee table. "But I'd give the world to see her right now. I need her so much." She blinked hard and rubbed her face with her hands.

As soon as the door closed behind them, Lydia grabbed Al's arm and led him down the sidewalk. Anna followed. "Ethel's daughter was in Dawson a few days ago," said Lydia when they reached the street. "She attended that protest meeting about the mine."

Anna nodded. "I recognized her from an old photo Ethel showed me once."

"Even more interesting," said Lydia, "when Beatrice Sherman left that meeting, she left with Jack Marsh."

Al gave a low whistle. "Marsh, eh? That man keeps turning up."

"I wonder where Beatrice met him," said Lydia. Then she snapped her fingers. "Red said Beatrice got her crazy ideas from a course she took at the community college. I wonder if Marsh taught that class. Yukon College offers some short summer courses and they hire part-timers."

"How would we find out? You're the expert on colleges," said Al.

"All it would take is an official call to the registrar's office. I assume that the course would have been taught six or seven years ago. It had something to do with Indian history. I'd start with Marsh's name as instructor and see what you come up with."

"Let's go," said Al. He turned and started walking toward the car.

Anna stood with her hands on her hips, glaring at Al's back. "Thanks so much, Anna," she said in an unnaturally deep voice, "for bringing all this to my attention. Without you the RCMP wouldn't know shit about Northern Fire. You've been so very, very helpful."

Al stopped and retraced his steps. He put a hand on her shoulder. "Sorry. I really do appreciate you steering us to Mrs. Haugen. This may be a real breakthrough."

"I think you're welcome," said Anna, "but I won't know for sure until you bring me a six pack of Bass Ale to assuage my hurt feelings."

"I'll bring the beer tomorrow if you can assure me that your feelings will still be hurt."

"Oh, they will be. This is a wound the size of the Grand Canyon."

"Excellent," said Al. "I do apologize for being brew-tal."

As soon as Lydia and Al reached the house, Lydia limped into the living room and gingerly lowered herself onto the couch. Al headed for the kitchen where he put on a pot of coffee and then picked up the phone. Any official request for information had to come from the RCMP detachment; Al called Wilbur Rogers and gave him a list of instructions. Lydia was almost asleep when Al shoved a steaming cup of coffee under her nose.

Lydia had finished her second cup when the phone rang. Al went to the kitchen to answer it, talked for a few minutes, and then was silent for a long time. Through the pass-through, Lydia could hear the scratch of a pencil on paper. Finally Al said, "Thanks a million." He walked back into the dining room and plopped a legal pad on the table in front of her. On it he had written *Anthropology 213, Genocide in Western Canada, Tuesdays 6:00-6:50 PM, 1 credit. Instructor: Professor John Marsh.*

"Now we're getting somewhere," said Lydia.

"The Registrar is faxing me the class list," said Al five seconds before the fax phone rang in his office. The transmission was a single sheet—a list of names.

Al ran his finger down the column. He jabbed his finger on the page toward the bottom and gave a low whistle. "Here she is, Beatrice Sherman."

Lydia took the list from Al and perused it herself. She touched the second name on the page. "And here's Emily Amos, the woman who joined Northern Fire when Beatrice did."

Al pushed his chair back and sat looking at class roll for a long time. Lydia could see frustration in the set of his mouth and discouragement in his eyes. "What's wrong?"

"Marsh really bothers me. He may have an alibi for the time of Teddy's murder but he's all over this Fleming case." Al screwed up his face. "Damn, I'd like to interrogate Marsh about Northern Fire, but I don't want to put him on his guard just yet."

"Maybe I can help," said Lydia. Al lowered his eyelids and groaned. "There will be no B and E, I promise." Lydia leaned forward. "Look, battered and bruised I may be, but I'll be able to handle a leisurely drive to Whitehorse in a few days. I don't need my left foot to drive. Why don't I go down and talk to that Amos woman? I'll tell her that I'm a friend of Mrs. Haugen and I'm helping her look for her daughter. It's true enough and it might get us some info about Marsh."

Al frowned. "I don't know. I ...."

Lydia interrupted him. "Come on. I won't be doing anything illegal and I'm already involved. It'll be perfectly safe. There's no evidence whatsoever that Emily Amos is connected with any of the bad stuff."

Al nodded very slowly. "I guess no harm can come of it. Ms. Amos is the only Northern Fire link we've got besides Beatrice Sherman and she appears to be unavailable. But remember that I know absolutely nothing about this."

"Okay but I'll need her address, your car, and your grandfather's cane." She paused and smiled. "I like this plan. There's lots of big box stores down there and I'll be able to buy that cool Leatherman tool I've been coveting."

"How will you walk around twenty acres of concrete with a

mangled foot?"

"I'll use one of those little scooters," said Lydia. "I've always wanted to try one. I wonder how fast they go."

"God help Walmart," said Al.

CHAPTER 20

Three days later Lydia threw a change of clothes and a novel into her day pack and threw the day pack into Al's Ford Explorer. She headed south toward the Yukon's capital city. Lydia enjoyed going to Whitehorse now and then. At 23,000 people, it is the largest city in the territory and its service area is enormous.

Lydia stopped at Pelly Crossing at lunchtime. A tiny First Nation village, Pelly had no real restaurants. The only food on offer at the Selkirk Center was pre-made sandwiches from the cold case. She snatched a ham and cheese and bought a bag of potato chips. She filled her thermos with coffee the consistency of molasses. The sandwich did not assuage her hunger and the coffee was undrinkable.

Finally, Lydia turned off the main highway and onto Two Mile Hill, the major commercial strip in Whitehorse. Emily Amos worked as a physician's assistant in a medical office on Wood Street in the heart of town. Lydia planned to catch her immediately after work. That gave Lydia over an hour to kill.

Unfortunately, there was no way Lydia could take in the many attractions Whitehorse had to offer. The Beringia Interpretive Center with its ice age mammoth and camel; the fish ladder that carried migrating salmon around the hydro-electric dam; the McBride Museum, home to gold rush relics and Sam McGee's cabin—all of these would have to wait until she was mobile.

She limped around downtown for ten minutes in an attempt to loosen up. The cane wasn't much help. Now her battered body was protesting both the drive and the exercise. Caffeine addiction and hunger finally trumped physical therapy.

Lydia found a small café near Emily's office and slipped into a booth next to a window. Equipped with a large cup of dark roast coffee and a scone dripping with jam, she pulled her O'Brien novel from her daypack. She was trying work up an interest in mast configuration when a couple walked into the cafe. They were having a quiet but intense argument. Here was real life drama. Lydia closed her book. She suddenly realized that one of the voices was very familiar. She looked over just in time to see Gretchen Lawler and her companion sit down at a table at the other end of the restaurant. Lydia could no longer hear them but Gretchen's gestures were animated and her face was suffused with anger. The man's body was rigid and he kept opening and closing his hands as they lay on the table. He seemed to be working hard to control himself. It looked like a lover's quarrel.

Gretchen banged her hand on the table and her voice rose. Lydia could hear her say, "No more. It's over."

The man put his finger to his lips and glanced around the shop. He saw Lydia staring. Gretchen followed his look and when she caught sight of Lydia, she put her hand to her mouth.

Lydia smiled and waved. Gretchen returned her wave with a tight smile and expressionless eyes. This was not the right time to go over and engage Gretchen in small talk. Lydia finished her coffee and asked for the check.

The cash register was just past Gretchen's table, which gave Lydia an opportunity to get a good look at her companion. As Lydia hobbled toward the cashier, Gretchen focused her eyes on the wallet in her lap. She was fingering its contents as if looking for something. Lydia smiled at the man and he smiled back. He looked vaguely familiar. He was tall and his face bore a tropical tan. He couldn't have been more than forty five but his thick hair was snow white. Lydia didn't know much about fashion, but his clothes looked expensive and so did his haircut. The stone in his earring sparkled like a diamond in the artificial light. She caught a glimpse of the Rolex crown on his gold watch and noted a broad, gold band on his left ring finger. No wonder Gretchen had been upset to see Lydia.

When Lydia opened the restaurant door, she turned and waved at Gretchen. Gretchen gave her a weak smile and waggled a couple of fingers.

The medical office in which Emily Amos worked was one of a string of small store-front businesses. Lydia was greeted by a receptionist with a bright blue steak in her long black hair and two inch fingernails which reprised this color scheme. As the young woman filed a damaged thumbnail, Lydia explained that she had come to take Ms. Amos to dinner. She quickly added that there was no need to announce her presence; she'd simply wait. She took one of Emily Amos's business cards, which, along with those of the doctors, sat in a plastic holder on the receptionist's desk. The receptionist invited Lydia to sit in a hard plastic chair under a print of a Florida seashore lined with curving coconut palms, lush seagrape bushes, and purple bougainvillea. It was a little fantasy for patients to enjoy during the cold dark of winter. The only magazines in the wall racks extolled the joys of golf and parenting. Since Lydia indulged in neither, she pulled out *HMS Surprise* and tried to remember where she was.

At 5:05 PM a plump First Nation woman emerged from an interior office. Lydia stood. "Emily Amos?" she asked. The receptionist looked up, undoubtedly surprised by Lydia's failure to recognize her own dinner date.

"Yes," said the woman. "I'm Emily."

On the spur of the moment, Lydia trotted out an alias, her mother's maiden name. If Emily was still in touch with Jack Marsh, Lydia's real name might prove problematic. "I'm Jean Stringfellow, a friend of Beatrice Sherman's mother. Ethel Haugen remembered you from your Northern Fire days and gave me your name." At this, wariness flitted across Amos's face and she took a small step backward. Lydia pressed on. "I'm here on Mrs. Haugen's behalf. She's very anxious to find Beatrice." Lydia put on her most dazzling smile. "Please let me take you to dinner? We can eat and talk at the same time."

"I don't know. I don't know where Bea is and I'm uncomfortable talking about her with a stranger."

"I understand that I'm a stranger to you but I'm not to Bea's family. I know her mother, her husband, and her son. Troy and I are good friends."

A wistful smile appeared on Amos's face. "I haven't seen Troy since he was little. He was so cute."

"He still is and he's a great kid. I'd like to talk even if you don't know where Beatrice is."

Amos pressed her lips together and thought for a moment. "Okay," she said, "I'll go but I don't have much to say."

"That's fine," said Lydia.

Her foot throbbed as they walked the block and a half to the Edgewater Hotel Bar and Grill. When the hostess seated the two women in a corner booth, Lydia smiled at the restaurant's eclectic decorating scheme—horizontal pine paneling, etched Plexiglas, mirrors, lots of brass, and a ceiling done in shake shingles. It was as if an English pub had collided with a backwoods cabin.

Lydia ordered a bottle of Merlot and poured two glasses. She made small talk until Emily had polished hers off. As she poured Emily a second glass, she launched into her presentation. "Now, let me tell you what's going on." Emily nodded, her face grave. "Beatrice's mother is distraught over the recent death of her foster father, a priest who raised her. She's in need of a lot of moral support right now. She really wants Bea at her side. If you have any idea of where she might be, please tell me."

Emily shook her head vigorously. "I don't. Really. She cut me off when I left the organization."

"That's too bad. I really would like to help Ethel. She's desperate."

Emily shrugged her shoulders. "Sorry."

Lydia tried a different tact. "I heard from Ethel that you and Bea took a course with a guy named Jack Marsh." It was only a small lie.

A glint of anger sparked in Amos's eyes. "Yeah, we did. He got us both into Northern Fire. I had issues with him but he sucked Beatrice in hook, line, and sinker."

"What do you mean?"

Emily was well into her second glass of Merlot and her inhibitions were weakening. "Bea was always a searcher. When I first met her, she was a vegetarian and into yoga and transcendental meditation. But more important than that, she was frustrated with her old life. She and her husband fought a lot and her job bored her. Bea's real smart and she needed more stimulation than she could get in Dawson. Marsh is a charismatic guy and when he started talking about cultural genocide and Northern Fire, she was captivated by his message. I do think Marsh cares about native people and he's certainly right about the destruction of our culture. But he's all talk. When we held demonstrations and sit-ins, he was never there. He always had some bullshit excuse. It bugged me. I figured if he didn't have the guts to be out front, I couldn't trust him. I left. Bea stayed."

"I've actually met Jack Marsh," said Lydia. Emily's eyes widened in surprise. "I live on the Yukon River and he's got an archeological dig up there."

"Ah, yes. I remember reading something about that project in the paper."

"So do you think Beatrice might be with Jack?"

"I told you; I don't know *where* she is." This time Emily's tone was hostile.

Lydia changed the subject. "What can you tell me about Northern Fire? I know very little about the organization."

Emily sighed. "God, that all seems like ancient history." She gazed at the ceiling for a moment and then continued. "Northern Fire was formed about eight years ago. It started in B.C. and then a year later some students from the community college began a chapter in Dawson. I got involved then. Marsh told his students that he'd give extra credit to anyone who joined the organization. That seemed like a bogus way to get points but I needed them, so I joined."

"As did Beatrice."

"Yes. We were both very taken with the idea of doing something positive for native people and we did, at least for a while. When I first joined, all our activities centered on projects in the Dawson area. We got more money for the abused women's shelter; we started an after-school reading program for native kids; we even offered a taxi service to old folks who had to get to town for medical appointments.

"But then the original organizers down in British Columbia decided that we should all live together. They formed a commune near Johnson's Crossing. It was a bad idea. Everybody became disconnected from their communities. A lot of time was wasted arguing about stupid stuff. It seemed to me that everything we did after the move was symbolic, not real. I think that was Jack Marsh's fault. He was big on symbolic gestures. I haven't had anything to do with the organization since I left."

"Jack Marsh says he's part First Nation. Do you believe him?"

Emily sighed and shifted in her chair. "That's a very touchy issue. I hate to question anybody's identity, but when I asked him about his nation, he said that his maternal grandmother was Squamish. When I asked about her clan, he hemmed and hawed and said it was Deisheetaan. The Deisheetaan clan is Tagish, not Squamish."

Just then the server arrived with two plates piled high with Alaska king crab and bowls of melted butter. The next twenty minutes were spent in near silence as the two women cracked crab legs and extracted meat with tiny forks. Lydia knew she was dripping melted butter on her shirt and she didn't care.

Lydia paid for the meal in cash so that Emily wouldn't see the name on the credit card. When they were about to depart, she asked for Emily's home phone number. Then Emily asked for Lydia's. Lydia tried hard not to grimace. She hadn't considered this when she decided to come to incognito.

"I don't have phone at my cabin of course, but you can reach me through my friend Anna. Here's her number." Lydia scribbled it on a scrap of paper and vowed to herself that she'd call Anna as soon as possible to warn her about the alias.

It was after 7:30 PM when Lydia and Emily left the restaurant. Lydia was too tired to shop but too wired to go to the motel. She decided to take in a movie. In Dawson the only movie option was the second-run films shown once a week at the Odd Fellows Hall. Lydia wanted the full experience—a real screen, gum under the seat, and a concession stand purveying popcorn and Jujubes. The movie was a soppy, maudlin romance but a giant package of licorice Twizzlers more than made up for deficits in plot and character development.

The next morning Lydia drove to Max's Fireweed Bookstore to stock up on reading material for the next few months. The next stop was a hardware store, where she bought a new pump for her Coleman stove, gaskets for her pitcher pump, and a Leatherman tool to replace her lost Swiss Army knife. Now she needed to stock up on cleaning supplies, toilet paper, and non-perishable groceries.

The Real Canadian Superstore was Lydia's favorite shopping venue, despite its hyperbolic name. Unfortunately, by the time she got there, her foot was killing her. She snagged one of the scooter/shopping cart combos lined up at the front of the store. She was very disappointed to find that the little vehicle had a top speed of three miles an hour. Even so, she managed to side-swipe a free-standing display of corned beef hash, sending twenty cans rolling down three different aisles. The teenage old boy assigned to round up the hash gave Lydia a sour look and muttered, "Spaz," under his breath. Lydia resisted lecturing him on his insensitivity to the handicapped.

Finally everything on her list was bought, bagged, and stowed in Al's Explorer. Lydia was about to put the car in drive when she remembered that she hadn't yet given Anna a heads-up.

Lydia groaned. Had she known she'd be spending most of her summer in civilization, she would have purchased a new cell phone. The one she had bought in Fairbanks had disappeared in a five foot snow drift. Fortunately, pay phones are still common in the towns of the north. She limped back to the store and called Anna collect. As soon as Anna heard her voice, she started yelling. "What's the hell's going on? I got a phone call this morning from someone asking to leave a message for Jean Stringfellow. I was about to say she had the wrong number when I remembered that was your mother's preposterous maiden name. Where are you and what are you doing?"

"Sorry," said Lydia. She explained.

"Well, your forgetfulness was almost fatal. She said to call her right away. It's urgent."

Lydia hung up the phone and stood a moment to collect her thoughts. What could have happened between supper and breakfast to make Emily call? Lydia pulled Emily's business card out of her pocket and punched in the numbers. The receptionist answered and said Emily would call her back; Lydia said it was an emergency, she was at a pay phone, and she had to talk to Emily now. The receptionist put Lydia on hold and she waited impatiently as canned music blared in her ear.

Finally, Emily picked up the phone and said, "Jean. Thank goodness." Her voice was tense. "Beatrice wants to talk to you. Today."

"My God, you *do* know where she is."

"Yes, but I couldn't tell you before I checked with her. She made me promise I would tell no one without her permission. She wants to see you. She's very upset about her foster grandfather."

"Is she at Johnson's Crossing?"

"No, she's close by." Emily gave her directions.

Lydia had no trouble finding the bright green mailbox that stood in a turnout next to the highway. A long driveway led to a new, two-story house sitting on a gentle knoll. There must have been two acres of lush grass. She could see the heads of a built-in sprinkler system. The house was painted white, while the decorative shutters and all the trim were a glossy, dark green.

Four green Adirondack chairs graced the wrap-around front porch. The white BMW sedan in the driveway was new. As Lydia approached the porch, she could see that the back yard sloped down to the river. A sleek red boat was tied to a dock.

Lydia knocked on the forest green front door. Lydia heard heavy steps and the door flew open. She was astonished to find herself looking into the blood-shot eyes of Professor Jack Marsh. His face reflected both surprise and anger. "What the hell are you doing here?" he asked, blocking the entrance with his body. The gracious Jack Marsh of Fools Gold Creek was gone.

"Beatrice invited me."

"Beatrice! How the hell do you know Beatrice?"

A soft voice from the other side of room said, "Let in her in, Jack." Reluctantly, Marsh withdrew into the room and Lydia entered.

Beatrice Sherman was sitting on a couch. She was wearing old jeans and a plain white T shirt. Her long hair was pulled back in a rubber band. Her face was pale. It was clear that she'd been crying. She patted the space next to her. "Please, sit down." Lydia sat.

Marsh threw himself into a leather chair across the room. A dirty tumbler and a nearly empty bottle of Dewars sat at his feet. His face was pinched and his body was tense. He grimaced, cracked his knuckles, and fiddled with his watch band. Finally he folded his arms in front of his chest. "Why the hell are you here?"

"I want to hear what Jean has to say about my foster grandfather," Beatrice said. "Jean told Emily Amos he was dead and Emily called me."

Marsh scowled at Lydia. "Jean? I thought your name was Lindsay." Lydia neither corrected him nor explained.

Beatrice touched Lydia's hand. "Please tell me what happened to Max. I have to know."

As Lydia described the scene that Al had laid out—the bible on the floor, the polished apple in the stained glass, the drag marks across the sanctuary, Beatrice pressed her lips and hands together. When Lydia explained Max Fleming's failure to save himself, she emitted a tiny groan. "Oh, Max," she whispered, "I didn't know. I didn't know."

Then Beatrice's hands clenched and her body stiffened. She fixed her eyes on Marsh. "You promised me Max wouldn't be targeted. Nobody will be hurt, you said. We'll scare people just a little bit, you said. People will see the error of their ways, you said." Then she screamed, "Nothing bad was supposed to happen, but Max is dead and we're responsible. Who did it? Who killed him?"

The leather creaked as Marsh leaned forward in his chair. "We are *not* responsible," he said, his voice staccato and harsh. "The old fool could have saved himself but he just sat there. We are *not* responsible."

"We are," said Beatrice, her voice low now. "I can't even remember why I thought this was a good idea. Targeting old men. Where's the honor in that?"

"Those people were part of a corrupt and brutal system. You know that," said Jack.

Beatrice fixed her eyes on him. "Of course, I know that," she shouted. "I know plenty of people who suffered in those schools. They were my people."

Jack stood up. "They were my people, too."

"Yeah, sure," said Beatrice. She stood, too. "What are you, Jack? A sixteenth, a thirty second Indian? Did you ever live as an Indian, eat Indian food, or wear Indian clothes?"

"Did *you*?" said Jack, jabbing his index finger in her direction. "Did you do any of that before you met me?"

"Fuck you," screamed Beatrice. "Fuck you." She sprinted across the room and slapped him hard enough to leave the imprint of her hand on his cheek. "I hate you," she yelled, as she ran out the back door. Lydia ran after her.

Lydia found Beatrice huddled on the bank of the river next to a tiny inlet filled with soft green horsetails and stiff, segmented reeds. Scores of luminescent damselflies danced across the still water. Some clung to the plants on legs no thicker than a hair. Others flitted around Beatrice, occasionally landing on her head or shoulders or shoes. The wings of the males were a cobalt blur as they darted in every direction, looking for receptive demoiselles.

Beatrice was oblivious to this beauty. Her arms were wrapped around her legs and her head was resting on her knees. Her whole body was shaking. Lydia squatted down next to her and put her arms around her. Beatrice's sobs and the sound of the rushing current joined in a heart-breaking duet—the river a soft, mellow baritone, Beatrice a high keening soprano. Suddenly there was the roar of a car engine and the squeal of a steering wheel turned to its limit. A cloud of dust rolled down the riverbank as Jack Marsh took off at high speed down the gravel driveway.

"Will you go back to Dawson with me, Beatrice?" said Lydia softly when the sobs had finally subsided.

Beatrice shook her head. "No, no. I can't." She gulped air. "I can't face my mother yet. I need to sort this out. Will you take me to Emily's place?"

"Of course," said Lydia. "Do you need to get anything?"

"Yes, I have a few clothes and some books. It won't take me long."

The two women went back into the house. Beatrice disappeared upstairs and Lydia took the opportunity to look around. The living area was tidy, nicely decorated, and perfectly ordinary with its leather furniture, shiny maple end tables, and flat-screen TV. There was a small collection of miniature Tlingit totem poles in a display case, some Gwich'in beadwork on the wall, and a Navajo style rug on the living room floor. Nothing about the place suggested a radical command center. The only political touch was a framed poster next to the back door. It featured an old photo of Geronimo and three other armed Native Americans; the legend read *Fighting Terrorism Since 1492*

Lydia perused the books and magazines in the bookcase. There was some fiction, two archeology textbooks, three histories of the Canadian First Nations, a book about residential Indian Schools, and one book co-authored by Marsh. A random collection of anthropology and ethnic studies journals lay at the end of one of the shelves. One brand new volume lay on the bottom shelf next to a small cardboard box. The book was titled *A Guide to Arrowheads in Western Canada*. The cover was a painting of an arrowhead. It was emerald green; its surface bore tiny scallops and a triangle had been inscribed in the middle. It was a lovely piece of art.

Lydia picked up the book and opened it. It was filled with color plates of artifacts that had been unearthed from the Northwest Territories south to the U.S. border. Some were so primitive that they barely resembled arrowheads; others had the perfect configuration of the cover painting. The book contained detailed discussions on the materials from which the arrowheads were made and techniques for shaping them. Some of the pages were smudged and some of the paragraphs were highlighted with yellow marker. Lydia read a few passages and frowned. Then she took in a sharp breath and shook her head. "Could he be that stupid?" she whispered. Lydia put the book back and picked up the cardboard box. She shook it. The contents rattled sharply. She stood still for a moment and listened for Beatrice. When she heard her walking around in the room above, Lydia removed the lid. The box was filled with small pieces of stone. Some looked like the flat rocks one might find on a river bank but others had been worked by a sharp tool. These were in the process of becoming arrowheads. Five of them seemed to be completed.

Lydia picked one out and examined it. It was a pretty piece of work with a sharp point, a shallow channel carved into each side, and rectangular chunk carved out of the base. Lydia grappled with her conscience for a second or two and then slipped the finished arrowhead into her shirt pocket along with one that was nearly done and one that was barely started. She returned the box to its resting place. Sam Avakian was absolutely right. She *was* a nosy bitch. And now she was a thief.

Lydia had reclaimed her chair when Beatrice came down the

stairs carrying a small duffle bag. "I'm ready. Let's get out of here before Jack comes back."

"Agreed," said Lydia. "A pissed off college professor is a danger to himself and others. Believe me, I speak from experience."

CHAPTER 21

Lydia would have very little time to quiz Beatrice about Northern Fire, but she needed to begin with something non-threatening. As she drove, she asked, "Does Jack own that house?" Beatrice nodded. "How come he has a house here if he lives in Vancouver during the school year and stays at Fools Gold Creek in the summer?"

"Jack can't stand being at Fools Gold Creek. He likes to be comfortable and he wants to be entertained. He spends way more time here than there."

Aha, thought Lydia. That explains why he never saw Teddy at the dig. "Three places to live. That seems excessive."

Beatrice gave Lydia a tight smile. "Jack's a trust-fund baby. He doesn't deny himself much."

"Do you live in that house?" asked Lydia.

Beatrice shook her head vigorously. "God, no. I would never live with Jack. I'm only there because we were doing a panel at Yukon College in Whitehorse tomorrow."

Lydia took a big breath before asking a question, the answer to which she knew. "Did Jack recruit you to Northern Fire?"

Beatrice hesitated and then nodded. "In a way. He mentioned it in a course I took with him at Yukon Community College in Dawson. He was very high on the organization. It sounded interesting so I joined, but I didn't plan to be active."

"But then you got sucked in," said Lydia, echoing Emily's words.

Beatrice frowned and shook her head. "Sucked in makes it

sound like I was a victim. I wasn't. I was ready to reclaim my First Nation heritage. Here I was—a half-breed with a white husband, a nearly white son, and a mother who might as well have been white."

"What do you mean?"

"My mother attended a residential Indian school from the time she was seven and then she went to a white college. She never really experienced Indian culture. And neither did I. Jack's right about that. I wanted to know what it was to be First Nation.

"Everyone in my old life, especially my mother, was a product of assimilation and assimilation is destroying the First Nations. Gwich'in life is crumbling. Young people are moving off the land; they don't hunt or fish or sew caribou clothing. Instead they wear designer clothes and work in restaurants and boutiques. They're losing the language. And worst of all, big money is coming in and destroying the environment. The oil pipelines, the gas pipelines, and the mines are all a terrible threat to the caribou. The Gwich'in in the bush, the unassimilated Gwich'in, they can't survive without caribou. I wanted to save my culture and my people."

Beatrice's words had taken on a regular cadence. Her voice rose and fell in a predictable rhythm. This wasn't conversation; it was a well-rehearsed speech. "I knew that if I was going to save anybody, I had to start with myself. That meant undoing my life, the life had lived for thirty three years. It meant giving up college; I loved college even though I never had enough time and never got enough sleep. It meant giving up my cushy white woman's job."

Then Beatrice paused and took a very deep breath. She started to speak again but her voice caught. She cleared her throat and looked away from Lydia. Her fingers began to tug at a loose thread on the sleeve of her T shirt. Her voice was strained when she said, "Worst of all, it meant giving up my family." She swallowed hard. "Leaving my husband wasn't so difficult. We were fighting a lot." She paused. "But leaving my mother and my little boy.

That about killed me." Beatrice was no longer declaiming. Lydia watched her face collapse as she relived that pain.

"Yes, that would be very hard," said Lydia. She worked to keep her tone neutral.

Beatrice nodded and was silent for a long time. Then she gathered herself and resumed her oration. "But I wasn't just leaving. I was going toward something, too. When I went to the commune, everyone there was First Nation. Not everyone was Gwich'in. A lot of them were Kaska, Tagish, or Tutchone, but they were all Indian except one mixed race man. I felt like I'd gone home."

"Couldn't Troy have visited you there?"

Beatrice lowered her head and spoke so softly that Lydia could barely hear her. "No. Children weren't allowed in the commune."

"I know Troy, Beatrice, and he barely remembers you. You must have dropped out of sight completely."

Tears came to Beatrice's eyes. "I did. I thought …." She emitted a small sob. "I thought it would be easier for Troy if I didn't flit in and out of his life. He's always been close to Red and Red's a great father."

"I still don't understand …."

Beatrice interrupted. "Don't," she said. Her voice was hoarse. She raised her hand palm out. "Please don't. I can't make you understand. I'm not even sure *I* understand." She covered her eyes with one hand and sat very still.

Lydia offered Beatrice three or four minutes of silence and then said, "Why was Reverend Fleming targeted by Northern Fire? I gather he was a kind and good man." The Explorer was approaching town and the time for questions was running out.

Beatrice intertwined her fingers and clutched her hands together. She almost whispered her words. "Because Max scared a First Nation boy to death."

Lydia scowled. "You'll have to explain that."

"A little boy was brought to Stony Creek who had always lived in the bush. He had never lived in anything bigger than a one-room cabin. The school dorm was huge and it scared him. At night he got panic attacks. The principal decided that the boy needed to face his demons head on. Max Fleming locked him in that storage room in the church one night. He gave him a cot, food and water, a chamber pot, and one candle. Of course when the candle burned out, it was pitch black in there. When Max opened the door the next morning, the little boy was dead. The doctor said he had a congenital heart defect, but all the kids knew that he had died of fright."

"How did you find out about this?" asked Lydia.

"That little boy's older brother was at the school, too. He kept the story alive. Everyone in his village knows what happened."

"So even the most benign of the Indian Schools destroyed children," said Lydia more to herself than to Beatrice.

"There were no benign Indian schools," said Beatrice sharply. "Some were less awful than others. That's the only difference." Lydia nodded.

The two women were silent for a long time and then Lydia asked, "Do you know anything about Jack's work at the dig?"

Beatrice shook her head. "No. He never talks about it."

"Have you ever seen any of the artifacts?"

"Oh, I saw him fiddling with some arrowheads the other day but I didn't take a good look at them or anything."

"So he never talks about his finds?"

"Not to me he doesn't." Beatrice paused and frowned. "He doesn't talk much at all anymore. And he's been drinking heavily for the last year. He's a very bad drunk."

Lydia turned right onto Robert Service Road, which led into downtown Whitehorse. Traffic was getting heavier. As she prepared to change lanes, she checked her review mirror. She was surprised to see a white BMW close on her tail. She frowned, turned to Beatrice, and pointed behind her. "Is that Jack's car?"

Beatrice turned around and looked through the back window. When she turned back toward Lydia, her face was pinched. "Yes, it is. I never should have slapped him. He's got a terrible temper."

Or, thought Lydia, he knows I stole his arrowheads.

Lydia glanced in the rearview mirror again. The BMW was about two feet from her bumper now. Jack laid on his horn and waved at her to pull over. "Bullshit," said Lydia. She sped up. Jack blasted his horn again and then there was a sharp jolt as he rammed the back end of Al's meticulously maintained Ford Explorer. Lydia's seatbelt tightened hard against her chest and her head bounced on the rest. The muscles in her lower back screamed.

"You son-of-a-bitch," she yelled as she pressed the accelerator. The BMW sped up, too. Jack rammed Lydia's vehicle again and then backed off. In the rear view mirror, Lydia could see a deep gash in the hood of the BMW, compliments of Al's trailer hitch. This wasn't going to improve Jack's disposition. He moved to the right and broke Al's tail light with his left front bumper.

"Enough of this crap," said Lydia. She entered the roundabout that funneled traffic onto various downtown streets. She circled it twice and made a sudden exit on Fourth Avenue. With a squeal of its tires, the BMW followed. Watching Marsh in her rearview mirror, Lydia made an abrupt right turn onto Hawkins and quick left onto Third. Marsh was right behind her. Lydia turned right into an alley. Jack hadn't anticipated this move. He was going too fast and his reflexes were dulled by Dewars. He ran head-on into a telephone pole. Beatrice turned around and reported that the pole was embedded in the BMW's front end. She couldn't tell if the car was still drivable."

Lydia turned left onto Second Avenue. "Does Jack know where Emily lives?" she asked, her eyes darting from the road to the rear view mirror and back.

"He might. I don't know."

"I'm not comfortable leaving you there then. The man's in a rage."

"I don't have any other friends here. Where else am I going to go?" That was the million dollar question. Al's place was out and Anna lived in the same building as Beatrice's mother.

Lydia scowled as she tried to think of an alternative. "I've got it," she said. "Hold on tight. Keep an eye out for Jack and watch for Mounties." Beatrice hooked her arm over the back of her seat and kept her eyes peeled on the back window. Lydia sped through a series of residential streets, past the cluster of chain stores on Two Mile Hill, and finally reached the other entrance to Highway 2. She headed north, holding the speedometer at 120 kilometers per hour and praying that all the local Mounties were eating donuts at Tim Hortons."

"Where are you taking me?" said Beatrice when she finally straightened out in her seat.

"I'm taking you to Dawson."

"I'm not ready to go to Dawson. I already told you that." Beatrice's voice was sharp.

"I'm not taking you to your mother. I'm taking you to someone who is always willing to offer sanctuary."

"Who?"

"Katherine Jenkins."

Beatrice breathed in sharply as she put her hand to her mouth. "George Jenkins's daughter," she said through her fingers.

"Yes," said Lydia.

"I can't stay there," said Beatrice.

"Because Northern Fire targeted George Jenkins."

Beatrice's mouth opened wide. She stared at Lydia. "How do you know that?"

"Katherine and I are friends. I know about *the apple doesn't fall far from the tree* notes."

"George Jenkins has every reason to hate me."

"George is dead, Beatrice."

"Oh, my God," she whispered. "How?"

"He was a recovering alcoholic and drank himself to death after he got those notes."

Beatrice emitted a low groan and covered her face with her hands. A moment later she turned to Lydia with panic in her eyes. "How can you take me to Katherine then? She'll hate the very sight of me."

"I'm taking you to Katherine because I know she will take you in. I'm taking you to Katherine because it's the last place in the world that Jack will think to look for you."

Beatrice turned her face to the window and kept it there. About forty miles south of Dawson, Lydia put her hand on Beatrice's arm. Beatrice turned toward her. "There's something else you need to know," said Lydia. "Jack got my name wrong. It's Lydia. Lydia Falkner. Jean's my middle name. I do know your mother and I am a friend of Troy's. But I also have a good friend who's a Mountie and he's going to want to talk to you about Northern Fire." Beatrice's eyes registered alarm and she shrank away from Lydia. "Max Fleming wasn't murdered but he *was* assaulted. The Mounties have to investigate."

Beatrice's nostrils flared; her voice was angry. "Is that the real reason you came to get me? To help the cops."

"No," said Lydia. "Mostly I came for your mother's sake. She thinks Northern Fire was involved in Max Fleming's death but she's convinced you weren't. Hearing that from your own lips would mean everything to her. But most important, she's needs for you to be with her right now. She's grieving hard."

Beatrice turned her eyes from Lydia, closed them, and clasped her hands in her lap. Then she grew very still and began to breathe, slow and deep. She did this for a long time. Lydia glanced at her periodically, worried that she might be having some sort of breakdown. But then she realized that Beatrice was meditating. Soon Lydia saw a change in her taut, tense body. First her shoulders dropped and the muscles in her neck relaxed. Then her jaw loosened and her back lost rigidity. Finally her face softened and her hands unclenched. She opened her eyes and looked at Lydia and said, "I can do it. I'll go back to Dawson. I'm ready."

She was silent again for a while and then she said, "I don't know anything that will help, but I'll talk to the Mounties. I owe Max that. I loved him." She took a deep breath and her lips quivered. "I don't trust Jack and I've been thinking about leaving Northern Fire for a long time. But I was afraid. Afraid to go home. Afraid my mother and Red would reject me. Afraid Troy wouldn't know me. I was afraid to face everyone I had abandoned." She touched Lydia's arm. "But you came and now it's over and I'm glad." She gave Lydia a tearful smile. With that Beatrice Sherman laid her head against the headrest and closed her eyes. Within five minutes she was asleep. Lydia shook her head in amazement. Would that she could exercise that kind of control over her own unruly subconscious.

The Explorer reached the Klondike River Bridge at 8:00 P.M. Lydia hadn't seen any sign of the BMW since they'd left Whitehorse but she wasn't taking any chances. After she turned off Front Street, she made a number of quick turns onto various side streets. The motion awakened Beatrice. "Oh, God, we're home," she said softly as she looked out of the car window. Almost instantly, her shoulders hunched and her hands clenched again. "Maybe I'm not ready after all." She turned to Lydia and grabbed her arm. "I'm scared."

"I know you are," said Lydia. "And it'll be hard. But not any harder than what you've already been through."

Lydia made one last quick turn and pulled into a driveway next to small frame house. The yard was a riot of color. Three beds of miniature rose bushes sat in the front yard. Terra cotta pots filled with petunias lined the sidewalk that led to the porch. The window boxes lined up on the wide porch railing were a riot of red, white, and purple flowers. Two recently planted conifers stood sentinel in the front yard. George Jenkins had loved gardening and this yard was part of Katherine's inheritance.

Lydia looked up and down the street, before she got out of the car and opened Beatrice's door. Beatrice was unsteady as she stepped onto the driveway. She wobbled and put one hand on the car roof to steady herself. Her face was pinched. Lydia took her elbow and helped her up the porch stairs.

When Katherine Jenkins opened the door, astonishment

registered on her face. "My God, it's Beatrice Sherman! I haven't seen you in years. How great that you're here." Beatrice looked down at her own shoes and offered no reply.

"We've got a story and a problem," said Lydia. "We need your help."

"Of course I'll help. Come in," said Katherine, stepping back and waving them forward.

The next hour was filled with outrage, yelling, and tension. But in the end Katherine and Beatrice agreed that each of them had lost a significant piece of herself to Northern Fire. Katherine invited Beatrice to stay for as long as she liked and Beatrice accepted.

When Lydia pulled back onto Craig Street, she looked right and left and then did it again. There was no sign of a white BMW. She headed for Anna's. Anna met her at the door with a beer in her hand. She secured one for Lydia and they sat side by side on the couch, feet on the coffee table.

"So what happened in Whitehorse? Did your cover get blown?"

"Not until I revealed myself to Beatrice Sherman."

"You found her!"

"I found her."

Anna tucked her feet under her legs and settled in. "Tell me everything. Don't leave out a single detail."

"Wow," said Anna when Lydia described the theft of the arrowheads. "Lying *and* stealing. You've come a long way from your provincial, goody-two-shoes roots."

"Wait 'til I describe the chase scene," said Lydia. "It was right out of *Bullitt*, minus Steve McQueen of course."

But in the end, it wasn't the chase that amazed Anna; it was the fact that Lydia had taken Beatrice to Katherine Jenkins's house. "Are you nuts! Beatrice is probably lying dead in Katherine's dining room as we speak, poisoned by arsenic in her sherry."

"Bea is perfectly safe. Katherine takes her moral and social responsibilities very seriously. St. Katherine, remember? It's clear that she thinks of Bea as having been victimized and Katherine responds to the needs of the downtrodden."

"Do you think Beatrice is a victim?" asked Anna.

Lydia sat quiet for a moment. Then she said, "No, I don't, largely because *she* doesn't. Northern Fire offered her something she needed at the time."

"Do you think she'll stay in Dawson?"

Lydia shrugged. "I don't know. But she's through with Jack Marsh and through with Northern Fire. She's agreed to talk to the Mounties.

"Wow. Marsh will be apoplectic. Does Al know that Marsh trashed his car?"

"Yeah, I called the detachment from Katherine's. He's not going to pursue it, at least not now. He doesn't want Marsh to know we're connected in any way."

"So what will happen to Beatrice?"

"The Mounties will interview her, but my guess is nothing. She hasn't done anything illegal. They're far more interested in whoever grabbed that priest."

"This has been a friggin' soap opera," said Anna. "We've got murder, terrorism, betrayal, alcoholism, and a family scorned." She paused and cocked her head. "Hmmm. Do you think Northern Fire *is* a terrorist organization?"

"Hell, I don't even know what the word means anymore. As far as I know, Northern Fire hasn't bombed any buildings or killed anyone. Guilt killed George Jenkins and Reverend Fleming."

"But their guilt lay dormant for fifty years and then Northern Fire rekindled it," said Anna. "It bears some responsibility." Then she grinned. "Of course, if having the capacity to generate guilt makes you a terrorist, my mother should be on the most-wanted list."

Fatigue, frustration, and hunger hit Lydia with a one-two punch. "I need to go home. I haven't eaten since this morning, I'm wiped out, and my foot is killing me."

"I've got stale cornflakes and sour milk. You're welcome to

it," said Anna, who rarely shopped and never cooked.

Lydia declined the offer. She had anticipated making a giant peanut butter and jelly sandwich at home, but when she walked into the kitchen, she found a note on the counter. It said *Sliced pot roast in the frig. Enjoy. I'll be home late.* Lydia grinned as she opened the refrigerator door. She laughed out loud when she saw the note Al had taped on the Pyrex bowl. *Candy is dandy but brisket is quicker.*

CHAPTER 22

The next morning over breakfast, Lydia presented Al with the three stolen arrowheads. "What the hell are these?" he asked. "Have you taken up archery?"

"No, but I broke my promise, or at least half of it." She had a self-satisfied look on her face and there was no apology in her tone.

"What promise?" asked Al, but before Lydia could answer, he emitted a low groan and clutched his head. "Oh, God. *That* promise! Who did you steal these from and why?"

Lydia told him. Al sat, calmly stroking his chin as she talked. When she was done, he said, "You obviously don't think arrowhead making is just a hobby with Professor Marsh."

"No, I don't. I have an idea and I think those pictures of his site will confirm it. Do you still have them?"

"Yeah, I downloaded them to the computer here."

"Let's go look at them again."

Al shrugged. "Okay, but Wilbur and I have looked at them at least five times."

"Humor me," said Lydia.

They went into the office and Al brought up the thumbnails again. They clicked through the photos of the archeological site; then Lydia went back to the first one and enlarged it until it filled the screen.

"There's a couple of weird things about this. First the place looks empty except for Marsh and the photographer, presumably Teddy," said Lydia. "No grad students around."

Al rolled his eyes at her. "Believe it or not, Wilbur and I did notice that Marsh was alone."

Lydia ignored him. "Second. Look at that shadow and the quality of the light. It looks like it's late."

"Yeah. We figured it was between ten and twelve at night."

"A strange time to be working, don't you think?"

Al gave Lydia a dismissive wave of his hand. "Professors don't work normal hours. Even I know that much."

"All right, all right. Here's my clincher. Click through all the photos really fast,." Al scowled but did as he was told. What had looked like slight changes in Marsh's posture were transformed into jerky movement.

"Does it look to you like Marsh is digging something up?" asked Lydia.

Al frowned and ran quickly through the photos again. He turned and stared at Lydia. "No. No, it doesn't. It looks like he's burying something."

"Exactly." Lydia lingered over the last photo. Marsh held a trowel in one hand and the other was splayed over the dirt. "Look," she said. "He's finished now and he's patting the dirt down." She looked up at Al and nodded at him. "Jack Marsh has been salting his archeological site with artifacts of his own creation."

Al gave a low whistle and nodded. "And the arrowheads you pilfered were to be buried at a later date. But wouldn't that kind of behavior get Jack Marsh fired from the university?"

"Undoubtedly," said Lydia. "Research fraud is a major deal. But if no one knows—" She let the conditional hang. "I think we need to talk to an archeologist. Find out what kind of a reputation Marsh has among his colleagues."

She paused and frowned. "Hey, I just thought of something. Remember Liz Nguyen out at the mushroom camp?" Al shifted in his chair and nodded. "Liz said that Marsh has detractors who argue that his dating of First Nations migrations is not supported by the data. Maybe he's manufacturing new data that will support those claims. I'm gonna Google Professor Jack Marsh and see what's out there in cyberspace."

When Lydia entered *John Marsh, archeology,* and *Simon Fraser University* into the search engine, scores of web sites came up. One was his own University web site, which listed his degrees (a BA from the University of Alberta and an MA and PhD from the University of California-Berkeley), his publications (three books and sixteen articles) and his teaching schedule from the previous spring—*Pre-contact Aboriginal America* and *Archeology in the Arctic and Subarctic.* His books were all published by reputable houses and, as far as Lydia could tell, the articles appeared in real academic journals.

She shook her head at Al. "He doesn't look like a fraud." Just to be sure, she checked the web sites of his publishers. His books were there along with glowing testimonials from reviewers. "There's nothing suspicious here."

Then Lydia frowned and returned to Marsh's publication list. "Wait a minute. Most of these articles and all the books were co-authored with two other people from Simon Fraser, Veronica Smythe and Marcus Weiss. But that stopped years ago. No more co-authors, no more books, and just one article. I wonder if these people left the University, if there was a falling out, or if they changed research interests."

Lydia returned to departmental web site and found Smythe and Weiss. They were both still members of the Archeology Department, the two of them had continued to publish together, and there was no evidence that they had changed research areas.

"I think you should phone one of these co-authors and find out why they don't work with Marsh anymore," said Al. "I can't do it. As far as I know, salting an archeological site isn't a criminal offense. Furthermore, I don't want Marsh to know that the Mounties are interested in him."

"Let me get this straight," said Lydia as she fixed her eyes on Al. "You are now urging me to meddle in police business. You are urging me to concoct a story in order to solicit information that might be used against Jack Marsh. You are urging me, dare I say it, to search for evidence."

"I am," said Al. "I do so without shame or apology. You're a professor. You can think of some pretext for calling. I'll even be an accomplice. Here." He shoved his cell phone into Lydia's hand. "I'll sit in the corner and bear witness to your crimes."

Lydia thought a moment, then dialed Smythe's number. The phone was picked up on the first ring by someone with a deep, loud voice. "Veronica Smythe here."

Lydia had barely begun her rather thin story about needing some information on Jack Marsh for an article she was writing, when Smythe interrupted her. "You want information about Jack Marsh? I'll tell you all you want to know and more." Her voice boomed. There was no need to put the phone on speaker. Al moved in close.

"Marsh is a parasite. He lived off my data for fifteen years and didn't contribute squat. He's a lazy son-of-a-bitch." The testier Smythe got, the louder her voice became.

Lydia was caught off guard. "Uh, really. Um, that's awful. How did that happen?"

Veronica Smythe offered Lydia a humorless chuckle. "What you really mean is why were we so stupid as to put his name on our papers if he didn't contribute. We did it because Jack was Mr. Moneybags. He got the big government grants and his grants supported our digs. He got the grants because we were looking for First Nation artifacts and at least one member of the team had to be First Nation. Jack claimed he was Metis. Said one of his grandmothers was Squamish. That's complete bullshit of course. He's less Indian than the Lone Ranger."

"So why didn't you tell the granting agency that he was a fraud?"

Smythe snorted. "Short of a DNA test, I couldn't *prove* that Jack had no Squamish blood. Besides, grant money is tight in our field and Marcus and I knew our project would end if we cut Jack off. Call us greedy, but that's the name of the game in academe."

"But I've looked at his curriculum vitae. You did stop publishing with him," said Lydia.

"We had to. Our own reputations were at stake. Jack's field work had become increasingly sloppy. He's too lazy and disorganized to set up a dig properly. The upshot is that none of Jack's data can be trusted. His research techniques are flawed and everybody knows it. As a result, he can't get anything published in a reputable journal. That last article of his is utter codswallop. No decent journal would have accepted it."

Lydia took a deep breath and then asked, "Do you think Jack Marsh is capable of deliberate research fraud?"

That silenced Smythe for a moment. "I don't really know," she said at last. "He's lazy and sloppy but I don't know if he would stoop to that or not. Why? Do you think he *is* involved in fraud?"

Lydia scribbled a quick note to Al. *Okay to tell her about the arrowheads?* Al nodded.

"He might be," said Lydia.

"What makes you think so?" asked Smythe.

"I've got some arrowheads that I'm sure he made himself. I also think he might be salting his dig with them."

"Jeezus!" yelled Smythe. "That would be an incredibly stupid thing to do."

"If I sent you digital pictures of these arrowheads, would you be able to tell whether they're fake or not?" asked Lydia.

"I might," said Smythe. "It would depend on how good they are. If Jack made them, my guess is not very."

"Give me your e-mail address and I'll take some pictures and send them to you in fifteen or twenty minutes. I'll give you half an hour to look at them and then call you back."

"Deal," said Smythe. "Nothing would give me greater pleasure than exposing Dr. John Marsh."

It took Lydia and Al a few minutes to set up the shoot. Lydia placed the arrowheads on a dark pillowcase and lit them with two desk lamps. Then she placed a ruler next to each of them. Al took close-up digital photos of both sides of each arrowhead and then Lydia held them as he photographed the edges and the points. Ten minutes later the pictures were in cyberspace.

When Lydia called Smythe back, the other woman didn't even say hello. "I can't believe this," she shouted. "Jack is a moron. No one can make credible Folsom points. He should know that."

"Slow down," said Lydia. "Start at the beginning. I don't know what a Folsom point is."

Smythe took a deep breath. "Folsom points have a very unique design. They were made roughly ten thousand years ago. None have ever been found in northwest Canada. The northernmost Folsoms were discovered in Southern Saskatchewan and Alberta. The chances of finding them in the Yukon are about zero. If these were real, they would be the archeological find of the century. But they're clearly fake. Everyone screws up stage six. Even expert knappers have a hell of a time getting that single thin flake on each side and Marsh is no expert."

Lydia laughed. "I'm afraid I don't know anything about flakes and knappers but you're absolutely sure those arrowheads are fake."

"As fake as Pamela Anderson's breasts," said Smythe. "If you were to send them to me, I could expose Jack Marsh once and for all."

Lydia cleared her throat. "Unfortunately, I can't do that in good conscience. I, um, Jack, um." She blew out air. "Let's just say that while I'm sure Jack made these, I can't prove it." She cleared her throat. "And he doesn't know I have them."

There was a moment's silence at the other end of the line and then Smythe bellowed, "There's more than one way to skin a cat."

Lydia grimaced at Al and then turned back to the phone. "Please don't tell Marsh about this. It could get me in professional trouble. I don't want to be the target of a defamation suit."

"I won't say a word to him, I promise," said Smythe. "But if you get any more dirt, let me know." She paused and took a deep breath. "I cannot believe what an idiot Jack March is." She gave a dry chuckle and hung up.

Al grinned at Lydia. "Well, that was productive. You're not bad at undercover work. Maybe you ought to think about a career change."

But Lydia wasn't listening; she was running hers fingers over the finished arrowhead. "Maybe Jack Marsh killed Teddy to hide this dirty little secret. He knew she had those photos and he knew that they could destroy his career. Research fraud is a big deal."

Al looked at her long and hard and then he sighed. "If you refuse to believe Marsh's alibi, you have to believe that Liz Nguyen would protect a murderer."

"Liz! What are you talking about?"

"Nguyen was Marsh's lady friend."

"Oh, shit," said Lydia. "But Marsh's alibi still isn't water tight. He could have slipped off, killed Teddy, and gone back to Liz. How long does it take to push a woman into a cellar?"

"Both Marsh and Nguyen say they were together every minute from the evening before until noon on the day of the murder. According to Nguyen, the only time Marsh was out of her sight was the middle of the night when he went out for three minutes to use the biffy. Marsh dropped her off near the burn around noon."

Lydia's shoulders slumped.

"But there is another possibility."

"What?"

"That Marsh killed Teddy and Nguyen knew it. They concocted the alibi before she left."

"Jesus, Al. Do you think that's what happened?"

"I don't know."

Lydia blew out air. "Liz does have a bad case of academic hero worship, but I can't imagine her lying to protect Marsh against a murder charge."

"Infatuation is a great corrupter of judgment."

"I hope to God that Liz isn't involved."

"It's gotta be somebody," Al growled. "And I want to know

who that somebody is. I want to know soon. This whole case is giving me a headache." He put his hands to his temples.

He clutched his head even harder when a loud pounding commenced on the front door. With a weary sigh he got up to answer it. When Al returned to the living room, he had Anna in tow. She was holding a white envelope. "This is for you," she said handing it to Lydia.

Lydia eyed it warily. A lot of notes had been received in her little world over the past few weeks, all of them ugly. On this envelope someone had written *Lydia c/o of Anna Dawson Dolly's*.

"How'd you get this?" asked Lydia.

"A fisherman showed up at the restaurant and gave it to me. He said a man named Red gave it to him to deliver."

Lydia opened the envelope and pulled out the note. As she read it, a broad grin spread across her face. "It's from Troy. You have to see this to appreciate it. It's priceless." She passed it to Al, who read it and passed it to Anna.

The note read:

> *Dear Lidea The mushroms are all pickt and the pickers are leeving soon. we are having a big goodby party on sunday at lunch time and you need to come. It will be a party to say goodby to Teddy and each other. Karl is cooking hungary food. If you dont come I will be sad. Bring your fishing pole.*
> *Troy Sherman*

"Will you go?" asked Al. "I know you're desperate to get to your cabin."

Lydia was quiet for a moment. Then she nodded. "Yes, I'll go. I need a chance to mourn Teddy properly. It will be wake, a celebration. Besides, I'd like to see those folks one more time. It would make Troy very happy if I showed up." She turned to Anna. "You should come."

Anna shook her head and sighed. "I can't, damn it. Sunday's

a big day at Dolly's and we're already short-handed."

"I agree that memorials are healing, but goddam it, woman, you log more miles than a long-haul trucker," said Al.

"Yeah," said Anna. "I only get to see you when I agree to crawl through the underbrush on some lunatic quest." She checked her watch. "Gotta go. I'm late." Anna headed for the hall.

When the door slammed, Al motioned Lydia into a chair. "I have something interesting to tell you. I received an e-mail just before Anna burst in. Remember the mysterious dead woman at the mine site?' Lydia nodded. "She's been identified. She was Vera Ladue of the Kaska First Nation. She lived alone, up in the Cassiar Mountains. Here's the important part. She was a member of Northern Fire."

"Wow. How did the Mounties figure *that* out?"

"She had an apple tattooed on her thigh, but no one realized its significance at first. Its importance finally dawned on someone and when the Mounties showed her picture to the folks at the Johnson Crossing commune, they identified her. Apparently Northern Fire was planning some actions that they hoped would lead to a shut-down of the Bad Axe Mine. Ms. Ladue had volunteered to penetrate the mine's perimeter and collect samples of soil and water. Northern Fire was looking for concrete evidence of toxins before they organized their first demonstration."

"How did she get in?" asked Lydia.

"No one knows."

"Do the Mounties still think her death was an accident?"

Al nodded. "It seems unlikely that the driver hit her deliberately. There's more to this sad tale. The Northern Fire people also admitted that it was Vera Ladue who dragged Father Maxell Fleming into that closet. She was the niece of the little boy who died there. Her father had never recovered from his brother's death and he passed his bitterness on to his daughter. According to them, she had no intention of physically hurting the old priest. When she learned of his death, she was devastated. She actually volunteered for the Bad Axe job. A couple of the

Northern Fire folks think she laid down in front of that truck on purpose, her life in return for Maxwell Fleming's."

"The ultimate penance," said Lydia.

CHAPTER 23

The morning was cloudy and cool. Ground fog hung in the alders and steam rose in waves from the surface of the river. The sun was pink and diffuse behind a gauzy curtain of moisture. Tiny droplets fell from the tapered ends of the cottonwood leaves. Across the water, a few ghostly black spruce cast undulating reflections on the river's surface.

A stiff headwind tried to push Lydia's little skiff back upstream. Lydia's butt bounced on the aluminum seat whenever river boils grabbed the bow. The brim of her hat flapped in three directions at once. But the wind brought beauty, too. The cottonwoods along the riverbank sent showers of white fluff to dance on the waves. Golden grasses bowed and brushed the copper colored water. Coal black ravens rode the thermals, spiraling higher and higher until they disappeared into a bank of clouds.

The sky finally cleared and the wind abated. Lydia removed her fleece jacket and baked happily in the sun. As she approached Fools Gold Creek, she was startled to see a plume of thick, dark smoke rising high over the forest. Damn. A forest fire. It would be terrible if the historic village were threatened. But as the smoke began to waft toward the river, she took a deep breath and grinned. This wasn't wood smoke; it had a light, skunky smell. The Mounties were burning the Bullock's crop.

When Lydia arrived at the mushroom camp, there were four boats lined up side-by-side on the bank. *High Arctic* was conspicuous by its absence. As she pulled her skiff between the Alaska Department of Fish and Game boat and Karl's battered old Lund, she noticed an arctic hare having lunch in a stand of scrub willow. The hare was still wearing his brindle summer coat and sported substantial cotton ball tail. His ears were edged in white but the tips were still black, enhancing that rabbit look of perpetual surprise. His nose and whiskers were in constant motion as he ran his teeth up and down the branches. When he finished with one bush, he hopped once on his big back feet to the next. Hop sit, chew; hop sit, chew—an interesting variation of eating on the run. Periodically his ears rotated slightly as he listened for signs of danger. He knew Lydia was there and glanced back at her a couple of times. He seemed comfortable with her presence.

Lydia saw the shadow moving along the ground the same time the hare did. The golden eagle was flying low and had his eyes fixed on the little creature. His buff head feathers stuck straight up like a war bonnet. His heavy beak was half open and his powerful talons were curved. He, too, was thinking about lunch.

The hare emitted no sound as he launched himself straight up in the air and then bounded across the tundra on his hind legs. His jumps were prodigious, four feet high at least. Periodically, he would land on all four feet and then bounce upright again. Lydia lost sight of him when he jumped into an alder patch. The eagle dropped into the same patch. Lydia waited. All was silent. A few moments later, the eagle reappeared above her and let out a hoarse cry. His talons were empty. He climbed into the sky, one bent tail feather cocked above the others. It was the eagle from Teddy's photograph. The hare reemerged from the scrub and bounded up the embankment. He made a wide detour around the little boy who was running in the opposite direction.

"It *is* Lydia! I told you she'd come," Troy yelled over his shoulder. He almost knocked Lydia over with his bear hug. Lydia hugged him back and then put her hands on his shoulders and held him at arm's length. She looked him up and down and grinned. The child was transformed. His clothes were clean and his hair shone copper in the intense midday sun. His face was pink from a thorough scrubbing and his fingernails were almost dirt-free. He was wearing a shirt with buttons and a collar and khaki pants that were just a little too short. His well-worn hiking boots had been brushed clean.

"How handsome you look," said Lydia.

"Pfff," said Troy with a sour look on his face. "My dad made me do it. He said everyone should know that I don't always look like a raga ... ragafin." He shrugged.

"Ragamuffin?"

"Yeah, that's it."

Troy scrutinized Lydia. "You look nice, too, but you need to comb your hair. It's all sticky-outy." Lydia ran her hand along her braid; the rubber band had loosened and long strands of hair had escaped. She pulled the band off and shook her head. Her hair fell over her shoulders and down her back in rows of loose waves.

"Wow," said Troy. "I didn't know your hair was so long. It's like Gretchen's. It's real pretty."

"Troy," said Lydia. "You have the makings of a lady-killer."

Troy gasped. "That's not true. I would never hurt a lady." Lydia explained and Troy grinned at her. "Oh, that's okay then. Maybe I will kill ladies when I grow up."

As they trudged toward camp, Lydia told Troy about the golden eagle. "Oh, sure" said Troy. "That's Hotel California. He lives in the woods behind camp."

"Hotel California! That's a famous song."

Troy shrugged. "I don't know nothin' about a song. I always thought it was a stupid name. It was Sam's idea."

Troy accompanied Lydia to the research tent and helped her unload her day pack. She had brought Nanaimo bars for all the men and bags of Dove chocolates for Gretchen and Liz. Since Red monitored Troy's consumption of sweets, Lydia had brought him a book instead of candy. Troy squealed with delight when she extracted a brand new copy of *Harry Potter and the Deathly Hallows* from the pack.

"This is so cool. It's the only one I haven't read."

"I know. You told me."

Troy hugged the both to chest with both arms. "I love Harry Potter. I think it would be cool to be a wizard but I'm not sure you can be a Canadian wizard."

"What do you mean?"

"Think about it. All the great wizards are from England— Harry Potter, Professor Dumbledore, Merlin, Morgana. She was a lady wizard. She was real evil."

"What about the Wizard of Oz? He's not English."

"Phooey," said Troy with a disdainful wave of his hand. "He ain't even a real wizard. He's just an old, bald guy behind a screen. Didn't you read the book?"

The English teacher flushed and grimaced. "Um, oh, I think so, but it's been a long time since I was a kid."

"Well, you better read it again," said Troy as he pulled out a second volume out of Lydia's day pack. "What's this?"

"That's a cookbook for Karl."

"A cookbook. That must be what people use when they cook books."

Lydia laughed. "People use cookbooks when they cook food. It tells them how to do it. No one actually cooks books."

Troy threw her an indignant look. "That's not true. Gretchen does."

Lydia looked hard at the boy. "What do you mean?"

"I heard Teddy say so. She said, 'I know you're cooking the books.' And she was real mad at Gretchen when she said it." Lydia frowned. "It's true," insisted Troy. "I'm not making it up."

"Is that exactly what Teddy said, Troy?"

Troy nodded vigorously. "Yes. I have a very good memory."

"Good, because this might be important. Do you remember when Teddy said this to Gretchen?"

Troy closed his eyes tight and scrunched up his face. "It was the day we had macaroni and cheese for supper." Troy paused. "No, it was the next day." He bit his lip. "It was the day before she died."

"You're sure?"

Troy nodded. "I know it was that day because I got ketchup all over my shirt at lunch time. I was down at the river trying to clean it and that's when I heard them."

"Do you remember anything else Teddy said to Gretchen?"

"Teddy said she was a stupid idiot for not figuring it out sooner." A spasm of grief crossed Troy's face. "But it's not true."

"What's not true?"

"Teddy was never a stupid idiot."

"You're right. Teddy was never stupid." She gave his arm a squeeze and then continued. "What did Gretchen say to Teddy? Can you remember that?"

"Yes, but it has bad words in it."

"That's okay. Tell me exactly what Gretchen said."

"She screamed at Teddy. She said she was full of shit and she should shut up. She said, 'Just shut the fuck up.' I didn't like it when she was talking to Teddy that way. It wasn't nice."

"No it wasn't. Did Gretchen she say anything after that?"

"No. She ran to her tent and didn't come out until supper time."

"What did Teddy do?"

"She left. I think she went for a walk in the woods."

"Did anyone else hear them arguing?"

Troy shook his head. "They were down by the river and everybody else was up by the tents."

"Did Gretchen know you heard their argument?"

Troy shook his head. "I don't think so. I was behind the boats."

"Did Teddy and Gretchen stay mad at each other?"

"They hardly talked to each other at all that night. But the next morning they talked at breakfast time and then Teddy took Gretchen out in the boat."

"And that was the day Teddy died." Troy nodded his confirmation.

"I need to talk to Karl," said Lydia. "Why don't you start your book?"

"You bet. I've been wanting to read this forever." Troy scooped up *Harry Potter* and let the screen door bang behind him as he trotted outside and headed for one of the lounge chairs.

When Lydia stood up and turned to look for Karl, she heard movement in the alder patch nearby. She held her breath. A moment later she caught sight of Charlie disappearing into the privy. Had he overhead the conversation? It seemed unlikely. Thank God, it hadn't been Gretchen.

When Lydia opened the door to the kitchen tent, Karl was standing at one of the tables, cutting potatoes into quarters. He had already assembled bowls of diced onion, shredded cabbage, and sliced carrots. A cutting board was covered with small chunks of beef.

"What are you making?" asked Lydia.

"Vegetarian Hungarian goulash," said Karl.

"Vegetarian! There's at least seven pounds of meat here."

"Yup. There's three kilos of meat and four kilos of vegetables. That's vegetarian by Hungarian standards." He rolled his eyes and sighed. "Do you think real *gulyas* has cabbage or carrots in it? It does not. But Bob and Lloyd are always worrying about their cholesterol, so I have to compromise my culinary principles. It's a crime."

"I'm sure the goulash will be wonderful."

"Of course it'll be wonderful. But it won't be right." Karl whacked an unpeeled garlic clove with the flat side of a cleaver. It lay smashed and partially disrobed on the cutting board.

Lydia pulled her contribution to the celebration from her daypack, three big loaves of rye bread made from her grandmother's special recipe. Three sticks of sweet butter lay nestled in a tiny ice pack.

She handed Karl his new cookbook. He grinned when he saw the title, *The Art of Manliness: Cooking Wild Game.* "I know you don't need this, but I thought you'd get a kick out of the premise."

"Actually," said Karl, "I could use a new moose stew recipe." He started paging through the book.

Lydia removed it from his hands and laid it on the table. "I have something to tell you," she said "I'm not sure what it means but it's serious. Smile while we talk. Make the conversation look casual. If Gretchen comes by, I'll change the subject instantly."

Karl frowned. "What's going on?"

Lydia looked around to be sure they were unobserved before she told Karl what Troy had reported. It was hard maintain a cheerful demeanor.

Karl's fake smile cracked instantly and he breathed out slowly. "Damn. It sounds like Gretchen was fudging the data on the salmon count somehow."

"It does," said Lydia, "but why would she do that? Look happy."

"Probably because someone is paying her to do it."

"Is Gretchen really that desperate for money?"

"I think she is. She worries constantly about her autistic boy and whether she'll be able to keep him that school."

"Why would someone pay her to alter the data? Smile some more."

Karl effected a cadaverous grin. "The salmon count drives national and international fishing policy up here. Hundreds of millions of dollars are stake. There's commercial fishing interests on both sides of the border that would love to control those numbers. A low count on this side of border just before they start renegotiating the salmon treaty would be especially hard on the Alaskan interests. My guess is that she's being paid by some Alaska outfit with a big fleet."

Lydia looked around, laughed merrily, then took a deep breath. "Do you think Gretchen would kill Teddy to hide her activities?"

Karl was beyond faking it. "That's hard to believe. What would she risk if she got caught faking data?"

"She's defrauding the government. Two governments, in fact. She'd lose her job. I suppose, she could lose her whole career." Lydia paused and blew out air. "And if she loses her job, Timmy won't be able to attend that school."

"And," said Karl, "if she went to jail, her husband might get those kids." He put one hand over his eyes. He was silent for a long time. Finally he shook his head. "I just can't see it," he said. "Her story about being stranded at the fish wheel was totally convincing. She was a mess when she got back to camp. And she went white when I told her about Teddy. She almost fainted, remember?"

"Yeah. I've probably constructed this whole scenario out of tissue paper. But I am going back to Dawson tonight. I'm not comfortable sitting on this for a day."

Karl nodded. "Yes. Sergeant Cerwinski needs to hear about the cooking-the-books thing." He picked up his cleaver. "And I need to finish my goulash."

"I'm going to see if Troy is enjoying his book."

Lydia found the boy flopped in one of the lounge chairs, his nose deep in his new Harry Potter saga. She looked over his shoulder. He had already finished twenty three pages. Lydia was surprised that Troy could navigate these J.K. Rowling books, especially the later ones. Troy may have been weak in geography and spelling but his reading skills were outstanding. Maybe that was the plus side of living for months at a time in a world without television and video games.

"Hey," she said. "How do you like it so far?"

"I just love it."

Lydia lay on the ground, cocked her elbow, and propped up her head with her hand. "What do think it would be like to go to a boarding school?"

Troy grinned. "I'd love to go Hogwarts." But then his face grew serious. "But a real live boarding school, I don't think I'd like it. It would be cool to have other boys to play with, but I wouldn't be able to see my dad or my grandma except on vacations. And I'm used to living outdoors." He looked up at the sky and then shook his head. "No. I'd hate it."

Lydia nodded. "That's what I thought."

"Shall I read to you?" asked Troy.

"That would be lovely. No one has read to me in forty years."

By the time Karl rang the dinner bell, Harry Potter had fled Privet Drive, been attacked by Death Eaters, and watched Mad Eye die. Lydia and Troy raced each other to the kitchen tent. Troy beat her by two yards.

The kitchen had been transformed. A big jar of pink wild roses sat at the center of each table, and a long garland of deep green alder leaves ran down the middle of each white paper table cloth. The roll of paper towels used for ordinary meals had been replaced by individual paper napkins. Liz had whipped up a batch of Sangria and fruit, which she had poured into plastic wine glasses. Troy had a bottle of orange pop, which was a special treat.

When everyone was seated, Karl proposed a toast to Teddy. Troy grabbed his pop bottle and everyone else picked up a plastic glass. "As Troy has told us many times, Teddy was special. She was smart, funny, whimsical, and kind. She didn't tolerate fools but she loved us all anyway. She was the glue in our little community. She never took herself too seriously and she wouldn't let us do it either. She brought us music, laughter, and fun. She brought us together and made us better people. We miss you, dear friend. Godspeed."

"Godspeed," echoed around the table.

Then Karl pulled his harmonica from his pocket. He took a deep breath and began playing *Amazing Grace*. He played chromatically, one note at a time. It was poignant and joyful and exquisitely sad. The grace notes sounded like tiny sobs. Karl repeated the melody in a minor key and Lydia's eyes filled.

When Karl was done, no one spoke. There was a lot of eye wiping and nose blowing. Red pulled Troy close. Bob was the first to compose himself. "Let's eat," he bellowed.

The almost-vegetarian goulash was lovely to behold. Each pot had been topped with blanched circles of green and red pepper. Paprika gave the contents a rosy cast and snow white sour cream swirled throughout the stew. The feeding frenzy was punctuated by stories of Teddy. Some were sweet, some were outrageous, and all of them were funny. Lydia snorted sour cream when Bob recounted how Teddy had mooned the Yukon Queen while bathing in the river. Liz talked about the time Teddy fashioned a rabbit trap out of an old bra. After snaring an enormous hare, Teddy had said, "You guys should be grateful for my ample bosoms. If they were A cups, we'd be eating field mice."

Despite the reminiscing, it took those assembled less than half an hour to polish off the three kilos of meat and four kilos of vegetables. They mopped their bowls with Lydia's bread. Lloyd said it was the best meal he'd ever eaten. Bob winked at Karl and said it wasn't half bad for foreign food.

Dessert was a special treat. Karl and Troy had found an enormous patch of wild blackberries the day before. Karl had managed to bake shortcake in two cast iron skillets on top of the propane burners. Each diner was presented with a tower of pastry, fruit, and whipped cream. There was near silence as those assembled ate every crumb. Then one by one the pickers and researchers pushed back from the table and groaned. Bob loosened his purple suspenders. Liz and Gretchen raced for the lounge chairs and stretched out; Charlie retired to his tent for a nap. Karl pulled a deck of cards from his pocket and he, Red, and Lloyd began game of euchre. Lydia sat down with her back against a log and closed her eyes. She knew she had to get back to Dawson, but she couldn't move just now.

She was almost asleep when she heard, "Hey, you can't do that. We're going fishing. I told you to bring your pole. Don't you remember?"

Lydia sighed. "I'm afraid I have bad news."

Troy's eyes widened. "What," he said breathlessly.

Lydia smiled. "It's not that kind of bad. But I do have to leave for Dawson very soon. I have a boyfriend."

"You do?" he said with incredulity.

Lydia laughed. "Why does that surprise you?"

"Because you're a teacher."

Lydia suppressed a giggle. "It's our anniversary. A long time ago, before I knew about this party, we planned to go out for a fancy dinner tonight." She bit her lip. She hated lying to Troy.

"But you brought your fishin' pole. I saw it."

"I did and I even put a lure on it, but I didn't realize that the party would last so long."

Troy's face fell. "Phooey." Then he gave her a look of resignation. "I know a boyfriend is real important, so I guess it's okay. What's his name?"

"Steven." That was Al's middle name.

"Where does he live?"

"On the river." She looked away. Lying to Troy was difficult work.

"What does he look like?"

"Oh, he's a regular guy. He's got hands and feet and a head."

Troy giggled. "If he didn't have a head, he wouldn't have any place to put his hat." He grew serious again. "I want to see you some more. Will you visit me at Grandma's house?"

"Of course. And maybe your dad can bring you to my cabin."

"That would be real cool."

"We'll plan on it."

"Good," said Troy. "You're my friend and I don't want to lose you." He looked down. "I already lost Teddy."

"You won't lose me Troy. I believe in friendship."

"Me too," said Troy. Then he leaned down and whispered into Lydia's ear. "What's a bosom?"

CHAPTER 24

It took Lydia half an hour to say her goodbyes. Liz promised to visit Lydia's cabin before she headed back to school. Bob invited her to go mountain sheep hunting with him in the late autumn. Red promised to bring Troy up to her place soon. Lloyd and Charlie said they'd be heading home in September, Lloyd to Edmonton and Charlie to Seattle. Lloyd gave her a warm hug and Charlie offered a limp handshake. Karl promised to stop by her cabin on a more regular basis but refused her whispered invitation to come to Al's in October for Canadian Thanksgiving. "Too crowded in Dawson," he whispered back. Gretchen, who had been working in the research tent, opened the door and gave Lydia a big smile and a quick wave.

It was almost 5:00 PM when Karl and Troy helped Lydia push her boat off. The light was soft and golden. The river reflected deep shafts of copper and bronze. Lydia settled back onto the seat, lifted her head, and watched wispy, cirrus clouds move quickly across a deep blue sky. She was delighted to see Hotel California circling lazily above her. When she gunned her engine, the eagle picked up speed, too. He followed her upstream for more than two miles and then soared up and over a rocky ridge. His bent tail feather waggled as he gained altitude, whether in salute or by chance Lydia couldn't tell.

This was a poignant journey for Lydia. She bit her lip as she passed the logjam that had captured Teddy's boat; she sighed as she passed the mouth of Fools Gold Creek and inhaled the lingering scent of cannabis; she shuddered as she passed the island where she and Anna had huddled after the capsize. These were difficult memories but, nevertheless, it saddened her to realize that it would be a long time before she came this way again.

Lydia had been on the river for an hour when she became aware of another boat behind her. It was coming up fast and then suddenly it slowed. Lydia was moving over to let the craft pass when she heard a distinctive boom. A scream caught in her throat. It was unbelievable. Inconceivable. Impossible. Then there was another boom and a plume of water erupted about five yards from Lydia's right hand. It was not impossible. It was a stone cold fact. Someone was shooting at her. Again. This time it was a shotgun. Shotgun slugs don't carry far. Her assailant was right behind her.

Lydia was as outraged as she was scared. "Stop screwing with me," she yelled as she dropped to the bottom of the boat. A shot skimmed the water beside her. Lydia twisted to look backwards over the gunwale. There was no mistaking the shooter. Gretchen Lawler was standing in the stern of the Alaska Department of Fish and Game boat, holding a shotgun to her shoulder. Her eyes were reduced to slits, her lips were pulled back, and her teeth were clenched.

"*You* did it," screamed Lydia. "You killed Teddy!"

Staying as low as possible, she reached over the stern seat and grabbed the throttle arm. She wrenched the handle sharply and the boat turned right, its gunwale just inches from the water. She wrenched the handle in the other direction and the boat went left. She zigzagged upstream as fast as she could go without capsizing. Gretchen's engine was bigger but her boat was less nimble. She nearly ran aground when she tried to follow Lydia's path.

As Gretchen struggled to back her craft out of shallow water, Lydia was able to widen the gap between them. But ultimately Lydia's 25 horse power motor was no match for the new Johnson 70 on the Alaska Fish and Game craft. As the two boats sped past the ruins of an old cabin, Gretchen sent a shot directly over Lydia's head.

Lydia was close to panic. She could barely breathe. She was underpowered and unarmed. Even if she could beach the boat, there was no way she would be able outrun Gretchen on dry land. Besides, there *was* no dry land. On the right bank there was nothing but muskeg, huge unstable clods of dirt and sedges sitting in ankle deep water. The left bank was high and severely undercut by the raging waters of spring breakup. A mountain goat couldn't manage that angle of ascent.

When Lydia turned around again, she could see that Gretchen was right behind her. She had lowered the gun and was jamming fresh ammunition into it. Lydia couldn't just wait for Gretchen to pick her off. She had to defend herself. But all she had was her new Leatherman tool and its three inch blade. Then Lydia's eyes fell on her fishing rod. The bright pink #3 Pixie was still attached to the swivel and one barb was looped over the bail. If she could hook Gretchen's clothes, her hat, anything, she might be able to distract her and buy some time.

Lydia grabbed the rod and unhooked the barb. The Pixie twirled in the wind. She turned to look at Gretchen and saw that she was still fiddling with the shotgun. Lydia stood, released the bail, threw her arm back, and made a wild cast in the direction of Gretchen's boat. Her heart sank when she saw the lure fly high over Gretchen's bow. With the rod still in her hand, she dropped to the bottom of the skiff. The barbs caught on something and Lydia heard a faint *whir* as the monofilament unspooled.

Every muscle in Lydia's body tensed as she waited for the firing to commence. But nothing happened. All she could hear was the rumble of Gretchen's big engine and the weak whine of her own. Moments went by. Lydia raised herself to her knees and peeked over the gunwale. Gretchen was no more than twenty feet away, almost parallel to Lydia. She was still standing in the stern but now the shotgun was hanging loosely from her right hand, the barrel pointed at the bottom of her own boat. Her neck was craned forward and she kept clawing at her cheek with her left hand. Then her left hand grabbed at the front of her pants.

Gretchen's face was contorted and her mouth looked unnaturally wide. There was blood flowing down her chin and neck.

Lydia frowned, stared hard, and then gasped. "Jesus Christ," she whispered. There was a bright pink lure hanging from Gretchen's lip; its silver edge winked in the afternoon sun.

Suddenly the spool went silent. The line had run out. The rod was jerked from Lydia's hand and dropped into the river. A few moments later, the handle was captured by a small piece of driftwood and the eight pound test line went taut. Lydia thought she heard Gretchen scream as she was pulled sideways. She lay folded over the gunwale, half in and half out of the boat. Her hand opened and the shotgun dropped into the river. Her long blond braids nearly brushed the water.

The driftwood released Lydia's rod, but at almost the same instant Gretchen's boat ploughed onto a gravel bar. She was catapulted over the side as her bow cut a large V in the sand. The engine chattered and then died. Gretchen lay motionless with legs splayed, arms out, and her face in two inches of water. A sandpiper that had been probing the gravel bar for crustaceans hopped over and inspected her outspread fingers.

Lydia's first instinct was to flee. Gretchen had undoubtedly killed Teddy and had tried to kill her. But if Gretchen was unconscious, she would drown in that shallow pool. Then again Gretchen was a marvelous actress. Her histrionics after Teddy had been found had been very convincing. *It's not true. It can't be true. Teddy's the sweetest person in the world.* Was this another splendid performance? Seconds ticked by and Gretchen didn't move a muscle. Lydia couldn't tell if she was breathing or not. Could she really stand by and let Gretchen die?

Lydia picked up her prop and poled her own bow onto the gravel bar. She watched Gretchen closely as she climbed over the gunwale and dropped into the mud. As she approached the immobile woman, Lydia pulled her Leatherman tool out of its pouch and opened a blade. When she was a few feet away, she called Gretchen's name; there was no response. She stood above her and touched her back; Gretchen didn't move. Only then did Lydia hold the knife one hand, grasp Gretchen's shoulder with the other, and turn her over.

She had to fight a wave of nausea when she saw Gretchen's ravaged face. Two barbs had penetrated her bottom lip and a third had caught the corner of her mouth. Every time the monofilament had tightened, more flesh tore away. The Pixie had peeled Gretchen's bottom lip down to her jaw bone. Two bloody flaps moved in and out as the rod bobbed up and down in the current. Lydia cut the line.

Gretchen's shirt was covered with saliva and blood and the tip of one of her long blond braids was stained copper. Lydia put her fingers on Gretchen's wrist and felt a strong pulse. She lifted her into a sitting position and whacked her back between the shoulder blades. At first Gretchen was dead weight but then, without warning, her chest heaved and she gagged, expelling a small amount of water and bile. Her large blue eyes opened but it was clear that she wasn't seeing anything. She lay in Lydia's arms, staring at the sky for ten or fifteen seconds and then she groaned. When her eyes finally focused, they fixed on Lydia's face and went wide with fear. She shrank away and tried to speak. But without a bottom lip, Gretchen could articulate no consonants. Her language was a series of ragged, guttural vowels, which quickly turned into a low wail.

Lydia tightened her grip on Gretchen's shoulder. "I need to get help. There's no way I can lift you. I'll take my boat out and try to flag somebody down. If that doesn't work, I'll go back to camp and bring some people to help me." Gretchen moaned. Her face puckered and tears coursed down her cheeks. "I'm sorry," said Lydia. "It's the only way." She laid Gretchen down, took off her own hat, and gently placed it on Gretchen's head. "That'll keep the sun off." When Lydia stood up, Gretchen began to scream, desperate, chilling animal noises.

As Lydia headed for her boat, she heard another noise, a long, low hum. She frowned and then recognized the sound. The

Yukon Queen. It was late afternoon and that meant the Queen was heading for Dawson. Lydia pulled a bandana out of her pocket and waded into the river as far as she dared. She waved her red flag wildly. At first it seemed that the Queen was going to speed by, but suddenly it slowed and headed toward shore. Then the engines dropped to idle. Someone in a uniform came out on the bow deck and yelled, "Are you in trouble?"

Lydia waved her bandana up and down and yelled, "Yes. Yes. Someone is hurt here. It's bad. You need to take her to Dawson." The woman disappeared and soon Lydia saw a small inflatable boat coming over the side of the catamaran. Two men climbed in and paddled and poled it onto the gravel bar.

It took over an hour to prepare Gretchen Lawler for travel. The Yukon Queen had a comprehensive first aid kit and one of the officers was a trained EMT. She determined that removing the barbs would be dangerous but she was able to staunch the bleeding and cover Gretchen's wounds. Pumped full of antibiotics and pain killers, Gretchen was finally carried onto the Queen.

Lydia came aboard to radio the Dawson RCMP. The captain stood next to her, mouth agape, as she told her story to Wilbur Rogers. She was surprised when Rogers asked her to stay on the catamaran. "I want to get your official statement as soon as possible and I'd also like you to keep an eye on Lawler."

"I can guarantee you she's not going anywhere," said Lydia.

"Nonetheless, I want you there."

"Will you send someone up to get my boat?"

"Of course. Put the captain on and he can give me the GPS coordinates."

One of the Queen's mates helped Lydia stow her skiff in a sheltered cove and in less than half an hour the Yukon Queen docked in Dawson City. A doctor, an ambulance, and three Mounties were there to greet Gretchen Lawler. Lydia Falkner was greeted by Sergeant Al Cerwinski, who couldn't decide whether to kiss her or slap her into protective custody.

CHAPTER 25

It was after 1:00 AM and the purple twilight was fading. The only light in Al's living room came from a small stained glass lamp on a low table. The only noise was the squeak of Al's soles on the hardwood floor as he paced from one end of the room to the other. His fists were jammed in his pockets and he was lost in thought.

Lydia sat on the couch with her chin in her hands. Her body was tense and her face was lined with fatigue. Her head moved back and forth as she watched Al pace. Finally she stood up, grabbed his hand, and pulled him down next her. "Please stop. You're making me crazy."

"Sorry."

Lydia put both her hands on Al's face and turned it toward her. "What if Gretchen dies, Al? Then I'll be a killer, too."

Al put his hands over Lydia's. "She won't die. The jaw area is mostly bone and she didn't lose that much blood. She'll be disfigured but she won't die."

"You know how spawning salmon swim along with their mouths open and sometimes catch a lure just because it's there?" Al nodded. "That's exactly what happened to Gretchen."

"You did what you needed to do, Lydia. I'm just glad you've got a terrific casting arm."

"She did kill Teddy, you know."

Al nodded. "It's the only thing that makes sense."

Lydia dropped her hands and stared at the floor. "There was no reason to suspect her. Not until today. Everything she did, everything she said seemed right." Lydia paused. "She even said, 'I feel so goddam responsible.' Jesus."

Al sighed and then checked his watch. "Constables Snowshoe and Kuptana should be at the mushroom camp by now. We'll have more information in the morning."

"Troy and I were talking about the *Wizard of Oz*," said Lydia, "and I feel like I'm living in Oz. Nothing is what it appears to be. The miners don't mine, the famous archeologist is a fake, the ancient arrowheads are new, and the fish count isn't counting fish."

"It's all fool's gold," said Al.

"You guys burned the Bullock's pot, didn't you? I smelled the smoke from the river."

Al shook his head. "No, actually the Bullocks insisted on burning it themselves. Rogers watched them do it."

"Will they be arrested?"

"No. They promised they would leave the Territory within three days. They plan to go back to B.C. where they're from. Mr. Bullock said the Yukon had brought them nothing but disappointment."

"I'm glad Wilbur didn't bust them," said Lydia. "I'd hate to see them go to jail for pot. Half the people up here grow it, for God sake."

"That may be an exaggeration, but given my own youthful indiscretions, I'm not inclined to be judgmental.

"I do have a piece of good news. Beatrice Sherman has reconciled with her mother. Ms. Sherman is taking an apartment in her mother's building."

"Hey, that *is* good news." Lydia paused. "I wonder how Troy will handle all of this."

"It'll take time for everyone to adjust," said Al, "but maybe, over time, the boy will learn to forgive her. His father can help a lot on that score."

"If *he's* willing to forgive," said Lydia. "Beatrice has put him through a lot, too."

"If he cares about his son as much as you say he does, he'll come around," said Al as he stood up. "I'm beat. I'm going to bed. You coming?" Lydia nodded and hauled herself off the couch. She followed Al through the bedroom door.

When Lydia reached the bed, she pulled off her belt. In the process her knife sheath slipped off and hit the floor with a clunk. Al reached down and picked it up for her. "This is new, isn't it?"

"Yeah, it's one of the new versions of the Leatherman tool." She gave Al a rueful little smile. "Gretchen Lawler had one of these and it looked perfect for my needs. I bought it when I was in Whitehorse. I wanted something bigger and stronger than my old knife in case I ever get trapped in the river again."

Al shuddered. "God forbid." He bounced the sheath up and down on his palm. "It feels like it weighs five pounds. How many bells and whistles does this thing have anyway?"

Lydia took the sheath from his hand, unsnapped it, and extracted the tool. She spread the handles apart and began pulling out implements. "It's got everything—a file, two knife blades, Phillips head and slotted screw drivers, little scissors, a ...." Lydia stopped when she saw a strange look on Al's face. "What's wrong?"

"Let me see that." He grabbed the Leatherman and pressed the handles together in the opposite direction; this action turned the tool into a heavy, sharp needle-nose pliers. He clutched the handles in his fist with the working end down. Then he slashed the air three times.

Lydia gasped. "Oh, my God. You think Gretchen killed Teddy with her Leatherman." She closed her eyes briefly and blew out air. "Al, I picked up Gretchen's tool at camp one day. She didn't flinch; she didn't bat an eye. I asked her if she liked it and she said it was very useful. Useful! Can you believe it!"

"It's the murder weapon. I'm sure of it. The shape's exactly right. The coroner said the wound was almost triangular with two little semi-circles cut into the skin at the margin. It's been a mystery until now." He ran his index finger around two heavy steel rivets. "She jammed the pliers into Teddy's skull all the way up to these. She must have applied incredible force."

"Gretchen is a tall, strong woman," said Lydia.

Al nodded. "I remember. I wonder if she had that tool on her today."

Lydia frowned as she tried to recall Gretchen's clothes. "I don't think she had it on her belt. If she had, she would have tried to cut the fishing line." And then Lydia remembered Gretchen grabbing at her pants just before the line ran out. "Oh, my God. The knife was in her pocket. She was trying to get it when she went over the gunwale. I hope to God it didn't fall in the water when she flipped out of the boat."

Al headed for the hall. "I've gotta call the detachment. Let's just hope that knife is in Lawler's property bag."

"But surely Gretchen would have washed it after the murder," said Lydia.

Al turned and nodded. "Of course. But there's a lot of nooks and crevices and edges on this thing. There could be microscopic bits of flesh, tissue, or hair hidden in there that she never saw."

Lydia flopped on the bed and waited for Al. He returned a few minutes later. "The tool was still in Lawler's pocket. We've got it and it'll be sent to the lab in Whitehorse in the morning." He laid down next to Lydia and hugged her hard. "Up until now we were clueless as to the murder weapon. Thank God you coveted her Leatherman."

"Easy for you to say. The damn thing cost me a hundred and fifty dollars."

"Hey," said Al, grinning as he reached for his wallet. "I'm good for a reward."

Lydia grabbed his arm and pulled him toward her. The wallet dropped to the floor. "I prefer a different sort of currency," she said. She slowly unbuttoned his shirt and released his belt buckle. She crawled to the foot of the bed and untied his shoes. He kicked them off. He raised his hips and she pulled off his regulation greys and threw them toward a chair. Next came the boxers. Then Lydia stretched herself on top of Al and buried her face in his neck. He pulled the rubber band from her braid and ran his fingers through the waves in her long, thick hair. "It's so soft," he murmured. "Like silk."

Lydia lay perfectly still as the tension in her jaw, her neck, and her back slowly melted away. Then she looked up at Al and smiled. He put his arms around her and began to move. Within minutes all thoughts of murder, murderers, and murder weapons had evaporated. Lydia's consciousness was filled with the softness of Al's caresses, the urgency of his kisses, and the intensity of a physical release that seemed to go on forever.

The next day Al and Wilbur Rogers took the jet boat to the mushroom camp to interview the remaining denizens. Everyone agreed that when Gretchen had left in her boat, she had told them all she was going down to Dawson for the night. She had left camp a half an hour after Lydia and no one had imagined that Gretchen was stalking her.

Al talked to a group of Alaskan salmon counters whose camp was forty miles downriver from the border. When he asked them how someone could *cook the books*, they assured him that it was easy. If you wanted to make the count look higher than it really was, you would remove fish from the wheel and not enter the data.

"Why does removing fish make the count look higher?" asked Lydia. "I would assume it would be just the opposite."

Lydia was surprised when Al went to the cupboard. She was mystified when he collected two empty bowls and two Mason jars filled with beans. One jar contained black beans, the other navy beans. He led her to the dining room table. He poured the entire jar of navies into the large bowl. Then he counted out fifty black beans and dropped them in, too. He shook the bowl to mix the beans. Then he had Lydia remove thirty beans. He spent the next ten minutes attempting to explain how sampling works. When Lydia scowled, groaned, and put her head on the table, he gave up. "English majors," he muttered.

He dropped the beans back into the jars. "Okay. I'll cut to the chase. If Gretchen was removing fish from the wheel and disposing of them, that would make the total population of salmon in the river look larger than it was."

"So that probably means that Gretchen was working for someone in Alaska," said Lydia, "someone whose fishing would be curtailed if there were a low salmon count on the Yukon side. That was Karl's theory."

"Yes," said Al. "And we have to find out *who*. This person may have paid other researchers along the river to produce fraudulent data as well."

Lydia frowned. "You know, when I was in Whitehorse, I saw Gretchen with some guy in a café. They were having a fight. She said something to him like, 'We're through.' I assumed it was a boyfriend and they were breaking up, but maybe he was a fleet owner.

"Well," said Al, "I'm gonna forget about it for an hour or two. I'm off to read the paper."

Lydia got up, too. "I'll check my e-mail while you do that."

Lydia hadn't checked her in-box in five days. She found forty messages. Some were from friends, one was from her mother, and a few offered prescription drugs and cell phone service at rock bottom prices. She was scanning through them rapidly, deleting as she went, when one caught her eye. It was from *vsmythe@sfu.ca* and the subject line read, WE GOT THE BASTARD!!

"Holy shit," muttered Lydia. The message was succinct. *Go to the website of the Society for Historical Archeology. Click on* **Other News**. Smythe provided the URL.

Lydia did as Smythe instructed and grinned when she saw a familiar name in bold face type. **Dr. John Marsh Accused of Research Fraud**. "Al, come here," she yelled as she quickly scanned the article.

"What's up?" he said as he trotted into the study.

Lydia pointed at the screen. "Look."

The article described how one of the graduate students at

Dr. Marsh's dig at Fools Gold Creek had unearthed artifacts that she knew to be fakes. This student had only recently arrived at the site to replace a student who had been taken ill. While the other students at the site were first year master's degree students, the new arrival was a Ph.D. candidate with expertise in North American arrowheads of the early period. When she realized that some of the artifacts being uncovered at Fools Gold Creek were fake Folsom points, she contacted the Canadian Anthropological Society. The Society sent investigators to Dr. Marsh's site and they confirmed the allegation. The article went on to say that Dr. Marsh had been suspended without pay from Simon Fraser University, pending an investigation. His dig had been closed down.

Al grinned. "How in the hell did Smythe pull that off?"

"I assume the doctoral student was hers, but how did she make that other student sick. Salmonella in the stew? Chocolates filled with ground glass?"

"I'd love to know but I ain't askin'," said Al. "This'll destroy Jack Marsh's credibility with Northern Fire. I suspect that the members won't take the manufacture of First Nation artifacts lightly."

"Beatrice should know about this," said Lydia. "Is it okay if I tell her?"

"Not yet. Wait until we get that lab report and, God willing, a confession from Lawler."

"Why?"

"I want be absolutely, one hundred percent sure Marsh had no involvement in the Gianopoulous murder before Beatrice Sherman talks to him".

Lydia pressed her lips together. "Stop it. We know it was Gretchen Lawler."

"We *think* we know it."

"*I* know it," said Lydia. Her voice was low and tight. "I saw her face when she lowered that gun. There was nothing there but rage. Pure, simple, murderous rage."

CHAPTER 26

The lab report came in three days later. Gretchen Lawler's Leatherman tool held significant traces of organic matter. There was smoked ham, peanut butter, and onion, as well as microscopic bits of Teddy's flesh and hair. The Mounties arrested Gretchen Lawler for the murder of Theodora Gianopoulous and the attempted murder of Lydia Falkner. She was charged as she lay swathed in bandages in her Whitehorse hospital bed.

Assistant Superintendent Carmichael had authorized a laptop computer so Gretchen could communicate with her caretakers and the Mounties. Gretchen's confession to murder had come quickly, but she refused to say why she was shooting at Lydia and refused to implicate anyone else.

"So," said Al, "we still don't know who was paying her or if she was being paid at all. We've subpoenaed her bank records to check for any large deposits. And there's more bad news. We've talked to experts about the statistics from the other fish counting sites. Their numbers all seem reasonable. The numbers from Fool's Gold were somewhat low one month, but nothing suggests on-going manipulation."

"So it's not a conspiracy to make the count look higher."

"Apparently not and that makes no sense at all. Why would Gretchen cook the books if a fleet owner wasn't paying her to do it?"

"I keep thinking about that guy Gretchen was talking to in Dawson. I think he's *somebody*. I'm sure I've never met him but he looked familiar. Maybe I saw him the newspaper or on TV at some point."

"What did he look like?"

"He was tall, handsome, and expensively dressed. I'd say he was under fifty but his hair was snow white and thick. He was wearing a Rolex or a really good knock-off."

Al was staring at her. "What else?"

Lydia shrugged. "That's about it." She thought a little longer. "Oh, and he was wearing one earring. It looked like a real diamond, maybe two karats."

She was startled when Al grabbed her hand and pulled her out of her chair. "Come with me." He pulled her into the study and shoved a second chair in front of the computer table. He pulled up a search engine and typed in a name. A head-shot of a smiling man popped up.

"That's him!" said Lydia. "Who is he?"

"That, my dear, is Maurice Gardiner, the president of Bad Axe Mine."

"Why in the hell would Gretchen be talking to him?" Then Lydia's body grew rigid. Her mouth opened wide. She spread her fingers over her sternum. "Oh, my God. I *know* why," said softly.

Al stared at her. "What!"

"That research site did more than count salmon. Teddy told us it was also charged with assessing the health of the fish. Remember? It was the only fish counting site charged with that responsibility."

"That's right," said Al. "They were checking for signs that the salmon were affected by pollutants." Lydia nodded. Al continued. "Gardiner must have been paying Gretchen off so she wouldn't report the results. Which means there *are* pollutants, pollutants from the mine. Burying that data would be worth a bloody fortune to Bad Axe."

"Which probably means they're paying a Gretchen a bloody fortune to hush it up," said Lydia softly. Lydia put her fingers to her temples. "This is unbelievable. Gretchen was willing to risk the health of hundreds of other children to protect her own sons.

What a perversion of mother love."

"But wouldn't the other researchers know that the fish were sick?"

"I'm not sure. Teddy did have to cut the heads open to find that ear bone, but I don't know if she looked at anything else. The only one working directly with Gretchen on the health issue was Charlie." Suddenly Lydia smacked the arm of her chair. "Goddam. When Troy was telling me about Gretchen cooking the books, I saw Charlie going into the privy. He must have heard us talking. I'll bet he was in on it and told her."

Lydia covered her face with her hands. When she finally looked up, she said, "Troy knew Gretchen's secret and at that point she knew it. Thank God she didn't hurt *him*. Thank God."

Al heaved a sigh. "I need to get moving. We need to corral Charlie Stafford before he leaves for the States. I'll send a boat up right now."

Five and a half hours later, Constable Bonnie Snowshoe walked into Al's living room, wearing a smile and waving a clipboard. "Stafford was there," she said. "He was sitting in the kitchen, drinking coffee and eating doughnuts. He was astonished to find out that he might be in trouble. He seemed genuinely shocked and angry to learn that Ms. Lawler had killed Ms. Gianopoulous. He said that he had liked Ms. Gianopoulous and had always believed that the fall was an accident. Yes, he knew that a few of the fish were sick. Yes, he knew that Ms. Lawler had fudged—that was his word, *fudged*—some numbers. He even buried some sick fish for her. In return she gave him two hundred bucks. A tip, she called it. None of this seemed like a big deal to Stafford."

Lydia flashed on the foul odor she had noticed during her walk with Troy on that first day in camp.

Al looked hard at Constable Snowshoe. "So he never realized that he was an accomplice in a high stakes game."

"I don't think so. Lawler's bank records came in just before we left the detachment, so we used that information as leverage.

When we told Stafford that over the last two years Gretchen Lawler had deposited three hundred thousand dollars into her money market fund from an untraceable, off-shore account, he went absolutely nuts. I thought he was going to have a coronary. He was far angrier about that than he was about Ms. Gianopoulous's death."

"He didn't get his fair share. What a shame," said Al. His voice was thick with disgust.

"Charlie was the perfect patsy," said Lydia. "Insecure and passive, he probably did whatever Gretchen asked without question." She frowned. "Did you ask Charlie why no one else saw the damage to the fish?"

Constable Snowshoe nodded. "He explained that the fish *looked* fine. There weren't any lesions or growths on the skin or the eyes. The problem is the roe. One of the pollutants affects the sexual development of the fish. Stafford called it a *gender-bender* chemical. The male's sex organs take on some female characteristics. The female's eggs are smaller than usual and she lays them too soon. Many of the eggs aren't viable. Apparently, scientists have known about this problem for a long time. The manufacture of plastics uses chemicals that can cause it. But the chemical used by Bad Axe is a new and different compound, and no one knows much about it. It has the same result though."

"A cycle like this would deplete the salmon population very rapidly," said Al.

Lydia sighed. "It's already happening. When we were discussing the salmon wars, Lloyd O'Hara told me that the king population on the river has plummeted over the last two years." She paused and gave Al a humorless smile. "Jack Marsh was right about Bad Axe. He was right about all of it. I hate that he was right."

"He's a bastard and a fraud, but he did the Territory a favor when he held that meeting. It got the community riled up about the mine. That will make it a harder for Bad Axe to sweep this under the rug," said Al.

"Do you think testimony from Gretchen and Charlie could get the mine shut down?" asked Lydia.

Constable Snowshoe and Al shook their heads simultaneously. "No," said Al. "The tar sand mines in Alberta have been polluting for years and they're still going strong. But the Territory may be able to force the Bad Axe to engage in serious mitigation." He sighed. "The Yukon's been through this before and we'll go through it again. And again. And again."

The next afternoon, Assistant Superintendent Carmichael gave Al a full report on the Mounties' meeting with Gretchen Lawler. When they had confronted her with Charlie Stafford's statement, her face had gone white and then red. She gave a low, guttural moan when Maurice Gardiner's name was mentioned. She waved her hands in the air, tried desperately to speak, and finally grabbed the laptop. *He is dangerous*, she wrote. *He said he couldn't let me go. He said if I left the project or told anyone, he would hurt my boys*. Then she had grabbed Assistant Superintendent Carmichael's arm with her left hand. *You have to save my boys,* she had typed with her right. *Please protect them.*

Lydia closed her eyes briefly and shook her head. "I still find it hard to believe that Gretchen killed Teddy. It was such a personal and violent attack. How could she have been *that* desperate?"

"Her world view was badly distorted." Al was silent for a few moments. Then he looked Lydia in the eye. "Could you kill someone in self-defense or in defense of someone you love?"

Lydia flashed on the previous summer when she had trained her shotgun at the head of a man and released the safety. She nodded slowly. "Yes. Yes, I could."

CHAPTER 27

Charlie Stafford had been told to stay in a Dawson hotel and not to speak to anyone about the situation at the research site. So of course this quiet, insecure young man who rarely drank went to a local bar, got plastered, and talked to anyone who wanted to listen. Needless to say, everyone wanted to listen. This was the juiciest scandal to hit town in a long time.

By the next afternoon, the story about the polluted river and damaged salmon roe was all over town. The local press and TV stations were having a field day. Al clicked on the TV. Channel 11 was covering a noisy, disorganized rally at the Dawson gazebo. A reporter was approaching a tall, disheveled man whose back was to the camera. He tapped him on the shoulder. When the old man turned around, he shook his fist and shouted something in an incomprehensible mix of English and Scots Gaelic. The camera man moved in and focused on his weathered face, the sawdust in his beard, and the woodchips in his hair. The reporter tried to ask a question, but Mick MacDougal never stopped yelling. Lydia shook her head in amazement. The sawyer must have put down his tools and hit the road the minute he heard about the fish. But how the hell did he hear? He had no radio, no TV, no phone.

Channel 11 switched its feed to Whitehorse where sixty pickets were marching in front of the Bad Axe Mine offices. The reporter noted that agents from the Department of Energy Mines and Resources were on their way to mining site, and representatives from Environment Canada were on their way to the mushroom camp. In the middle of this report, Assistant Superintendent Carmichael called Al to tell him that a *Yukon News* reporter had managed to get past a dozing guard and into Gretchen Lawler's hospital room. Gretchen, who had been a pitcher on her college softball team, had thrown her laptop at him overhand. He had a cut on his forehead head and a concussion. Carmichael also reported that there was a wall of lawyers between Maurice Gardiner and the Mounties.

"I guess our part is over," said Lydia.

"*Our* part?" said Al, raising his eyebrows.

"Yes, *our* part,' said Lydia firmly. "You may remember that I was the one who learned about the fraud from Troy. I was the one who was nearly shot to death because of it. Meanwhile, you were safely ensconced in a cozy office, signing papers and drinking bad coffee."

The next morning Lydia carried a copy of Veronica Smythe's e-mail into the dining room. She re-read and said to Al, "It's time to tell Beatrice Sherman about the salting of the dig. It will destroy Marsh's credibility with anyone left in Northern Fire, and Beatrice will see that they hear about it."

Lydia folded the print-out and shoved it into her shirt pocket as she strolled slowly toward the Blue Moose Apartments. It was early and the streets were nearly tourist free. When she reached the sidewalk in front of the building, she almost collided with Troy Sherman, who was running in the other direction, arms flailing, face wet with tears. He pushed past her without pausing and disappeared around a corner. Red and Beatrice stood in the doorway of Ethel's apartment looking desperate. Beatrice was crying. She moved forward as if to follow Troy but Red took her hand and shook his head *no*. When he caught sight of Lydia, he came down the sidewalk to meet her. There was panic in his eyes.

"Troy is furious," he said. "We just told him that Bea is his mother. He refuses to believe it. He thinks Ethel and I have betrayed him somehow. He's been screaming and throwing things." His voice caught when he said, "He even punched me in the stomach. I don't know what to do. He hates all three of us right now. Please, please, will you try to talk to him?"

"I don't know if he'll listen to me but I'll see what I can do."

"Right now you may be the only person in his world that he trusts."

Lydia found Troy on the playground. He was lying in the sand in front of the swings. He had rolled himself into a ball, knees up, arms wrapped around his shins. His whole body shook with sobs. Lydia sat down and touched him. He ignored her. She remained silent and immobile, her hand resting on his shoulder. Finally Troy looked up at her, his face twisted with grief and pain. His T shirt was wet with tears and streaked with dirt. It was new and bore a silhouette of a bespectacled boy walking into an eerie blue light. The legend read *Difficult Times Lie Ahead, Harry.* Difficult times indeed.

Lydia pulled Troy next to her, put her arms around him, and rocked him. "Troy," she said finally, her voice low. "That lady is your mother. She really is."

"No," whispered Troy, his face buried in Lydia's shirt. "She ain't." He pulled his face away from Lydia's chest and his voice rose. "I know my mother. I remember her. That ain't her." Then he raised his face to the sky. "It ain't. It ain't. It ain't," he yelled. He began to cry again, big gulping sobs.

At that moment an older boy carrying a baseball started toward them. His plump face bore a challenging scowl. When he was a few yards away, he stopped and yelled. "Looky, there's Troy. Troy, the crybaby." His voice became sing-song. "Crybaby Troy. Crybaby Troy. Crybaby Troy."

Troy was out of Lydia's arms in a flash. Tears streaming down his face, he lunged for the other boy. "I'll kill you, Jared. I will."

Ah, yes, Jared Spolsky, the boy who had called Troy's grandmother a lazy Indian. Troy knocked Jared on his back and began pummeling him with his fists. The baseball fell out of Jared's hand and rolled under a swing. Lydia's conscience didn't bother her one bit as she sat there and let Troy pound on the larger boy. But once Troy had bloodied Jared's nose, Lydia stood up and pulled Troy off him.

"Go home, Jared," she said in her sternest school teacher voice. "And if you ever insult Troy or his grandmother again, you'll have to deal with me." She gave the boy a sharp slap on the rump. "Get going."

Jared whimpered and took off running. Soon Lydia heard him wail, "Mummy, Mummy, I'm bleeding. Troy beat me up and stole my baseball. I'm *bleeeding*."

"Do you feel better now, Troy?" asked Lydia.

Troy nodded as he wiped his nose with his fist and his eyes with his palm. "Yeah," he said. He rubbed his hand on his pants. "Are you going to tell my grandma what I did?"

Lydia shook her head. "No. Jared got what he deserved."

Troy nodded vigorously. "I shoulda gave him a black eye."

"A bloody nose is much more spectacular." Lydia put her hands on his shoulders. "Troy, you know in your heart that Beatrice is your mother. Tell me what's really upsetting you."

Troy swallowed hard and looked at the ground. "They'll make me live with her. I don't want to. I don't know her." His face collapsed again. "I want to stay with my dad. I don't wanna live with that lady."

Lydia touched his chin with her index finger and raised his face. "Did anybody tell you that you had to live with her?"

Troy drew a figure in the sand with the toe of his shoe. "No."

"So maybe that's not going to happen. Why don't we go back and you can tell your family why you're upset. They'll listen to you. They know it will take time for you to get used to the idea of having your mother in your life. It would make your dad very happy if you go back into the apartment and talk to her."

Troy grabbed Lydia's hand. "Will you come, too?"

"I'll walk you to the door but then I'll leave. This is about your family and I'm not a part of that."

"Yes, you are," said Troy, "because I love you."

"I care about you, too," she said, "but parents and grandparents are special."

Red and Beatrice were still standing in front of Ethel's front door when Troy and Lydia approached. Red put out his hand. Troy released Lydia's and took his. Beatrice smiled at Troy but didn't attempt to touch him. Red opened the door for Troy, who hesitated at the threshold of the apartment. Lydia saw his little shoulders rise as he took a long, deep breath. With a desperate backward glance at her, he stepped inside. Red followed him. Beatrice entered last. When she turned to close the door, she mouthed the words, "Thank you." Lydia nodded an acknowledgment and headed back to Al's place.

"So I never got the chance to tell Beatrice about Marsh," said Lydia to Al, after describing Troy's crisis. "I'm not sure this is going to have a happy ending. Troy sees his whole world tumbling down. He's terrified."

"How about his father?"

"I don't know. I didn't talk to anyone but Troy. The fairy tale ending would be Red and Bea getting back together and living happily ever after, but this is no fairy tale."

•

CHAPTER 28

At long last Lydia was going back to her cabin. Nothing would stop her this time. She would have than less three months to enjoy it before freeze-up. Anna had invited her over for a farewell lunch, catered by the second best Chinese restaurant in Dawson.

As Lydia strolled down Third Avenue, she stopped to admire an enormous geode in a gift shop window. The rock had been split in half, exposing a cave of iridescent crystal which dripped with jagged blue stalactites. When her eyes moved from the geode to a collection of fish fossils, she caught sight of a familiar figure reflected in the glass. She turned around and stared at Jack Marsh as he shuffled down the boardwalk.

Marsh looked like he hadn't slept in a week and he had lost weight. The skin on his face was loose and sallow. He glanced at Lydia but didn't seem to recognize her at first. He walked past her and then stopped and turned on his heel. He stared at her a moment and then breathed in sharply. He bared his teeth. "It's you."

"Yes, Jack. It's me. You still don't remember my name, do you?"

"I don't give a shit about your name."

"I have so many names they're hard to remember." She paused and smiled. "Say, how are things going at the dig these days?"

Jack's face contorted as he yelled, "The dig is finished, my career is finished, and you're a meddling bitch." Lydia gave him a quizzical look. "You're the one who told people I was salting the dig. You stole my arrowheads. You had the pictures that dead woman took."

Lydia nodded. "Actually, Jack, you're right about the pictures." She wasn't about to admit to burglary. Her eyes locked on his. "You knew that was Teddy's camera when you found it. You knew it, you took it, and you didn't tell the Mounties you had it."

Marsh hesitated. "No, I ...." He sighed and his shoulders drooped. "Oh, hell. Yeah, I knew it. There were pictures of the mushroom camp. There were pictures of you. I knew she'd been up to the dig. It had to be hers." Then Marsh's breathing became labored. His eyes bulged. He moved toward Lydia with an arm raised but pulled back when he saw two young men walking purposefully toward them. "But goddam it, you didn't have to destroy me. You're worse than a meddling bitch. You're—." He paused and groped for words. "You're a vicious cunt."

Lydia clenched her teeth, grabbed the front of Jack's shirt, and pulled him toward her. The two boys stopped and stared. Lydia's voice was low. "You heartless, soulless bastard. Do you ever think about the harm *you've* caused? Do you ever think about George Jenkins, Maxwell Fleming, or Vera Ladue?"

Marsh pulled back, his eyes wide. "Vera! How in the hell ...?"

But Lydia didn't hear the rest of the question. She was walking away from Dr. John Marsh. It had felt good to get in his face. Her steps quickened and she began to smile. The smile got bigger and bigger.

"What are you grinning about?" said Anna when she opened her front door.

Lydia flopped on the couch before she answered. "My status is rising. Sam Avakian called me a nosy bitch, but I just ran into Jack Marsh and he promoted me to a vicious cunt."

"You go, girl!" said Anna as she raised her hand in a high five. "My attempts to knock that small town reticence out of you have finally paid off."

"Have you talked to Ethel or Beatrice lately? How are things going with Troy?"

"I saw Ethel this morning. Things aren't good. Troy's withdrawn and sullen."

"That's hard to imagine."

"Isn't it? It's really sad. I'm beginning to wonder if Beatrice should have come back at all."

"Is Troy staying with her?"

"No, he's with Ethel, but Beatrice comes over every day to see him. She keeps the visits short. At first Troy wouldn't talk to her. He's talking a little now but it's still very tense."

"Where's Red?"

"He had to go back to camp to pack up his stuff. That's made things even harder."

"Poor little kid. He's been through a lot this summer. He needs to do something special. Unfortunately, I can't afford to take him to Disneyland." Lydia cocked her head and thought a moment. "Hey, it's not a theme park but I wonder if Troy would like to come up to my cabin for a while. A change of scene might do him good." She grinned. "And I could use some help tackling the accumulated dust and grime of many months."

"That's a great idea. Let's go down and suggest it."

"No, I'll call Ethel first. I want to ask her about it before I see Troy."

"Okay. Call her right now. Her number's on that list on the wall."

Ethel sounded tired when she answered. "Oh, I don't know," she said when Lydia proposed that Troy come to her cabin for three or four days. "Beatrice is working so hard to win Troy back. I hate to interfere with that right now."

"How is it going?" asked Lydia.

There was a long silence on the other end of the line, then a sigh. "Not well."

"A little break might give both of them time to regain emotional strength. I'm not competing with Beatrice for Troy's affection, Ethel. I just want to give him a little breathing room."

There was another long silence, then Ethel said, "You know,

that may be just what Troy needs. I'll talk to Beatrice and if she says yes, I'll ask Troy if he wants to go. I'll call you back in a few minutes."

"I'm at Anna's," said Lydia.

Five minutes passed and then ten. The delivery boy from the Chinese restaurant arrived with cartons of Kung Pow chicken and rice. Anna set the table in the kitchen with bowls and chopsticks and poured iced tea. Lydia scooped food into her bowl. Bright red hot peppers, sliced green onions, and peanuts nestled atop a mound of juicy chicken nuggets. "This is tasty," said Lydia, but she ate mechanically with her eye on Anna's cell phone, which lay on the table between them.

It was now twenty five minutes and still no phone call. Lydia shook her head. "He's not coming. His mother won't let him." She was surprised at how disappointed she was.

Lydia had finished her chicken was attempting to pick the peanuts out of the bowl when the phone rang. She dropped her chopsticks. A single peanut went skittering across the table and into Anna's lap.

Lydia grabbed the phone. A small voice said, "Is Lydia there?"

"This is Lydia, Troy."

"Grandma said you invited me to come to your cabin. Did you really?" His tone was tentative, as if he thought the whole thing was a hoax.

"Of course, I did. I really want you to come." She paused. "If your mother and grandmother say it's okay."

Troy's voice grew stronger and more animated. "They said I could come but I have to obey your rules."

"I don't have a lot of rules at my house."

"When will you take me there?"

"How about tomorrow morning at nine?"

All doubt was gone. Lydia had to move the receiver from her ear when Troy yelled, "I'm going to Lydia's house!"

The next voice Lydia heard was Ethel's. "You have given me my grandson back"

Lydia smiled into the phone. "He was in there all along. He just didn't know it."

CHAPTER 29

It was a beautiful morning on the Yukon. The sun created shafts of light beneath the copper tinted water. Bugs danced drunkenly on the surface. A flock of Arctic terms flew overhead on the first leg of their long journey to Antarctica. Troy was so excited he was literally bouncing up and down on his seat as Anna pushed the boat into the current. Lydia was excited, too, but she was also apprehensive. As soon as Dawson disappeared from view, she commenced her annual ritual of worrying about what catastrophes might have befallen the cabin in her absence. It was true that it sat empty during the winter months every year. It was true that nothing terrible had ever happened. It was true that Lydia's closest neighbors had promised to stop by at least once a month, to check things out. Finally, Lydia forced herself to relax and concentrate on the beauties of the sub-Arctic landscape as it slipped by.

The Territory was experiencing an early autumn. The long, drooping branches of the willow trees puffed out like hoop skirts and swayed in the wind—a cotillion of sashaying, golden ball gowns. The tall birches sported foliage ranging from pale green, to corn yellow, to eye-popping orange. Some of the big cottonwoods were resisting transformation. The result was a patchwork of green and yellow leaves which, at a distance, created a pale chartreuse canopy. The dwarf birch clinging to the rocky slopes above the river glowed deep red in the sun. Only the spruce and fir trees had escaped the seasonal re-costuming.

Suddenly Lydia realized that Troy was pointing at a moving

shadow high on the cliffs at river right. It was an osprey. The bird flew leisurely, his wings undulating slowly as if he were out for his morning constitutional. His eyes, however, were fixed on the riffles in the water below. Suddenly the osprey pulled in his wings and dove, a feathered MiG heading straight for the Yukon. There was a tremendous splash, and when he emerged, he was carrying a fish almost as long as he was. The bird's left talon was firmly implanted in front the sail-like dorsal fin of the Arctic grayling. The right talon was struggling to gain purchase behind it. It looked as if this giant bird were riding a shimmering rainbow surfboard. Without losing his grip, he shook the water from his wings, soared over Lydia's boat, and into the woods.

Troy turned to her, grinning. "He's having sashimi for lunch," he said.

"Do you eat sashimi?" she asked with surprise.

"Sure, I do. Dad makes it in camp. All you need is fish and soy sauce. It's easy. Dad says living in the wilderness doesn't mean we have to eat pork and beans and Spam."

At noon Lydia pulled into a little cove and slid the bow up a sandy bank. She tied the boat to an alder and pulled two big peanut butter and jelly sandwiches out of the cooler. She and Troy sat on a big cottonwood log on the bank and munched in companionable silence. A plump willow ptarmigan emerged from an alder patch and, with bright red eyebrows raised, scrutinized the bread crumbs that were littering the sand.

Suddenly Troy jumped up and ran to the river bank. The ptarmigan scooted back into the weeds. Troy looked toward the sky and pointed. Lydia heard a faint hum. As she walked to the bank a bush plane came into view. "Look," yelled Troy. "It's smiling." The plane flew low and waggled its wings. Lydia looked up and swallowed hard. There was indeed a smile painted on the nose. It was the plane Teddy had flown during their fishing trip.

She looked over at Troy. She was surprised to see that his mouth was turned down. "What's wrong?"

"Teddy was a pilot. Did you know that?"

"Yes, I did. I've been flying with her."

"I ain't never been in a plane. Never in my whole life. But Teddy said that after the salmon counting was done she'd take me for a plane ride over the Yukon Mountains. I want to see things from the sky like an eagle. Now I never will. I'll never see Teddy again and I'll never fly like a bird."

Lydia put her hands on his shoulders. "Yes, you will. When I come back to Dawson, I'll arrange to have someone take us for a long plane ride."

Troy put his arms around her and squeezed. "That would be real cool," he said with a small smile.

Lydia retrieved the cooler and strolled to the boat. "Let's go see if my cabin still standing." Troy climbed in and Lydia pushed off.

As they neared the cabin, Lydia watched for familiar landmarks—the ancient cottonwood with its grotesque burls, the pile of lumber that had once been a mining shack. She slowed so they wouldn't miss the mossy old moose skull that had graced the bank for years. She cursed softly when she realized that only a concave depression remained. Some jerk had dug it out as a souvenir. "Stupid tourists," she muttered.

Fifteen minutes later Lydia caught sight of her flagpole, naked without its Maple Leaf flag. She ran the boat up on the bank, climbed out, and took a deep breath as she gazed up, down, and across the river. The landscape was so familiar, yet every time she made the first trip of the summer, she saw or heard or smelled something new—a vixen and three kits peering at her from a hole in the river bank, the thin, insistent cry of a peregrine falcon, the faint scent of wild roses growing among the foxtails and sedges. The something new wasn't always pleasant. One year it was a dead moose lying in her front meadow; the next it was two piles of fresh bear scat in front of her door. This year nothing new greeted her from the riverbank. She would have to wait.

Lydia grabbed her shotgun and the cooler while Troy toted his duffle bag. They climbed the bank and stepped into the front meadow. It had not been scythed since the previous autumn and it was filled with wild flowers. Drooping columbines grew in clumps along the creek's edge, each purple base shading to pale lavender, then into white. Indian paintbrush stood tall, its stiff yellow-green flower so different from the scarlet variety that grew back in Colorado. The fireweed was past its prime, faded and blowzy; the air was filled with seed pods on silky, white parachutes. Beneath all of this, mountain avens hugged the rocky ground in tangles of white and green. Bees buzzed frantically in the grass, euphoric at all this bounty. Every step Troy and Lydia took trampled something delicate and lovely.

The cabin sat in the middle of the meadow. It was a simple one room affair constructed of local logs and topped with a steep tin roof. A storage shed and a privy were the only other structures on the property. Lydia had helped her father and Frank Johnson build this cabin many years before. It had been her late father's summer getaway and now it was hers. It was the only home she had ever owned and the only place in which she had ever felt truly content.

The cabin had always been hostage to the academic calendar. It was occupied from June through August, empty from September to June. Lydia's father had been a teacher, too. Lydia had been laid off from Mountain View Community College in Colorado over a year ago, which meant that, for the first time, she had been able stay in the cabin until just before freeze-up in late October. Then she had moved in with Al until her duties at the University of Alaska commenced in January.

As Lydia stood awash in reminiscences, Troy walked around the building turning his head this way and that. He looked up at the roof and down at the little slab that constituted the front porch. He circled the structure three times. Finally he said very seriously, "This is very well built. I think it will last forever."

Troy caught sight of the privy. "Hey, I have to go. Can I use that?"

"I doubt that there's any toilet paper."

"I always carry some in my pocket cuz you never know. I don't like using moss and leaves and stuff."

Lydia grinned and nodded. As he opened door, Lydia was reminded of her mother's reaction to the privy. She had come to the Yukon just once, right after the cabin was built. She lasted three days. She hated everything about the place—its remoteness, the mosquitoes, the bears, and, worst of all, the outhouse. "Never again!" she screamed at Otto upon confronting a giant spider who was happily spinning its web across the toilet seat. "I'm never coming back. Never!" Her parents were divorced a few years later. Lydia, however, loved everything about her three acres, even the spiders in the privy and the bears who left deep scratches on the dark green door.

When Troy emerged, he was carrying a large zip-loc bag. He seemed perplexed. He held the bag aloft. "Look, it's full of comic books. And there's a note." He handed the package to Lydia. She grinned broadly as she read the words scribbled on a scrap of paper.

With apologies from the brothers of KZB. We didn't set foot in the cabin.

"Who is KZB and why are his brothers giving you comic books?" asked Troy.

Lydia grinned. "KZB is a group of college boys who used my place last summer and made a terrible mess. They are making amends."

"Is that like mending a sock?"

"Exactly," said Lydia.

She flipped through the comic books. There was *Aquaman, the Fantastic Four, Superman, the Hulk, the Green Lantern,* and *Wonder Woman.* Enough bathroom reading to see her until freeze-up.

"Hey," said Troy. "I didn't have to use my own toilet paper. There's four big rolls in there. The really soft stuff, not the kind we use at camp. Is that mending, too?"

"It is, indeed. Let's see what kind of shape the cabin is in."

With great anticipation, Lydia slowly pushed open the heavy front door. The *something new* announced itself with a chorus of squeaks and a blur of fur as a family of short-tailed voles ran for cover. She sighed. "There's no place like home even if it is infested with rodents."

"Those ain't rodents," said Troy. "They're mice. They're real cute."

Lydia was too preoccupied to respond. She stood quietly in the middle of the room and took in every detail. The interior was unadorned. It was a log cabin inside and out. There was no drywall, no paneling, and no ceiling. The logs had been stained a rich brown. The seams had been chinked with wood chips and twigs which were then covered with a mortar made of clay, lime, and straw. Over time the mortar had turned to a soft grey. The steeply peaked roof showed off the building's support beams, long straight spruce trunks, which wore the same brown stain. Only the main floor and that of the loft had been made with milled lumber.

With the exception of a beautiful old rocker and a hand-built kitchen table, the furniture was a motley collection of thrift store fare. It was frayed, scratched, and stained—the work of muddy hiking boots, errant pen knives, spilled coffee, and sweating beer cans.

Lydia walked slowly through the cabin, savoring every detail. Then she did it again, this time marveling at how dirty everything was. Cobwebs floated under each horizontal surface. They cocooned the rungs of the chairs and the table legs. They crept up the coffee cups and glasses sitting on the open kitchen shelves. Every surface was coated in dust which in turn stippled with tiny paw prints and vole scat. Every window pane was black with grime and green with mildew. The effect was a grim paisley, Peter Maxx gone gothic.

Lydia slapped the brown corduroy cover on the old futon and

a cloud of dust rose. She traced the back of her grandmother's oak rocker with her index finger and then wiped it on her pants. She wrote her name and then Troy's in the dust on the table that Frank Johnson had built. She ran her hand over the edges of her beautiful, wood-burning cook stove, its enamel elegance compromised by a thick coat of grime and tiny brown droppings.

Frank had taught Lydia how to bake in this stove. The cabin had regularly filled with the aroma of baking bread and puffy, gooey cinnamon buns as Lydia experimented with yeast, salt, and a temperamental stove damper. She checked the oven for rodent nests but found only spiders and a mummified biscuit.

While Lydia took stock, Troy crawled around on the floor, looking for voles. When he finally stood up, his clothes were covered with dust and his hands were filthy. He had one curly cobweb hanging from an ear. He pointed to the pitcher pump at the sink. "Hey, you have indoor plumbing. I can wash my hands after we prime it."

Suddenly he put his index finger to his lips and pointed into the big porcelain sink. A baby vole lay in one corner. It was curled into a ball with its eyes closed. It was tiny, fat, and pear-shaped with small, round ears plastered close to its head. Its whiskers were long and its tail was short and nearly hairless. It was shaking. Slowly and carefully, Troy picked it up. He gently rubbed its neck and it burrowed deeper into his hand.

"He wants his mum," said Troy. Before Lydia could intervene, he put the vole on the floor and it scampered under the stove. Lydia groaned.

"Tomorrow is eviction day," said Lydia. "I don't care how cute they are."

Troy pointed to the built-in ladder that stood in the middle of the room. "Hey, can I go up there?" Lydia nodded. When he reached the loft, he yelled down, "Hey, can I sleep up here?"

Lydia hesitated. "Okay," she said finally, "but no jumping on my brand new bed." That bed had been a big investment for Lydia. The previous summer she had slept on the floor of the loft, nothing but a thin pad and a sleeping bag between her butt and the spruce planks. The pad was a mere twenty inches wide and when Al Cerwinski came into her life, this became problematic. After she bruised her coccyx during a September night of athletic passion, she decided that a real bed was necessary, no matter what the state of her bank account. It had taken four people to get the damn mattress up the ladder. Then it had taken Lydia two hours to assemble the damn platform. The pre-drilled holes didn't line up, three bolts were missing, and one of the planks was warped. But finally the parts morphed into a queen-sized bed. That night when she and Al test-drove it, the platform held. They bounced with abandon on eight-inch thick mattress without fear of concussion or bruising.

Lydia could hear Troy walking around above, as he inspected the crates that served as bedside tables, the footlockers which held her clothes, and Frank's beautiful, hand-turned pegs, which ringed the room. "Hey," he yelled. "I can see the river from here. But the windows are real dirty." Lydia grimaced. Washing those windows would involve performing a precarious ballet on an extension ladder.

Troy appeared at the edge of the loft and abruptly swung down the ladder hand-over-hand as if it were a set of vertical monkey bars. Lydia put her hand to her chest. Apparently, she didn't have the nerves for child care. "Next time you come down, use your feet. I don't have a lot of rules but that's one of them."

Troy gave her a sheepish grin. "Yes, ma'am."

"Let's haul those supplies up to the cabin and put them away."

With Troy's help, it only took half an hour to bring everything up. Lydia gave Troy the job of wiping the dust and vole scat off the kitchen shelves and then stacking the canned goods on them. She opened all the packages of dry food—flour, corn meal, pasta, beans, lentils, sugar, popcorn, nuts—and placed the contents in vole proof canisters or large green mason jars with zinc lids. Six, two pound cans of coffee were stowed in the place of honor on the top shelf above the sink. Once Lydia primed the pump with water from the creek, the kitchen was in working order.

"Hey," said Troy. "I'm hungry. Can we make supper now?"

"You bet," said Lydia. "We'll grill hamburgers. That okay with you?"

"I *loove* hamburgers," said Troy.

"Let's go make some coals," said Lydia, heading for the door.

Lydia's father had built a big fire ring in the meadow many years before. Four flat river rocks and a stainless steel shelf from an industrial refrigerator constituted the grill. Lydia put Troy in charge of collecting kindling while she split logs from last year's wood pile into quarter rounds. Some of these she split again. They piled the kindling and split logs next to the fire ring.

"Let me build the fire, okay?" said Troy. Lydia nodded. Troy took out his pocket knife and sat down with a small pile of kindling at his feet. He picked a twig up, held it between his forefinger and thumb, and cut into it diagonally. He did this again and again until it looked like a thin, wooden feather. He repeated this procedure eight or ten times and then built a tiny feather teepee in the middle of the fire ring.

"Do you want some paper?" asked Lydia.

Troy gave her a contemptuous look. "Real woodsmen don't use paper. But I do need a match."

"Just one?" asked Lydia grinning.

"Just one," said Troy. Lydia removed a small box of kitchen matches from her pocket and handed it to him. He picked out a match and flicked it against the striker. It flared and he lowered it to his teepee. The little feathers caught immediately. Troy dropped his match in the ring and brushed his hands together in a *that's that* gesture.

"Wow," said Lydia. "No paper. One match. I'm impressed." Troy slowly added more wood to the blaze until it burned high and hot.

"Great," said Lydia. "We'll let it burn down. Let's go in and you can help me make the hamburger patties."

Unfortunately, Troy's expertise did not extend to handling

ground meat. His patties were loosely constructed mounds and they fell apart as soon as he tried to lay them on the plate. "Phooey, I ain't a good cook," he said, slapping a gob of hamburger down on the counter in disgust.

"Tell you what. I'll repair these and you can set the table cloth."

"Don't you mean set the table?"

"No. We're going to have a picnic by the fire." She pointed to a piece of red and white gingham which lay folded on a kitchen shelf. "Spread that out on the ground and then put two plates and two forks on it. You can take the ketchup and buns, too."

Troy trotted off holding the plates with the table cloth, the forks, the ketchup, and the buns stacked on top. He stabilized the load with his chin. While he was gone, Lydia reworked the patties and laid them on a platter. She pulled tubs of potato salad and coleslaw from the cooler, grabbed a spoon and a spatula, and carried it all outside.

Troy was very conscientious about his fire tending. He moved sticks to maximize oxygen and pushed outlying embers into the pile of shimmering coals. After half an hour, he announced, "It's just perfect now."

Lydia picked up the fire grate with an oven mitt and rested its edges on the four strategically placed rocks. She laid four hamburger patties on the grill. They immediately began to pop and sizzle.

"Mmmm," said Troy. "My mum don't eat hamburgers. She's a vegetable person." Lydia was pleased to note that Beatrice was now *my mum* instead of *that lady*.

"A vegetarian, huh?"

"Yup, but not me," said Troy. "I love meat. One time I ate a whole half a chicken all by myself." Lydia would have been embarrassed to tell Troy how many times she had done that.

They sat in companionable silence and watched the grease flair up as it hit the coals. Lydia flipped the burgers once and waited until they were crisp around the edges. She checked one with a knife. She nodded at Troy and gave him a thumbs-up.

He watched expectantly as Lydia slid the spatula under a patty and plopped it on a plated bun. She added dollops of potato salad and coleslaw to the plate and handed it to Troy. He doctored the hamburger with ketchup and then took one big bite after another. "Hey, slow down," said Lydia, laughing as she prepared her own plate, "There's more where that came from."

Troy had barely swallowed the last mouthful of his first burger when he held his plate out for a second. He poured even more ketchup on this one. When he picked it up, a big red glob slid off the patty and onto his shirt. "Oh, no. Not again." Then his face froze and he fingered the stain. Lydia knew he was remembering the last time he'd soiled a shirt with ketchup.

Troy put the hamburger back on the plate and looked up at Lydia. His face was pinched. "Can I ask you something?" She nodded. "I know that Gretchen killed Teddy. I know she shot at you, too. Why did Gretchen do such awful things?"

Lydia blew out air. "Because Teddy and I both knew that she was doing something bad."

"Cooking those books, right? My dad explained about that."

"Right."

"Then it's my fault that Gretchen shot at you."

"No, Troy, no. It's not your fault."

"Yes, it is. You didn't know about the book cooking until I told you."

Lydia closed her eyes a moment as she thought about what to say. "That's true, Troy, but Gretchen didn't hurt me and you helped me catch Teddy's killer."

Troy looked down at his plate. "Yeah. But I don't want the killer to be Gretchen." He tore a piece from his hamburger bun and began rolling it around in his fingers.

"Because you like her?"

Troy shook his head. "Because she's Tommy and Tim's mum. What will happen to them when Gretchen goes to jail?"

Lydia took a deep breath and searched for reassuring words.

"Tommy will stay at his school and Tim will live with his aunt, just like he did this summer. Nothing bad will happen to them."

Troy shook his head. "That's not true. Losing your mum is very bad." Lydia didn't reply. There was nothing to say.

They sat in silence for a long time. Lydia was about to suggest that they put out the fire and take the leftover food inside when she saw the tall grass on the other side of the creek begin to sway. Lydia sat silent for a moment and then whispered, "Troy, look." His eyes caught the movement, too. He nodded and slowly stood up.

A black wolf stepped daintily onto a bare patch of ground. He stopped and stared at the humans. He was huge and magnificent. His coat was glossy and his eyes were amber with black centers. His gaze was steady without fear or curiosity. He crossed the creek and then trotted around the perimeter of the meadow sniffing the air and the ground. His circles got smaller and smaller. Finally, he lowered himself to the ground, but he kept looking around as if expecting something.

When he laid his chin on his front paws, a second wolf tiptoed into the clearing. She was white with black stripes circling her cheeks and one black paw. She offered the black wolf no greeting and paid no attention when the cotton grass behind her began twisting and bending. She ignored the barks and yips emanating from the weeds. Troy turned to Lydia, his eyes wide. "She has pups," he whispered.

A small grey wolf loped into the clearing, pursued by a black one. A few moments later two more pups emerged, one black and one brindle. They looked quizzically at Troy and Lydia and then began to dash around the meadow. The grey pup stopped and sniffed at the ground. He began to dig a hole with great energy and purpose. Dirt and grass flew. Whenever one of his siblings came over to help, he growled softly. Every now and then the brindle pup would stop running, raise her head to the sky, and emit a thin, high pitched cry. "Howl practice," whispered Lydia. The grey pup kept digging.

One of the black pups headed for the creek. "He's coming to see us," said Troy softly. The little wolf trotted to the edge and then lost his footing in the slick mud. He slid down the bank and hit the water face first. He wrinkled his nose and snorted. Undeterred, the pup waded across the creek toward Lydia and Troy. Mother wolf was not pleased. She jumped across the creek and grabbed her unruly offspring by the scruff of the neck. She half carried and half dragged him across the water and dropped him. He found his footing and dashed into the weeds. A moment the mother and other pups followed.

The male wolf stayed. His head still on his paws, he watched Troy and Lydia for a long time. As the last embers in the fire ring burned, he slowly rose, jumped the creek, and disappeared into the trees.

"That was so cool," said Troy. "Did you ever see those wolves before?

Lydia smiled and nodded. "Last summer the father came and sat with me on the river bank. He did it twice. I think he likes this place."

"So do I," said Troy. He placed more wood on the fire and came and sat next to Lydia. He scooted over until their hips were touching. He leaned against her arm. "Wolf mothers never leave their puppies when they're little. Did you know that?" Lydia nodded. "My mum left me when I was little and I never saw her for a long time."

Lydia pulled Troy close and put an arm around him. "I know. Are you afraid she might leave again?"

"Yes." His voice was small.

"I can't make any promises," said Lydia, "but I think she's back to stay."

Troy didn't respond. He sat in thought for a moment, then snuggled up against her, his head on her chest. Lydia put an arm around him. They sat and stared at the flames in silence. A few minutes later, Troy's chin dropped. Lydia looked down. His eyes were closed and he had a faint smile on his face.

Lydia didn't move. She inhaled the faint smell of wood smoke; she watched a bee wade into the sticky, yellow center of a wild rose; she felt the light evening breeze caress her face. And then she heard it. The howl started low, rose sharply, modulated into a minor key, then fell away and died. It was a mournful sound, like the far away whistle of an old steam engine. There was a moment's quiet and then another howl. Louder. Closer. It was a different voice, a different pitch, a different melody. It rose higher and higher until it spanned an octave or more. Then it cut off abruptly and all Lydia could hear was the rustle of the cotton grass, the rhythmic breathing of the little boy asleep in the crook of her arm, and the distant sound of the Yukon River as it rushed past her cabin to the Bering Sea.

*   *   *

Also by Lynn M. Berk in the Lydia Falkner series

The Yukon Grieves for No One

Made in the USA
Monee, IL
11 July 2021